TO CATCH A STORM

By Warren Slingsby

First published in Great Britain in 2014 by Warren Slingsby in association with Completely Novel.

Copyright © Warren Slingsby 2014

No part of this book can be reproduced, stored, or transmitted, in any form or by any means, without the prior written permission of the copyright owner.

Except for those in the public domain, all the characters in this book are fictitious and any resemblance to actual persons, living or dead, is coincidental.

ISBN No. 9781849145947

This book was written and edited by Warren Slingsby. More information about Warren Slingsby can be found at warrenslingsby.com

TO CATCH A STORM

Janet comes round in a strange hotel room, her memory almost erased by a drug and alcohol fuelled binge from hell. Unsure which hotel or even which city she's in and no idea how she came to be there. She is not alone; there is a dead man laying next to her. And there are some eye opening surprises awaiting her in the room. Surprises which will lead her to abandon her life as a successful banker and plunge her head first into the unspoken world of stolen art.

She inadvertently stumbles into a dangerous game of cat and mouse crossing the paths of thieves, thugs and oligarchs that will take her from Glasgow to Edinburgh and onto Barcelona and the Cote d'Azur. During her journey, she will unlock the secret to the location of most infamous and valuable stolen painting in the world. But there's a high price to pay for such knowledge and riches as the super wealthy who inhabit this secret world are not prepared to give it over without a fight to the death.

TO CATCH A STORM

Many thanks to Tom Gabbutt, Sam Burgess, Tracy Dyson, Adam Morrison, Steven Lucker, Catherine McGrath, Lottie David Jardine, Leah Burgess, James Butler, Andrew Woodhead, Shay Moradi, Lucie Warrington, Stuart Warrington, Dominic Howe, Kerry Dyson, Julian Kimmings, Nicholas Emms, Chris Dance, Roy Slingsby, Lajos Sovago, Kerry Kidd, Sally Slingsby, Lucy Butler, Karen Johnson, Vicky Swift, Debbie Quinlan-Lodge, Gill Wood, Jane Leah, Emma Bodger, Craig Richardson, Tom Thorpe, Nadine Slingsby, Mark Hendry, Sophie Whitaker, Jay Woods, Chris Cox, Richard Telford, Aran Wilkinson, Laura Campbell, Sara Strid-Coughlan, Oliver Kneen, Philippa Armitage, Edward Nolan, Aidan Nolan, Carla Stockton-Jones for support and encouragement in getting this book published.

Special thanks to Tom Gabbutt and Sam Burgess for their invaluable advice, patience and feedback whilst I lost myself creating the secret world of stolen art that follows.

For Mike, my life mentor

"Art attracts us only by what it reveals of our most secret self."

Jean-Luc Godard

PART 1

CHAPTER ONE

Day zero

Janet's left eye opened less than a millimetre, enough to take in a small section of the unfamiliar room through gloopy blackness. Her right eye, she guessed, was totally glued shut with mascara. Her eyelid certainly didn't have the strength to lift itself. It wasn't just her eyelid, the rest of her body felt odd, exhausted, unable or unwilling to communicate with her brain. She tried to move her head backward slightly to take in more of the room, but her neck just gave her a thump of pain. She could see the stitching on the quilt seam in super close up but couldn't quite get her eye to focus properly on it.

She closed her eye again. Then she was gone. Dropping heavily back into her black pit. Her body twitched with bad dreams. Dreams she'd be glad she would never remember. The fine hair on her back and arms stood on end from the chill in the room. It was April and the windows in the room were open, the curtains were pulled slightly back allowing some spring sunshine to flood in and shedding light on the other side of the bed Janet was in.

Two hours passed by and a message alert sounded as one of the phones in the room received its sixteenth text message of the morning. A few seconds after, Janet's eye opened slightly again. This time her head was a little lighter, her muscles a touch stronger for extra sleep. She thought she knew now why her vision was so heavy with blackness, she must have a ton of mascara on, plus falsies. Her left eye still remained steadfastly shut, but her right eye opened a little wider. She was in a hotel bedroom, a nice one. She could see a huge window which was floor to ceiling with grand dark red drapes. It was all slightly out of focus. She was laid on her left side with her left arm behind her, it was completely dead; the blood cut off by the angle of her shoulder. She brought her right leg forward and pushed herself backwards over her left arm onto her back. It freed up her dead arm. The movement forced an involuntary grimace from her lips. Her numb arm lay at her side now, but she couldn't move it. Seconds later, it filled with intense pins and needles as the blood began to flow back into it. She could literally feel the life running back into her dead arm and along with it, warmth and sensation. She lay for a while longer. She could move her fingers again.

Above her a huge chandelier glistened in the sunlight. A pair of knickers were dangling from it. They looked very much like her knickers. That was weird. She tried to clear her mind and think about where she was and what she had been doing. There was nothing, but she felt that maybe she wasn't in London where she lived. She wasn't sure why it felt different. Something to do with the light or the temperature of the air flowing through the curtains perhaps?

She was effectively blind in her whole right hand vision, but she studied her delicate ivory pants from her half open left eye. There was something not quite right about her knickers. They seemed to be torn at the sides, as if she or someone had ripped them from her. She felt her hip with her functioning right hand and found a sore a patch on her hip bone. Come to think of it, she was very tender. As though she'd been with a man who'd been pretty rough with her. She shut her open eye once more, but not to sleep, to think. To focus. She tried to force her mind to recall what she'd been doing last night, where she was, who she was with. Nothing. Whatever happened was now wiped.

Once enough blood had streamed back into her arm, she lifted it to her right eye to give her eye lid a helping hand to open. The mascara on her lashes had stuck fast, but her eye was also sore and scabbed. Like it was bloodied and the blood had mixed with the mascara to create a strange glue. Being as gentle as she could with her newly working hand, she peeled her eye lids apart and blinked a few times until her vision started to clear. It improved, but was still a little fuzzy. She moved her head to the left and saw more of her clothes around the room. Her dress was slung over a chair. Her phone lay on the floor. She looked the other way and a man was staring back at her. She started to scream but somehow she was still sharply inhaling at the point she should have been exhaling and nothing came out. She sat up and groaned as her stomach muscles complained. Pushing herself away from the man. He didn't move and continued to stare in a way which made her skin crawl. She reached out to him, then pulled her hand back. She didn't really know what she was going to do with her hand.

"Hello," she croaked, cleared her throat and then "are you okay? Hello." But she felt stupid as the words passed her lips, this guy was not responding and yet his eyes were wide open. He was definitely *not* okay. She reached out again, this time placing her hand in front of his mouth to feel if there was some breath. Held it here for a few seconds. Nothing. Then warily touched the skin on his shoulder with one out stretched finger and the coldness confirmed his lack of life. His skin could have been the leather on a handbag. The elasticity had gone. She'd been sleeping (or unconscious) next to a dead fucking man for God's sake. He continued to stare, now at her hand which propped her up. She found herself breathing heavily and had to tell herself to keep calm.

He looked Italian to her, but she didn't recognise him. As far as she could remember, she'd never laid eyes on him before, but here he was, naked and dead in a hotel room next to her. It suggested that something must have gone on between them last night. Whoever he was, he obviously worked out. He had a great body. He was handsome with short, dark hair, blue eyes and thick set eyebrows. He was clean shaven and wore a silver ring. This was so fucked up. He was on his back and there were no obvious signs as to what had happened to him. She tried not to and knew she shouldn't but she sneaked a look at the dead guys junk. It raised one of her eyebrows and she hated herself for that.

'Dead man in the room Janet, hello!?' She would try not to look at him any more.

She turned away from him, moved to the side of the bed and stuck her head in her hands. She ran her fingers through her hair, but it was matted with... oh, fuck knows what. Her bag was on the floor, upside down and its contents spread around. Makeup, cigarettes, money, cards, a hairbrush, plus a ton of other crap. There was a broken glass and a bottle of champagne on its side and a patch of the plush deep red carpet was wet underneath. Further around the room, a lamp hung off a table, still plugged in and hanging by its cord. It was still on and shone downward onto the carpet where it lit up more broken glass.

A mobile phone message alert sounded behind her. It wasn't hers and it sounded a long way off to her. There was another sound masking it, but she wasn't sure what it was, perhaps a shower or fountain. Definitely running water. She grabbed the sheet and put it around her shoulders. Suddenly very aware she was totally naked and even though, there was no one else (alive) in the room, it was not a good feeling. She didn't even know where she was. She went to stand up, but needed to help herself up with her hands. Like her legs were made from jelly. It was the same feeling she got two days after her trainer made her do his leg circuit. Her vision went blindingly bright for a few seconds and she thought she may faint, so she grabbed at the dressing table. She held herself there for a few seconds until it passed. Her focus regained, she took a few steps. Avoiding the broken glass, she walked around to the foot of the bed and took another look at the handsome naked man on it, but from this angle he still looked as unfamiliar as before.

There was a quiet knock on the door. It took a good five seconds for Janet to compute what the noise could be. Another two seconds for her to figure that she was in a room with a corpse and that it was probably best for whoever it was not to come in. She half ran, half limped to the door and opened it a few inches. She peeped around and looked who was knocking. It was a cleaner.

"Could you come back later?" Then she realised that wasn't a great idea either. "In fact, much later. In fact, I don't think we'll need any cleaning today at all."

"Ok, that's fine" The cleaner, who was Scottish and was about 16 years old, looked up at Janet with very worried eyes. "Are you okay? Do you need me to get you a doctor?" She had a husky Glaswegian accent that didn't fit her face. Janet computed what she had said for a few seconds. "What? No, no, don't worry." She touched her hand to her eye instinctively. "I'm absolutely fine. Just a rough night. Bumped myself in the dark. Thanks." She gave her her most calming smile. The cleaner lingered as she closed the door. Her eye was very sore. She didn't like the look in the girl's eyes and thought that it could spell trouble. She might go to tell her manager.

Janet grabbed the 'Do not disturb' sign from the inner door handle and transferred it to the outer door sneaking a quick look around, but the young cleaner was gone. Probably in another room now.

If the cleaner (or anyone) saw the inside of this bedroom with her in it, it could be the end of her life as she knew it probably. How would she explain the scene? 'Oh, I can't remember anything - I just blacked out.' Likely story.

She went to the bathroom. There was more broken glass in the doorway, so she stuck her shoes on and then crunched over glass to the mirror. The hot tap was running and the mirror was steamed up. She turned that tap off and wiped the mirror until a small patch revealed her face. Her eye was a dark reddish brown and her eyelid was swelled up and shiny. It looked sore. It was sore. Her hair was all over, but looked very different to how it normally did after a night out, like it had started off a different style to her normal style. She had dark grey eye shadow above her eyes and a ton of blusher. She never put so much make up on. She actually looked hot, in a slutty, trashy way. The black eye troubled her. Had the dead guy hit her or was she so drunk she'd fallen or had she been drugged maybe?

She needed to rest her wobbly legs again and sat down heavily on the toilet seat. She looked all around her unfamiliar surroundings. Confused and dizzy. She put her head in her hands for a second. She passed out and slumped off the side of the toilet against the wall and slid down. Fifteen minutes passed as she twitched and flinched on the bathroom floor. As she opened her tired eyes, she saw the room was on its side. She was light headed and just told herself lay down for a second. If you get up too quick, you'll go down again girl.

She studied the side of the bath and the tiles. They were spotless. Sign of a good hotel probably. Except something was not right here. The board which covered the first quarter of the tap end of the bath was slightly askew, like it had been removed and hastily put back. She reached up and pulled at the panel, it was indeed loose. She pulled a little more and it came away. She peeked around the panel and saw that stuffed into the gap was a tan leather overnight bag. She sat up. The bag filled the space completely. She stared at it for a second and looked around as if she expected someone to be watching her. Was this his she wondered or had it been here for longer than their stay? The bag was unmistakably Gucci with a red strip and two green strips running along its length. She grabbed the leather handles and pulled it out of the gap. The leather was beautifully soft and smelled wonderful. It was open and in plain view, stuffed into the bag was money. A lot of money. She pulled the sides to open it more and looked in. It was full of tightly packed bundles of twenties under a hundreds of loose ones. She took one out and fingered through it. She guessed that two hundred twenties wafted in front of her face. That made £4,000 in each bundle. She looked at the contents of the bag again. She guessed there must be at least a million and a half or possibly two here. Maybe a bit more. On top of the money was a dark grey gun with a black handle and a car key. She picked up the gun by the barrel, ensuring her fingers stayed clear of the trigger. She thought it would be heavy but was still surprised how solid it felt in her hand. It had COLT SUPER .38 AUTOMATIC across the barrel and a rearing horse (a Colt she guessed) protruded from under her fingers. She placed it back into the bag and then picked up the car key. It was a single black oblong with two buttons. Lock and unlock. Rather than a horse, this had a angry looking bull on it, but other than that, it looked the same as her car key. She pushed it back in for now.

She went back and looked around the wreck of a hotel room for clues as to where the hell she was, but non jumped immediately out at her. Usually you get a hotel information pack which would have told her, but she couldn't see one. She turned the TV on to see if that would help in any way. Maybe it would tell her what day it was at least. There were just ads on, no volume and she couldn't see the remote control.

A phone received another message. She found the phone on the floor and picked it up. On the lock screen, it said there were 12 missed calls, 6 voice messages and 16 text messages. It also said there were a heap of Facebook alerts and a Tweet. The guy had missed calls from several people. She pressed the button which dialled voice mail and listened to some of the messages. An agitated man was saying how they were at their lock up and asked what Joseph's E.T.A. was. So she knew his name now. The second sounded more concerned and said to get in touch if there were any problems. The third simply said 'Call me back Joseph'. The fourth was a different guy and he sounded really pissed off and babbled something about double crossing and to come clean. The fifth and sixth messages were the same guy sounding even more angry and upset and had other people in the background shouting at the same time.

She went to sit on the bed. Then after a second, sat herself down on the floor. It felt wrong to sit on the bed with the dead guy. Sorry, with Joseph. She looked at the text messages and they ran roughly the same as the voice messages. Starting out calm and enquiring as to the whereabouts of the owner of the phone (Joseph) and descended into vicious threats of violence. The final one said simply -

wen I find u I goin to mince u up
an put you in sausages an feed
u 2 yer mother. And my dogs

That made a shiver run through Janet's body. She guessed that this definitely had to do with the bag of cash and the gun. The phone started to ring again. Carl calling. Not good. She thought it best to not answer this time. After thirty seconds, it rang out. Carl didn't bother to leave a message this time. Then, shortly after that, Charlie called. Again, she let it ring out. She turned the volume down. There had been some text messages from Charlie. He seemed to have a more conciliatory tone than Carl.

Somewhere in the room her phone rang loudly and she jumped out of her skin, so much so she let out a mini scream. She scrabbled through the mess on the floor and located her phone next to a fat wallet. The face of a man showed on the screen and she recognised him. He was her ex. Gary. She couldn't speak to him in this state, she needed to figure out what was going on and where she was before she could speak to anyone from her life. She also had a lot of missed calls and texts. Ten in all. She'd listen to them later. She put the phone back on the floor next to the dead guy's.

She picked up the fat wallet from the floor and looked though it. There was a lot of cash. No surprise there. No credit cards, but a driving license. The driving license of Joseph Stocksbridge. She figured out his age was 32. His address was listed as Islington in London. A car park ticket for the THE 1862 HOTEL, GLASGOW. She went to the window and peeked around the curtain. She was surrounded by Georgian buildings, she must be in the middle of the city. She put the ticket and the wallet into her handbag.

She took another look at Joseph and a little shiver passed through her body. She squeezed her eyes shut and willed herself to think, to get her mind moving, but it was just like thick syrup in there. This was just not Janet. Janet didn't get into situations with men she didn't know in hotel rooms with bags of cash and guns.

She lived in London and worked in banking. She was successful in what she did. She worked hard. Long hours and didn't take all her holidays. She never really spoke about this sort of stuff to her friends, but she was really good at her job and was head hunted recently because she had performed so well. She earned a good salary but then she spent too much of it on clothes and handbags and shoes and holidays and anything else she could throw her credit card at. New phones as she seemed to be very good at losing them or smashing them. Smart phones were surprisingly expensive. As was her TT convertible. The list was long. Yes, spending was her little weakness. Spending; not getting into tricky situations with guys that ended up in hotel rooms with them dead.

She slumped back down against the foot of the bed and pushed her head back against the bed in anger. She pushed so hard, her head touched Joseph's foot and she jumped back up letting out a sickly yelp. She grabbed her bag and told herself she needed to get out of the room. She picked up her phone and shoved it into her bag and closed it. Screw the money, screw him and whatever had been happening, she needed this to end. She picked her dress up from the floor and threw it on over her head and zipped it up at the side. She recognised the dress, but couldn't remember where she'd bought it. She vaguely remembered the purchase. The dress was very simple, black with a halter neck and an attached slim red leather belt. The label said Donna Karen. She looked around to see if she had any other clothes but couldn't see anything. She went to take a look in the wardrobe, but it was totally empty.

"Get out of this room Janet." She looked over at the bed again. "Now!"

She went to the door and saw the key card in a slot next to the door. She took it out and slipped it in her bag. She took another look around the room, she went to the bathroom to check in there. The steam had subsided now. The bag sat half hanging out of the gap under the bath. Open and overflowing with cash. This seemed wrong. If she left the room as it was, someone was going to get this cash. She reached in and took the black car key and put it in her bag. It wasn't her money, she was sure of that. She couldn't remember what had happened in this hotel room last night, but she had not robbed a bank. She worked in a bank. She didn't enjoy it anymore, but she hadn't robbed it.

Someone was going to get their hands on this cash however. Someone was going to stick all this money into an off shore bank somewhere and live off it and not work another day in their life if they so wished. They'd be going and buying flash cars, taking gorgeous holidays to faraway and exotic places like the Maldives and Mauritius and the Bahamas. They'd be buying beautiful clothes and eating in the finest restaurants and they'd be smug about it all. And whilst they were doing this, what would she be doing? She'd be going back to work in banking? Sitting in an office. Back to her credit card debts. Awful... no that was wrong, she didn't have an awful life. She had a good life. She had a good job. She had good friends. She was comfortable. But what if it could be better? What if she could live without credit card debt. What if she could travel without sticking the whole thing on her credit cards? She didn't have a bucket list as such but she had a lot of things she wanted to do and see. She wanted to visit Las Vegas, Sydney, Goa, Barbados, Miami. The list was pretty long. She wanted to go to the top of the Empire State building, see the northern lights, see a whale, climb a pyramid. Now that she started thinking, there was a ton of stuff she wanted to do but possibly would struggle to do. Especially whilst she was young. You could do this type of stuff once you'd retired and paid off your mortgage. But what if she could do it all now?

  She zipped up the bag and grabbed the handles. It was heavy. You'd expect two million quid to be heavy though. She placed the Gucci travel bag and her hand bag next to the door. She looked around the room. Did she need anything else? The room was still a mess with broken glass and a lot of stuff on the floor but this was not a time to be worried about cleaning up. There was one thing she did not want to leave here for whoever would discover him. She gently stepped up onto the empty side of the bed and grabbed her knickers from the chandelier and crumpled them into a ball. She saw his phone and picked it up. One more text message had arrived. From Carl. She dropped both items into the Gucci bag.

"As popular as ever Joe." she told him. She suddenly felt very sorry for him. She was about to leave him in this room. Alone. How long would it take for them to ignore the Do Not Disturb sign and enter the room? A fair amount must have been racked up on room service, so they wouldn't leave it so long.

"Live fast, die young and leave a good looking corpse." she said almost in passing. "Someone said that, but I think you really did it Joseph." She grabbed the sheet she had worn earlier. It was dirty, but that didn't really matter now for him and placed it over his crotch.

"That's better isn't it?"

She found herself staring at him again, breathing heavily. Her chest tight. It was time to get the hell out of here before she was discovered. She had everything but oddly was as afraid to leave as she was to stay. She opened the door and peeped around the corner. All was clear. 'Look like you belong here Janet', she told herself and off she went. Walking fast, but not too fast following the sign to the lifts. Purposeful speed. A train to catch or a meeting to get to.

She called a lift and the doors opened almost immediately announced with a bing. She walked in and placed the bag on the floor whilst she got the stuff ready. Parking ticket, cash, keys. In the vain hope she was going to exit the hotel unnoticed, she jumped as a young, scrawny lad with dark hair walked past the lift. He looked her up and down briefly, gave her a friendly smile and continued walking. The doors slid closed.

. . .

Dan scanned the hotel's public areas methodically. Floor by floor, corridor by corridor. He'd started with the ground floor and was working his way upwards. He didn't know exactly what he was looking for. Joseph, ultimately but he knew that was unlikely. He walked the full length of each corridor listening intently to see if he could hear Joseph's voice or his name mentioned perhaps, but the hotel bedrooms were well sound proofed and he could hear nothing much other than his own Adidas Superstars brushing over the plush patterned carpets. The corridors looped, so you could keep walking from the open area by the lifts and get back to the same point. As he walked back to the lifts on his loop of the 2nd floor, he heard the ding of the lifts and saw a woman entering. He speeded up to the lifts and then eased back so he gave the impression he was generally walking past. He looked in and smiled at the woman in there. She was wearing a swish black dress but otherwise, looked quite unkempt. At her feet was a distinctive tan leather bag with the green and red stripe across it. The doors swept shut before the recognition hit him, but that bag looked very much like the description he had. He stood glued to the spot watching where the lift floor indicator went, whilst taking his phone out. He dialled Carl and hit the button to call another lift.

"Yep. Tell me some good news Dan."

"I think I just spotted the bag that had the cash in." Dan came back quickly.

"Did you see Joseph?"

Dan ignored Carl's question. "It's with a woman dressed in a... black dress... and it's... hang on... about to walk out into the lobby..." A second later, the floor indicator stopped at the B. "Actually, she's gone to the underground car park. Get the car and meet me at the entrance to the car park. Be quick!"

. . .

She didn't like the fact anyone had seen her. She had a rush of adrenaline coursing through her veins now making her short of breath. She paid the ticket by the entrance to the car park. There were only a handful of cars in the car park. She took the key, pressed the unlock button and a far corner of the garage lit up orange briefly. Whatever it was, it was small and completely hidden by a black Mercedes. She walked toward the light until she found herself looking down upon what seemed like the tiniest, lowest car she'd ever seen. It was white and only seemed to be hip height. She pushed the button again just to be sure this was the right car and sure enough, the indicators doubled flashed and the locks clicked. She looked around and was happy to see no one else around. It took a moment to see how to open the car's door as the handles were almost totally flush. She got in and read 'Lamborghini' written across the dashboard with joined up golden letters. She'd heard of a Lamborghini. It was an Italian sports car. Like a Ferrari. Very expensive. What the hell she thought. She stuck the key in the dashboard and twisted. The engine exploded into life behind her and she jumped, hitting her head on the roof. She'd never heard a noise like it. She pulled the door closed and it was dulled slightly, but still ridiculously loud, like a giant, angry, gurgling animal sat behind her. She was cocooned in black leather and suede. The seats were a black suede with criss crossed white stitching making up diamonds. The steering wheel was also suede covered.

She familiarised herself with controls - wipers, indicators, lights, they all seemed very similar to her little Audi. She grabbed the gear lever which felt very odd, bare metal. She wasn't sure what gear levers were normally made of or covered in, but this felt decidedly strange and cold. She stuck the car into first gear and pushed the throttle and moved the car very gently forward, she turned left toward the exit. It was easy to drive. The doors clicked as they locked themselves.

. . .

Dan looked all around. If she was going to drive surely, she couldn't have reached her car, started it up and exited in that amount of time. He walked toward the exit. Quick but at the same time trying hard to look casual. He didn't want to spook the woman in the black dress. From behind, he heard an almighty roar of an engine which sounded like something was right behind him, but he could see nothing. He doubled back toward the noise, but then thought better of it. She would have to go to the exit. He heard the growl grow louder and he looked behind to see a low sports car coming toward him. He looked away as he didn't want the driver to see his face. Surely that couldn't be her he thought. As it slowly passed him, he saw it was a Lamborghini and yes, she was driving. Weird. Odd choice for a car for a young woman. He thought he could see the tan bag was crammed into the passenger footwell.

She must have tapped the throttle because the exhaust snarled ferociously. Then the brakes lights came on as the car reached the exit barrier. Her window slid down as she went to put her ticket into the machine. He took his chance just before the barrier went up and tried the passenger door handle. If it was open he would just grab the bag. No questions asked, but it was locked. Damn. Clever girl.

. . .

The man reached the passenger side of the car as she was putting the ticket into the machine. She looked around to see him looking in. "C,mon, come on." she told the machine under her breath, it pulled the ticket in, pushed it out and then swallowed it completely.

"Nice car darling." the man said to her through the window. "What sort of car is it?"

She ignored him and stared at the barrier. He knocked on the window to try to get her attention. He'd definitely got her attention, but she was not going look at him. The barrier finally went up after what felt like a long, dragging minute but was just a few seconds. She turned briefly, blew him a kiss and set off to the left down the one way street. It had been the guy that walked past the lift which was odd that he would then be down in the car park when he was supposedly walking off toward one of the bedrooms two minutes before. She watched in the rear view mirror to see the man get into a Mercedes that pulled up from high speed. This was not good. This definitely seemed like it was bad. She took a left and then a right and then a left, but they stayed in touch and suddenly were right up behind her. Play it cool, she told herself, but this was not a coincidence. No way.

She pulled up at a T junction and waited for a gap in the traffic. She didn't go when she could have. She waited for almost two minutes, glancing at the people in the car behind her. The guy driving was huge and bald and looked pretty scary. She did not want to have to deal with him. A small gap came up and just before the first of a long line of cars, she floored the Lambo and flew off up the street leaving them stuck and awaiting a space to get out. She kept her eye on the traffic behind but didn't see them pull out. Half a mile down the road, she turned right and pulled up at a crossroads. Looked left and right and pushed on the throttle; the car howled straight ahead and every one stopped and turned to look around at the source of the howl. She'd better take it easy, this was the most outrageous car and she was going to get stopped by the police at this rate. Not a good move considering her current position. She eased off the throttle and took the pace right down.

Things were still fuzzy. She drove toward the edge of Glasgow vaguely aware she was following signs for Edinburgh. As she got toward the open road, she wound the driver's and passengers's windows down and let air rip through the car. She breathed deeply for the first time today. Fresh air after the confined atmosphere in the hotel room with its dead occupant felt invigorating and liberating. It tussled her hair around her face and out of the window as if she stood atop a huge cliff. It would have looked crazy to anyone who saw, but the roads were dead. With the noise of the engine, it was deafening, but it was starting to blow away the fuzziness. She could just hear her phone ringing above the cacophony, but still was in no mood to talk to anyone. What would she say? She didn't know why she was in Glasgow, how she got there, why she was with a dead guy and who the dead guy was. She drove for a short while following signs on a kind of auto-pilot. Before she knew it, she was on the M8 motorway. All she could remember for the last 10 minutes or so was looking at her blackened eye in the mirror and wondering if and how she could cover it with makeup. She stuck to the middle lane and tried to be as inconspicuous as it was possible to be in a white Lamborghini. At least, she didn't look like the typical type of person who would steal a car like this. She drifted along with the ambient traffic, passed a traffic police car driving at about 60mph in the slow lane and it made her panic. She needed to get off the motorway. Taking the next exit (after indicating precisely), she drove south along country roads until she hit the A71 and picked up signs for Edinburgh again (21 miles).

Hitting the countryside, the roads were empty, she pushed her foot down and the car shrieked forward toward Edinburgh. The car oozed raw power and she loved it. No police car could keep up with her if she decided she wanted to get away from them. She looked at the speedometer and it read 130mph. Way faster than she'd ever been in a car and yet she felt a sense of control over this unlike she currently had over her the rest of her life. She eased off the throttle and dabbed the brakes gently until the speedometer came back to read 60mph (the national speed limit, she reminded herself) and tootled onward. Had she left any clues behind? She was definitely in danger as she was involved with Joseph (somehow) and some bad people were after him, plus she'd nabbed the cash. She didn't think she'd left any clues should the police get involved. She was driving a huge great clue, but that was a different matter somehow.

As she drifted along the deserted roads, a fragment of a snippet of dream came to her. She was with a stranger, who could have been Joseph, in an unknown place. They were on their way somewhere, she wasn't sure where, but they were at the sea, yes on a cliff. It was incredibly windy there as it was in the car right now. Perhaps this is what brought the dream back to her. In fact, the place felt strangely familiar. Not like it was an actual place she had been but like it had featured in many of her dreams, a place she often went. It felt dangerous, but exciting and fun at the same time. Unlike many dreams where there seemed to be frustration or anxiety, this was a good place. He was laughing at her, but in a good way like she was making him laugh. Off in the sea, something was moving very fast like a powerful boat, leaving a jet stream of white water behind it. The boat was on its way to the same place that they were going. It seemed to be a place further along the coast, not a town but some type of a craggy bluff that stuck out into an ultraviolet ocean. They saw the boat arrive at the bluff, but they were still a way off. That was as much as she could remember for now. She tried to replay the chapter in her mind, but she could not remember anything before or after this walking along the cliff.

She jumped as a blue hatchback full of young lads overtook peeping the horn as they were alongside. They pulled in sharply in front of her and the car lolled from side to side on its suspension under its heavy load of testosterone fuelled occupants. The two teenagers in the back looked back through the rear window and were laughing like this was the funniest thing they'd ever seen. It brought her back from her dream and she focused once again on the road. I'll show you little dick heads she thought. She scanned the road ahead. It was clear for half a mile or so. She dropped the car from sixth to third gear, re-gripped the suede covered wheel hard and pushed down on the accelerator, not flat to the floor but enough to make the car jump, leap and howl forward past the teen filled Honda. They wanted to race and the driver also dropped several gears and floored his charge, however it wasn't really a fair fight in power or weight. Janet's white sports car flew up the road; spitting out white lines at the Honda Civic as she put an ever increasing chunk of space between them.

What was wrong with her, she'd never driven like this in her life had she? She had never overtaken anything before. It was addictive though. As she crested the next hill to which the boys had not yet begun climbing, a wide grin broke out. Then out of nowhere - chevrons and sharp corner. She was going far too fast. She'd never make it. She hit the brakes hard whilst steering into the corner. Any other car would have gone straight ahead on the corner and through the wall into the field. But the white sports car seemed to grip down onto the road with all its wheels and flew round the right hander with a screech of tyres. She felt she could have hit the corner even faster and the car would still have flown around it. Lapping it up. Almost like it was enjoying the challenge. It filled her with even more gusto. She adjusted her rear view mirror, so she could see how far back they were but they were out of view, probably at the bottom of the hill still. She came off the brake and squeezed the accelerator once again. As the speed increased, so did the width of the grin across her face.

"Bye bye little boys. Don't mess with girls in white" she looked over at the wording on the glovebox and reminded herself, "Lamborghinis."

Millions of pin pricks of stars cut into the sheet of twilight that was descending over her. Ahead of her lay Edinburgh where an ambient orange glow rose above the city. As she left the country side behind her, the pin pricks became fewer and fewer. Once into the slower traffic of Edinburgh, she was aware of people staring whenever she was at traffic lights. They were alerted to the car by the exhaust's popping and backfiring as she slowed (she wasn't sure if this was something it was supposed to do or if there was a problem). Then the deep bass burbling noise that counted for this car's 'tick over' would cause people to crane their necks to see who was driving such an outrageous car. Just Janet, a bank worker from London. She came into the city through Morningside which seemed lovely and vaguely familiar. She had been in Edinburgh before but wasn't sure if she had been in this part of the city.

What was she going to do once she arrived at her destination? She needed to regroup, get herself together. She also needed somewhere to stay. She opened her maps app on her phone and saw a lot of hotels, but a 5 Star one just ahead looked about right. There was no need to worry about expense considering the bag next to her.

She saw Edinburgh Castle lit up in the early evening dusk. As she passed it on her right, she saw the imposing looking hotel on her left hand side which corresponded with her phone's navigation and swept the car around to its front. The Caledonian. She killed the engine then rummaged in her bag for her sunglasses. She looked like (and was) a beaten women currently and it did not suit her. A smart looking man with a grey tartan kilt came and opened her car door. He also offered his hand to help her out of the car which she took as she was sat so low down. Once out, he reached in and got her her bags from the passenger seat and place them on a trolley. This made her panic slightly, but she told herself to be cool.

"Do you have any other bags to bring in Madam?" he asked.

"No, that's it thanks."

"OK, just let reception know when you need your car back and we'll bring it around for you." A group of teenagers stopped to look at her car and try to see what it was like inside. She was used to this type of attention now. One of the teenagers said 'nice Lambo' Missis'. She gave him the slightest, coolest smile possible and turned away. The valet's assistant turned the key and the cars engine shouted its angry growl. The teenagers were visibly shocked and recoiled.

She ignored them and entered the hotel trying to look like the sort of woman who turns up places in a white Lamborghini. And not doing a bad job (she secretly thought). At reception, she told them she needed a room and after a few questions about her 'needs' was offered a 'Queen Classic' double room with breakfast. She looked at the bag on the trolley for a second and turned back to the receptionist.

"Do you have something more like a suite?" She asked.

"Of course madam." The receptionist looked again at the computer screen and scrolled downwards. "I have a one Queen suite left." There was no mention of cost, but Janet didn't care. It had been a stressful day and she needed space (and time) to recuperate. She enquired about room service and was informed there would be a menu in her room (as well as a mini bar) and to dial 0 for service.

She sauntered away from the reception followed by the porter. She dropped the key into her hand bag and stuck her head into the bar area which was vast and busy with guests taking an early evening drink or snack. She liked this hotel much more than her previous residence. A few people looked over toward her direction, but generally she could blend in here in her new guise as high flying Janet. She realised she was the only person wearing sunglasses and it was indoors and it was dusk, but what the hell, she drove a fucking Lamborghini.

She continued on her way to the room with the porter. After he left, she immediately put the DO NOT DISTURB sign on the outer handle as she felt she would need a good, undisturbed lie in in the morning. Without looking at the menu, she rang 0 and asked for a Club sandwich, fries, mayo and a large bottle of sparkling water. She also asked for a carafe of Pinot Grigio. She was asked if she would like a newspaper delivered to her room in the morning and the man on the end of the line seemed a little surprised as she ordered 'the Times, Independent, Mail, Guardian and the Sun, oh and the Scotsman'.

By the time she was finishing her snack (which was huge), her eyes had become weary and sore, especially her blackened eye. She took a look at it in the mirror. It had gone a more yellowish colour now. She guzzled all the water from the bottle in an attempt to flush out her system of the drink and whatever else was in there muddling her up. Her wine was untouched and would remain that way.

"How did you get involved in this?" she asked her reflection. What was going on in that room with that man Janet? she thought and gently touched the bruising and inflammation around her eye. She laid on the bed and shut her eyes. She was tired beyond belief. What had she done to her body to be this tired at this time of night? She had't realised how sore her eyes had been until just now. The soreness you get when you've been up all night. The last time her eyes felt this way was when she'd been to Berlin with friends and they'd been to a club called Panorama? Panoramic? And they'd been there from 2am on the Sunday morning until midday on the Monday. She remembered coming out into the bright daylight and her eyes felt like they had salt rubbed into them. She flicked off the TV and the lights apart from a small reading spotlight which stuck out of the wall above her bedside table. The subdued lighting helped her relax. Her eyes felt much easier in this light.

Half sleeping, half awake. She remembered she was in a bar in... Edinburgh perhaps and someone bought her a drink. She had to find him, he was at the back of the bar on his own. She wandered through the bar with the glass of champagne and he was there. It was Joseph, but alive. Not dead and naked next to her on a bed. They talked and he was funny she remembered. Then she was gone. Fast asleep.

TWO

Two days before

They'd been tracking the painting for a while. It was a painting Joseph knew well. He didn't particularly like it, so wasn't too worried about the fact once he sold it on, it would disappear from public view for ever more. The art world was particularly excited about this art sale taking place in London as Rothko's work had been fetching record breaking figures over the last decade or so. Most Rothkos sold in the US though, he had after all been a US based artist and that's where most of his art subsequently ended up and came up for sale.

Joseph's contact, Matthew Weiss, was a private art collector whose family had an amazing collection of modern art, the bulk of it bought at art auctions around the world usually from up and coming artists. He'd been backed by his father in the 1970s and '80s as his father allowed him to use his money to buy and sell art on the proviso that he made a profit and found some interesting and valuable pieces for him. It turned out he had one of the best eyes for art in the business and had rewarded his father with excellent dividends buying art from artists whose art was increasing in value and selling their art as their value peaked. His father knew nothing of the art world other than he liked to make money from it. Their father and son relationship blossomed during this period of profit as he bought, kept briefly and sold art from Lichtenstein, Warhol, Wassermann among others.

The Weiss family had not been a close one. Victor Weiss had been a busy business man who rarely made it home through the week; mainly, this was attributed to running a business with offices in three distant cities across Europe and being a hopeless adulterer with a string of long term affairs which not surprisingly coincided geographically with his European offices. Carol Ann Weiss had been a society girl and was now a society lady, if such a thing existed, whose main role in life was holding parties, lunches and dinner dances with her girlfriends. Matthew had been sent away to boarding school from an early age and therefore had a fairly weak bond with his parents, in fact he resented them very strongly up until the age of 11 when he at least started to make friends and partly enjoy school. He felt a closer bond with his teachers and his housemistress, Miss Gemma, than with his parents. The bond that came from the business arrangement between father and son had therefore been very welcome and they came to love the time spent exploring their world of art.

Their relationship soured badly when Matthew sold Marcus Yakovlevich Rothkowitz's 'Untitled (Green on Grey)' from 1970. The painting was a simple green block on a grey background. He had bought the painting from a collector in a private sale and his father had held on to it and indeed cherished it in his collection for 15 years before Matthew advised selling it in New York. Even though he made a handsome profit of £1.5 million at the time, almost immediately after the sale, Rothko's work began fetching record breaking sums at auction. Victor Weiss berated his son for what he called 'the worst timed art sale in history'. Victor

Weiss had not cut his son off totally, but their relationship had regressed to what it was before, nothing more than a business arrangement. The invites to spend time at the weekends with his father on the golf course or the yacht or fishing at father's highland retreat had disappeared into thin air. His father had a tone with Matthew which cut deep. It played heavily on his mind. That damned painting.

The relatively unknown Rothko was likely to sell for £10 to £15 million and Matthew wanted the piece back. However, he didn't want to pay upwards of £10 million, he wanted it for a fraction of that. He was prepared to pay Joseph £2.5 million for it and he wanted Joseph to get it by any means after the auction. The only catch was that if the piece made less than £12.5M, the deal was off. It was always going to make way more than that though. The artwork was bought by an overseas telephone bidder. In the end, the bidding went to £16.7M which, as the auctioneer pointed out, reflected how rarely this artist's work came up for sale nowadays.

Of course, Matthew's father was all above board so he couldn't give the stolen piece back to his father, it had become a point of principle but in some odd part of his mind he daydreamed he would have liked to hang on to the Rothko and reveal it his father on his death bed. His father's smile returning as he held out his arms once more to embrace his son.

The reality was vastly different however. He did not have £2.5M 'spare'. He would be selling on the Rothko immediately and for a hefty profit. He had a private collector to whom he had passed several pieces of art that could not go through 'public' channels. The collector knew the score of course; he had his known collection and then he had his private collection amongst which there were several infamous works of art. Matthew also had other warm leads to some interesting pieces and one very hot lead to an extremely valuable piece. He would raise this with Joseph down the line. For now, he just needed to complete on this particular Rothko transaction. One thing at a time.

It was to make its way back over the Atlantic in the hold of a Virgin Atlantic plane from Heathrow. However, it would not actually get to the plane. In fact it would not even make it into the secure courier's van. It would make it into *a* secure couriers van however.

They had been unsure of some of the technical details of how the art courier worked, so five days earlier, they'd had a dry run. They had prepped a reproduction Warhol self portrait. It was unframed and covered in tissue paper and clipped flat in its A0 case. Arrangements had been made with their account handler at CST Couriers for pick up over the phone and then confirmed by email. CST Couriers prided themselves on being a modern, low carbon, paper-less company. This all played perfectly into the hands of Joseph and his little crew, especially in conjunction with the auction houses' ineptitude in modernising themselves technically.

Their armoured van turned up at 10,30am on the dot. Their vans were unmissable in bright red. The C and T in blue and the S in white emblazoned across a light blue shield that doubled as a padlock. The van was spotless as were the three men who arrived with it. One driver stayed put in the van and the other two came to the door of the office space they had rented. The men were well turned out and their shirts mimicked the van in bright red with the logo embroidered on the left chest pocket and the company's brand line across their backs - 'YOUR TRUST IN OUR HANDS'.

On arrival, they asked Joseph to confirm the collection reference number for security, adding it was on the email confirmation. He pulled up the email on his phone. They produced a tablet computer with a confirmation screen with the same number on. He was given a stylus and asked to sign in a box on the tablets screen. It all seemed secure. It wasn't. They were told they would be able to track the artwork to its delivery address from a link that would be emailed to them shortly. The men lifted the packed artwork carefully and carried it to the van where it was loaded and secured against the inside side wall. They said the artwork was in safe hands before they started up the engine and off they went.

An email duly arrived to confirm the artwork had been picked up, the time and location. A link took Joseph to a page on CST's website which showed the current location of the package.

Meanwhile, Carl and Dan were in Edinburgh for a few nights to find a lockup where they could lay low after the robbery. They wanted somewhere secluded and capable of holding two cars as well as being a place they could hide out for a while if needed. They bought the Edinburgh Evening News and scanned the classified ads for storage space. They looked at a few different places but this was the best in terms of comfort and seclusion. They may need to stay here for up to a month in the unlikely event the heat was on them.

The landlord, a man of around eighty with outrageous eyebrows and giant ears pulled the sliding doors back with surprising strength. He showed them the space and pointed out the toilet which was a bit grim, but would be useful. He asked a few questions about what they wanted the storage space for - cars (not a lie). He accepted this and told them the price per month and his terms. Three months up front in cash.

He'd only accept payment in cash and would arrange to meet them in person after the three months to extend the arrangement. This all suited them down to the ground. No paper trails. He gave them two sets of keys and informed them anything they stored here would need to be covered by their own insurance.

Happy with the lock up, they set off to Stirling where they planned to bag themselves a few cars. Joseph had instructed them to get some fast but inconspicuous cars. They wanted something modern and reliable and Carl had some Mercs' or Audis in mind. They had done their homework and knew the areas of the town to target. This is where Dan, who at a slight 5 foot and 4 inches was very well suited to stealing cars. And the way to steal cars in a day and age of immobilisers, alarms and deadlocks was to - not steal cars. You would struggle with a modern car to get into it, if you did get in, it would alert everyone within 200 yards within seconds and if you could stop that, you'd never get the engine started by traditional 'hot wiring'. No, the way to steal cars was to steal the keys. This way, there was no breaking of glass, you simply walked up to the car, blipped the key, started the engine and drove off as if you owned it; which you now did. Dan was very good at the 'sneak in'. Follow someone home in the car of your choice, allow them a little time to get in and get settled down for the night, then stealthily get in and grab the keys (usually from the hall or kitchen). Nothing else, just the keys.

First up, an old guy of about fifty in a Merc' E350 Sport in black. They followed him at a distance toward the countryside on the edge of town where he pulled onto the gravelled drive of a detached converted stable. He wandered around the side and into a door near the back as they slowly drove past and pulled up. Carl killed the lights and Dan slunk out.

"I could be a while" were his parting words. "Go a bit further up the road and keep the engine going just in case."

It could be tricky with the gravelled drive and the noise it would make but Dan knew what he was doing. Carl moved about a hundred yards further up the road and angled his rear view mirror to get the best view of the driveway of the target house. Time ticked away and Carl started to think it was going to be too tricky and Dan wasn't going to get a chance, but he was just biding his time. It was a clear but cold January evening and all the lights were on in the house making it very easy for Dan to see exactly what was going on. To make sure he wasn't going to waste his time, he so so gently tried the handle on the side door. It was unlocked.

Dan was just being thorough. He was noting all the people in the house firstly and then trying to figure out what everyone was doing and where they were doing it. This was far from a typical house set up though. The driver had come in and was straight into the kitchen and started cooking. The woman who was probably his wife was in the living room watching Dog the Bounty Hunter (trashy bitch) Dan thought. Upstairs, there were lights on in one bedroom and the bathroom. Dan understood the layout of the house now and thought there were probably four people home. He sat tight and continued to observe the household activity. He worked out that if the family were to eat together, they would more than likely eat at a table which was adjoined to the living room. The man he followed home was splitting his time between cooking and setting the table.

Fifteen minutes later, four people were sat at the table. Daddy, mummy, son and daughter. Aww, the perfect little family Dan thought. Soon to be lightened of their ride. He was no different to the kids around that table and yet he'd never had this a single time in his life. Some kids get brilliant families and some just end up with scum bags. Time to take his chance. The father had been back to the kitchen once to get what looked like butter. They chatted and seemed happy.

Quiet as a mouse, Dan opened the door, walked in quickly looked around. There were no keys in the small, dark hall, he walked further down toward the kitchen and without entering looked around. There were several bunches of keys across the kitchen in a bowl along with a light bulb and lots of general house junk. The chunky black Mercedes key stood out from the other keys in the bowl. Dan calmly tip toed across the kitchen, picked up the bunch with the Merc' key ensuring he made no sound and walked back to the door. He gently snook back out and just gave things a second to settle and make sure no one had heard or was following him out.

All clear, he blipped the car got in, stuck the key into the dashboard, depressed the brake pedal and pushed the illuminated Start button. The car was auto, so he stuck his left foot out of the way and engaged reverse. He immediately backed the car out and planted his foot to the accelerator, flashing Carl as he moved off at speed. The now single car family heard nothing and would remain unaware of their loss until midnight when they went to lock the door and call the cat in.

The night after was a similar set up. A detached house on the edge of town, out toward the countryside. It was dark, there were few streetlights around and they'd selected another German car, this time a smaller but faster Audi RS4 estate. Black and two years old. Dan checked the door had been left open and now looked through the windows and was going through his checks, logging who was home, what they were up to and where. This time, it was a single bloke and a teenage son. They were both in the living room playing on a racing game, flying along a city highway which fronted onto an ocean. They were totally engrossed. Dan waited for the current game to finish, the dad got up and left the room. Dan shifted his position so he could see the kitchen. All the time ensuring he remained in the shadows in case any neighbours should look out. The man got some drinks and stuck something into the oven. Looked like a couple of ready meals. He took two cans of coke back into the room and resumed his place on the sofa. A game was restarted and this was now Dan's time. He opened the door being careful to do it slowly so that there was no sudden change in the air pressure in the house that might move internal doors. He quickly discounted that the keys could be in the long hallway. To get to the kitchen, he had to pass the living room, but they faced the opposite direction. He glanced at them, move quickly past and was at the door to the kitchen which was a little further from the entry door than he hoped. Eyes darted around the work surfaces, but no sign. He couldn't have them in his pocket surely? He went to the cupboards and opened them carefully to see if they were possibly hung up in one. This was taking too long. He'd been in the house for a minute which was way longer than he wanted to take, but could hear the continuing sound of engines roaring in the background. They had paused the game previously if either of the two had got up to leave the room.

  Meanwhile outside, Carl watched as another car pulled up into the drive. He grabbed for his phone to text Dan but had no signal. He got out of the car, went in the boot for his balaclava and a piece of lead pipe and started toward the house at a brisk walk.

Inside the house, Dan heard the front door go and had no choice now, but to go further into the house into a darkened utility room. There was a gap where a washing machine or dryer should be under a worktop and Dan got into the gap and tucked himself into the corner as far as he possibly could. He didn't know who was now home, but he was too slight to take the man and his son on, let alone someone else. He had a knife, but really didn't want to start using that. This was supposed to be low risk. He heard the latest arrival walking into the kitchen and tried to figure what was going on. It sounded like shopping bags being unpacked, accompanied by whistling. It was a woman's whistling which was the best he could hope for. His ears picked up on a bunch of keys being dropped into something pot, either a bowl or something similar.

He stayed put for now whilst Carl watched (helplessly) from the dark shadows at the side of the house. There was lot's of activity in the kitchen now, it sounded like all three were in there chatting and laughing. People were rattling cutlery out of drawers and clanging plates out of cupboards. He would wait for them to go and eat, so he sat tight and hoped that no one would come into the utility room. After a while the kitchen became quiet once more and it sounded like they were all in the living room, they probably wouldn't be staring at a TV screen and away from the door to the hallway as they had when he came in, but the utility room led outside and there was a key in the door, so he could make his exit here once he had the car keys.

He went back to the kitchen and saw a pot hen on the worktop, something you kept eggs in he guessed. It was pretty much the only thing that could have made the noise he heard. He gently lifted the top off and there were several bunches of keys. He took the bunch attached to the Audi key. He was going to be ok after all. He started for the utility door, but was unaware Basil, family cat, was sat behind him waiting to be fed and his first step was straight onto Basil's paw. He was a big cat and made a funny noise. Half meow, half screech. Not good. He needed to act quickly. He went for the back door as he heard stirring in the living room. 'Basil's fighting again' the woman said. He pulled the door to the utility room closed behind him to buy a little time. The three people were now in the kitchen with the cat and trying to figure out what the noise was about. They asked if Basil had been fighting again or if he'd hurt himself. Keep your mouth shut Basil, Dan thought as he moved silently toward the back door.

Dan tried desperately to turn the key in the lock but it was really stiff. The utility room lightened and heard 'What are you doing?' from behind him, it was the woman's voice. The game was up. Before he knew it, the man and teenage son went to grab him as he finally pulled the door open. He jumped outside. Carl was at the door with his lead bar and wearing the balaclava. The man and his son got to the door shouting after Dan and saw Carl holding up the lead bar. Carl, a much more imposing figure, told them calmly to go back into their living room, carry on playing racing and prey they never saw the two of them again. They didn't need telling twice.

. . .

Even though Joseph considered himself to be the brains of the outfit, he conceded that Charlie was clever on an all together different level when it came to computers and

43

software. Charlie had studied computing specialising in networks and programming. He did well and had had a successful but very brief career as a network manager for a company who made accounting software. He'd had a very wide range of responsibilities at that company and was paid handsomely. They clearly valued him but he didn't value them. He was bored beyond belief being a salary monkey. It was one of those types of jobs where you set your own agenda. The people he answered to knew very little about what he did and certainly had no idea how long things should take. He occupied himself with extra curricular activities such as writing password breaking programmes, hacking the internal financial systems and stealing data. His skills were too good to be wasted making printers work, setting up mailboxes and telling staff to restart their computers. The company he worked for had three major competitors who all had similar products and all were hit by security breaches care of baby faced Charlie Caines. There was no trace of it back to Charlie, but he was responsible for two of the companies closing down their systems for 12 hours or more as they frantically fought to re-secure their login systems for their tens of thousands of customers. The third company remained unaware that their customers data was copied and sold to the highest bidder on a highly illegal website. That particular sale paid for Charlie's new kitchen and bathroom with enough left over for a new Ducati.

    Charlie knew Joseph from the local boozer they shared. Neither were full on loners, but didn't have many friends. They'd both been talked into playing for the pub's Sunday league football team and ended up chatting in the pub after a game. Joseph needed someone who knew their way around computers and email systems. He asked Charlie if he could 'intercept someone's email'? 'Tell me more' had been Charlie's exact words manoeuvring Joseph to a quieter area of the pub. He said he had a job for him where he needed to intercept some very important emails about a very expensive item and that he could earn enough pay off his mortgage with a few months work. Joseph pointed out that with any job where this type of money was involved, there was risk. A lot of risk.

Charlie gained access to the auction houses internal systems in around 3 days. Their fatal flaw was not only the simplicity of their passwords but more the guess-ability of them. *M0n3t123* and *P0llc0k321* were pretty simple even for someone like Charlie who knew few artists. Since he'd got in, he had been tracking emails which were being received by the auction house from CST Couriers and knew exactly when the painting was to be picked up. He had a copy of the paper work from a PDF which had been emailed. He had also created an exact copy-cat email template and was able to send emails that looked exactly as CST's emails. The emails Charlie sent came from cstcouriers.co as opposed to the emails and actual website of CST Couriers which originated from cstcouriers.com.

Charlie had been beavering away with some off line activities as well. He had bought a second hand and high mileage Mercedes Van and had it vinyl wrapped in bright red with the CST logo emblazoned across both sides and the back, split in two by the doors. He had also bought work wear which matched exactly with the CSTs employees - blue cargo pants and red short sleeved cotton shirts with the logo on the left chest pocket. The look was smart, but hard wearing.

The big difference between their fake Warhol being picked up and what the auction house had requested was the artwork would have the additional security of police motorcycle outriders. An additional cost of several thousand pounds which the new owner was happy to pay for on strong advice of the auction house. Again, Charlie had been very busy in this area. He had bought two second hand BMW R1200RT motorcycles. The bikes had been stripped back and painted white and looked like new. Charlie set about having the bikes made into police motorbikes with the help of his friend who worked for a vinyl wrapping company. The bikes and the van were done after business hours and cost Charlie materials plus two and a half grand for no questions to be asked. By the time he was done, they all looked brilliantly authentic. The final link were the two police outrider uniforms which came from a TV props and fancy dress company. These were hired for a film which was being shot in Manchester with the working title of 'Man Down'. The whole set up came in at a few quid under £32k. It would be cash well spent.

Joseph went through the plan with the group in minute detail with timing down to the last second. He omitted the part where he would screw the five of them over and leave them with nothing.

. . .

The auction house took the security of multi million pound artworks extremely seriously as well they should, or so their waffly website said. In fact the whole operation of getting the artwork to its new owner was meticulously planned down to the last dotted i and crossed t. The auction house was an especially secure building into which Joseph had no wish to attempt to break. The art would be transported by CST Couriers who prided themselves on their secure transport and storage of valuable art and jewellery. Obviously, they would not be armed as that wasn't allowed in the UK, but their men were well trained in the art of defensive driving, they carried mace and batons. Additionally, their guards could all handle themselves, actually, the website marketing called the CST guards 'sentries'. CST did take training deadly seriously. Their sentries took part in training exercises and team building on a quarterly basis and were encouraged to actively compete in combat sports such as boxing, Taekwondo and Judo. Training and success was taken into account in their work assessments. Joseph knew all this and knew he would need to minimise any contact with their sentries during the operation.

Joseph would be the one of the drivers for the job. He had a good background as he'd raced cars in the past. Carl would drive the van and Jim and Charlie would be the two guards. Dan and Kyle would be on the bikes.

Dylan Feather, the contact at the auction house dealing with the Rothko had received an email from CST Couriers (AKA Charlie) to say that as part of their risk assessments, they had seen that there was to be a protest march through London that morning. Even though it was to start later in the morning, people would be gathering and roads would be blocked off and therefore, they wished to pick up slightly earlier to ensure smooth transit to the airport. With the benefit of Charlie seeing all the other emails from CST, he was able to match previous emails from the formal way of writing to placement of logo and signature. He asked Dylan to reply and confirm receipt. Dylan duly did this.

9,27am

The CST Couriers van along with their two police motorcycles drove down the utility road behind the auction house. They pulled up at the trade entrance. Jim and Kyle stayed sat on their bikes though they lifted their visas so they were able to make light conversation with one another. They looked relaxed. They weren't.

9,30am

Wearing their CST outfits, Dan and Charlie knocked on the trade entrance door of the auction on the rear utility road in Mayfair. They looked immaculate. Their shirts washed a few times so they didn't look brand new, but at the same time, they looked clean. Their red CST peak caps serving dual purposes. Firstly, they made the men look smart, finishing the uniforms off. More importantly, in public places, so long as the men kept their heads tilted downwards, their faces were hidden from the vast amount of CCTV cameras dotted around. They looked like they took real pride in their work. They did. They entered and made friendly chat about the weather with Dylan and his assistant Bryan. It was a lovely bright day. They had spent time improvising this conversation. It was rehearsed but they came across exactly as they wished - friendly and professional.

Charlie asked Dylan to confirm the collection reference for security. He told him it was on all previous communications. Dylan turned to his assistant expectantly. Bryan pulled a colour printout of the PDF from his clipboard. The collection reference was highlighted in fluorescent orange highlighter. Charlie produced a tablet and stylus for Dylan. He brought up the admin page on the website which had their collection reference. Charlie asked Dylan to sign to confirm they matched. With that he handed over ownership of the artwork to CST Couriers. Charlie clicked a submit button below the signature box. The web page was set up to automatically fire off an email to Dylan with his signature on the document.

Charlie told Dylan and Bryan they would be able to track the artwork to its delivery address (a private collector in Houston) from a link in an email that they would receive shortly. Dylan and Bryan knew this to be standard procedure when using CST Couriers. The men lifted the packed artwork carefully and carried it to the van where it was loaded and secured against the inside side wall. Charlie shook hands with Dylan and bid him farewell. Dylan thanked Charlie for their efficient service. Charlie shook Bryan's hand as a slight afterthought. The tradesmen's door closed and bolted shut once more as the van set off toward its next stop which would not be a Virgin jumbo jet heading for US soil. An email did turn up in Dylan's email. He took no notice of it. He had other things to do that morning. Several paintings were being shipped out after the recent sale.

10,00am

A CST Courier van turned up at their utility road entrance. The CST Couriers knocked on the door. After a little confusion, Dylan at first accused them of being incompetent for sending two vans and wasting their time, CST Couriers ignored Dylan and his rude attitude and immediately called 999 from a company mobile. Police arrived shortly after. It would be 11,00am by the time detectives started to investigate the emails and the originating website. The website, database and mailboxes were all deleted remotely by Charlie by then. Only printed emails and PDFs existed as evidence by that time. Payments for the website hosting and domain would eventually be traced back to a card stolen from a middle aged lady in Cheshire. She didn't have a computer and had never been online.

10,15am

Carl reversed the van up to the rear of the Audi and Charlie and Dan carefully transferred the packed painting to its open rear hatch. Once it was laid flat in the Audi, they then pulled a ramp from the van up which they rolled the two bikes. The bikes weren't secured, but simply thrown on their sides. They shut the door of the van and drove away. The transfer took less than 90 seconds. Apart from Joseph reminding them to be careful as they 'had seventeen million quid in their hands', no other words were spoken. Carl, Charlie and Dan drove the van to a scrapyard near Edgware. The CST van and bikes would be a small block of crushed metal, rubber and plastic within the hour. Two of the men at the scrapyard would earn themselves £1k each for their speedy and discrete service. As they left the scrapyard in their Mercedes, they stripped out of their CST uniforms into their own clothes. They would make their separate way to Edinburgh before meeting back up at the lock up.

11,56am

Joseph, Jim and Kyle pulled into a country lay bay near Leicester. It was an unmemorable and untidy dead end road. There was no passing traffic. No one to witness the transfer of the large package. An 'associate' of Matthew Weiss awaited in Matthew's Mercedes 4x4. Jim and Kyle took a moment to stretch their legs. They had a long trip ahead of them. There was a brief exchange between the associate and Joseph as to whether the operation had gone smoothly and Joseph confirmed that it had indeed gone well.

"Excellent work." said the associate as he handed over a bag to Joseph. He placed it in the back of the Audi and opened it and examined the contents.

"Two point five. A nice mornings work." The associate confirmed. Joseph nodded graciously. "Well done boys!" the associate called to Jim and Kyle. Kyle really didn't like the 'boys' bit. Nothing more was said, the different parties got back in their respective vehicles. The cars turned around and went their separate ways.

"Patronising arse." Kyle said as they pulled away.

"Who cares Kyle? He just gave us a bag with two point five mill'." Joseph said. That was the end of the part they had all planned together.

Now it was time for Joseph's separate plan to kick in. Famished after their 5am start (plus massive amounts of adrenaline), Joseph went to drive through McDonalds at some nondescript services just off the M6. They all put in big orders. Big Macs. Super-sized meals. Doughnuts. Joseph took the liberty of ordering large coffees for the three of them on top of the large cokes they all ordered. They sat in the car park and ate and chatted about how easy it had all been. Joseph pointed out there were not home and dry as yet and would need to get to Edinburgh to lay low for a while. Jim opened his back door, swung his legs out and lit and inhaled deeply on a cigarette.

They were on the road a few minutes later. Before they reached Manchester, Jim and Kyle were begging for some motorway services to take a leak. Joseph barely sipped his drinks so did not need the loo but played along with them saying he was desperate too. As they hit the next services, they practically sprinted to the toilets. Joseph went into a cubicle. Two seconds later, he opened the door and sneaked back out. That was the last they would ever see of him. He slipped back out of the services, fired up the Audi and took off toward Edinburgh. He had no intention of going to the meet up point, but didn't see any worries being in the same city. Edinburgh was large and he knew it well. Another reason why he'd suggested to meet up there and once they figured he was not going to meet them, it was probably the last place they'd expect him to be. Charlie knew roughly where Joseph lived but he had emptied his flat out and his things were in storage indefinitely. The Manchester part of Joseph's life was now closed.

The Audi was now on its way to the auctions. In its place, Joseph had parked a 6 year old pearlescant white Lamborghini Gallardo Superleggera on the top floor of the Edinburgh Radisson's multi story car park. Bought from a prestige and performance car garage in Manchester. Cash. He was staying a short distance away across The Royal Mile at The Carlton. Coming round from a particularly peaceful snooze and feeling really quite smug with himself, he decided he deserved a drink. He knew a new little bar with many secret little alcoves not too far away. He'd be able to install himself in a far flung corner and drink a nice bottle of wine (or two perhaps). He knew he shouldn't drink too much. It had been a problem for him in the past, but he deserved it tonight. He'd royally screwed over five dumb asses to become a very rich young man.

He started with a glass of Tempranillo on recommendation from the bartender and found the deepest, darkest corner. He reflected on a brilliant day. All his plans had worked out exactly as he intended. He was now the proud owner of a Lambo and was starting to dream about what else he would spend his cash on. He would hang out in Edinburgh for a day or two and then would take a holiday somewhere far afield - somewhere hot and exotic.

He'd also like to find himself a new girlfriend. It was a lonely life on your way to the top. It was well over a year since he'd been in a relationship and that could barely have been classed as a relationship in most people's terms. Generally, the relationship thing didn't work with his way of life. Too many questions were asked. Girlfriends tended to want to know what you did for a living, where you went to work, details about holidays and so on. None of that applied to Joseph's chosen career path. His last few girlfriends were led to believe he was a freelance stock broker. Of course, that is not what he was but he knew it was cover enough.

He had had a small but stylish city centre pad where he had an office. He was even set up with the share dealing software so his computer really looked the part. Graphs and tickers all over his desktop. On the nights when girlfriends stayed over, he would make as if he was going to work at his home office on a morning as they went off to their respective jobs. In reality, he did a little dabbling on the stock markets as it was something he understood. Joseph was schooled at Etan and studied at Oxford. He had a degree in Economics but chose not to spend his time working for a bank or brokerage. He was actually quite good with his own stock investments and made money but making a return of between 5% and 9% was not something that really interested him. He wanted to make bags of cash and he knew this was best done by robbing very rich people.

Up until this point, he had worked with two groups of thieves. He kept the two groups well away from each other. To his knowledge, neither knew of his connection with the other group. This was the best way, especially as he now had an end game for his association with both. He had now disposed of one group. It was time to get several million banked and move away and live without worry or stress for the rest of his life. He had grown tired of Britain and wanted to live in warmer, more exotic climes. Once he had finished his little double crossing plan, he would have upwards of £6M banked across several

European banks and would get down the business of spending it in whatever footloose and carefree way he desired. The only thing you couldn't plan for was massive sudden heart failure.

THREE

The day before

Janet was sick to death of the conference she'd be sent on. Hour after gloomy hour of tedious financial lectures and workshops. Highlights included *Predicting Distance to Default*, *Global SIFIs, derivatives and financial stability* and not forgetting the thrill ride that was *OECD Sovereign Borrowing Outlook Q2-3*. How could they have sent her on this? It would have cost them a fortune too (four day conference in a five star hotel) and she'd learned no more than she could pick up reading a few select blogs, white papers and the FT. The people at the conference were not Janet's sort of people either. Well, it was probably more that Janet wasn't really that into banking and finance any more. She was very good at it and was considered senior management potential within the company she worked for. She'd recently been head hunted from JP Morgan where she'd had a six month stint in Singapore and several shorter stints in Europe - Frankfurt mainly. She was a bit of an oxymoron in the world of hedge funds - women didn't really get into this. It was a little like the bar at Muirfield or the board room at Shell. Men saw to it that women didn't get a look in most of the time. Testosterone generally ruled over oestrogen. But her bosses had found it hard to ignore her when she performed so well for them. Up until the financial crash in 2008, she had been one of their best performing hedge fund managers. Making great profits on the hundreds of millions she was given the responsibility to invest.

After the crash, it had been a different matter. The risks that Janet had once been allowed to take had been clamped down upon. Imagination was not encouraged any more. It was safety and reduced risk all the way now. And it was boring. Just like the conference. She'd been sought out by a more traditional bank now and was still a 'high flyer'. She'd requested a move into the consumer division of the bank. What was the point to manage hedge funds if the constraints were so rigid now that you had no freedom or creativity to go your own way. The bonuses were gone along with the risk. At the time, she had felt incredibly guilty about receiving the bonuses, but there was no getting away from the fact that vintage Chanel jewellery was a thing of sheer beauty.

She spent whatever she had and always had done. Right up to and sometime well past her limit. A penchant for Casadei shoes, Mulberry dresses and Gucci handbags was the source of the problem. She just liked the finer things in life. When she went shopping with friends, they would find bargains in the SALEs but she never seemed to be able to get anything in her size, but something expensive from NEW SEASON would always jump out at her. She had calculated she was taking home an extra £1.1k a month since her move and two subsequent promotions and still had nothing spare. All her friends in banking had stacks of savings but she had precious little. It was her guilty secret.

Consumer banking was a new challenge. There was a certain amount of creativity needed. The fact of the matter was however she liked risk. She liked seeing the value of the millions of pounds she invested jumping as a consequence of business deals and product launches around the world. Seeing funds she'd just pulled out from drop like stones. She knew she was a thrill seeker. Like a surfer, always making sure you're on the right wave at the right time to catch the best ride. Consumer banking was not giving her the thrill. She knew she would not be sticking in this job for long. But equally, she didn't know what she wanted to do as an alternative. Probably nothing in banking at all. She was young, there was no huge hurry to figure this out.

She sipped at her second large Hendricks and tonic in the hotel reception wondering if Elaine or Katie, acquaintances from the conference, would show their faces for a few drinks. They were good fun and she could pass the time easily with either of them. All three were from London and had a lot in common; all single(ish) high flyers in their early 30s with similar tastes in clothing, music and films. Being with them took her mind off the fact she was single again too. She'd broken up with her boyfriend just a few days before coming to the conference. He just wasn't her type, but she'd gone out with him because he was difficult to shake off. Ultimately, it wasn't going anywhere good. 'Rip the plaster off quickly' she told herself.

Her excellent tipping (a habit from her time in Singapore) meant the waiter was right on her whenever her drinks were running low. It also meant the waiters were very helpful. Whether she was asking where were good places to eat out or just wanted good measures in her drinks, they were very obliging. Right on cue, her drink was almost finished and her favourite waiter (Zach his badge said) was there for her. He pointed questioningly at her almost empty glass. She smiled and nodded. It must be the dryness of the days' lectures that was making her so thirsty as she took her first bitter sweet sip.

57

She flicked on to Facebook on her phone to see what was happening back home. Wednesday night, they'd be having a few mid week drinks after work no doubt. That was the thing she loved so much about living in London, pretty much any night she wanted to go out, she would have friends out. As she suspected, lots of friends were out in London. It was obviously a nice evening down in London from all the beer garden Instagrams popping up all over the place. She sent a few messages, finished most of her drink and made up her mind to take a stroll in the warm (for Edinburgh) evening.

If her friends from the conference weren't going to show, she was certainly not going to be staying in. She wanted some chat (attention). Actually this was more than attention. This was a man. She wanted a man. Someone to flirt with. And she knew how to get that, but she'd leave here and try some where new; once she'd done her little trick. She went to the loo and stood in front of the mirror. She took out some key make up tools from her hand bag - blusher, mascara and eye shadow. She'd learned quite a while back that her best look was very 'Eighties'. So she piled on the blusher high up on her cheek bones in diagonal strokes, stuck a touch more mascara on (just up top, never on the bottom lids) and quite a lot more eye shadow. Then finished it off with glossy pink lipstick. She looked like a girl from a ZZ Top or Meatloaf video, but even though it was an old fashioned way to wear make up. It would do what she wanted, it would get her some attention. She walked back out of the toilets with a different walk to the one she went in with, the way Clark Kent walked differently when he came out of the telephone box in his cape. Her cape was her copious amounts of blusher and eye shadow.

Janet found herself feeling a little tipsy when the fresh air hit as she walked over the North Bridge toward the Royal

Mile. She liked the feeling and decided a couple more drinks would be in order. She hung a left, then a right and found herself sitting at a bar. It was early still and the bar was quiet. As she looked over the cocktail menu, a glass of champagne arrived. Nice champagne at that (thank you blusher and cheek bones). Someone with taste she thought (or plenty of money), though she couldn't see who'd sent it. She sipped at it and chatted on Facebook with Karen back home; stalling for time really. Toward the end of the champagne, she stood up and decided to go thank the 'gent in the far corner'. Never know, he might be a catch. She was feeling confident after a few drinks and was wearing her latest Donna Karen dress which she picked up yesterday on George Street after skipping a workshop on yawn-filled Foreign Tax Compliance and Avoidance. Ironic that she skipped a workshop on saving money to go and buy a £750 dress.

The waiter who had brought her drink over directed her toward the far back right corner with a subtle flick of his eyes. The lighting was down way low back here (good) and music (trip hop mixed with lounge jazz) was deep and seductive. She couldn't see anyone and walked a little further. Still no one. Eventually, she saw an Italian looking man in his mid thirties. There was no one else back here, so it had to be him.

"Do I have you to thank?" she said holding up the half drunk champagne tentatively. He nodded with a smile that said 'yes' and 'pleasure'. "So who are you hiding from back here?"

"Oh, I just robbed a few million pounds from some rather unpleasant types." he told her with a wink "How about you? Also, drinking alone, in a bar in Edinburgh, when you're clearly not from these parts." She tilted her head in slight mock confusion.

"What makes ye say that?" she asked in her best Scotch accent.

"Haha, well your terrible Scottish accent for a start."

"Got me. Haha. . . I'm not hiding from anyone, just a little bored and looking to escape from the financial conference I've was forced to go on this week."

"Would you like to grab a bite to eat?" He asked thinking this is a long shot. Drink was one thing but a meal...

"Gosh you don't waste time... do you have equally good taste with food?" she asked holding up the champagne once more, "This was lovely, so you've set the bar at a fair height." She sat her self down on the other side of the booth and tried to look relaxed and at home approaching men in bars.

"Well if you *really* want great food and you *really* want to escape your conference, I know a great restaurant in Glasgow." He twinkled his eyes at her.

"Well, you're pushing your luck aren't you?"

He was pushing his luck he knew but he was brimming over with confidence right now.

"And what's so much better about this restaurant than all the restaurants in Edinburgh may I ask? I take it there's a good reason to take me half way across Scotland."

Janet knew deep down that this was it for the night. She had little self control and was bored with not just this conference, but her career and even her life in general. Someone that wanted to whisk her off her feet; to the other side of the country in order to buy her a lovely meal would be difficult to say no to.

. . .

Carl, Dan and Charlie were six hours late as they reached the meeting point. The lockup. The Mercedes had broken down on the M6. Not what they were hoping for from German engineering. None of them had any breakdown cover. They had managed to get a local garage to come out and tow them back to the garage. In the end, one of their mechanics had managed to fix the worn fuel line by replacing it with a spare piece of tube that was lying about. They had maintained their 'forced radio silence' as Joseph had put it. 'Doesn't matter how long it takes us to get to the lock up, just get there.' Once there, they could debrief and chat as much as was needed.

As it was daytime, they wished to draw attention from no-one. This was the second time they'd passed the meeting point, but Carl was not in the habit of getting caught out nowadays. This was just his way of being cautious. There were very few people around apart from the odd person working in the docks, but he wanted to be 100% sure that it wasn't being watched by anyone. Charlie had a final discreet look about, unlocked the padlock and pulled the door to the side slightly and peeped in. He could see no one. He guided Carl driving the Merc in. The place was quiet and peaceful. He pulled the door back behind and looked around. He was expecting to see other members of the gang in jubilant mood. They had successfully taken the Rothko after all.

Joseph, Kyle and Jim had gone their separate ways, as planned, but had not showed up. Charlie thought if they had taken an extra six hours to reach the lockup after breaking down, they should definitely be the last to arrive, not the first. Charlie smelled a rat. Carl did too. It was Joseph who planned the whole thing out including them leaving the scene of the robbery in two different groups of three. Carl told them to stay put for the time being. He trusted them to show up, he said.

But it was a lie and right now, he could not for the life in him understand why he would allow himself to get into a situation where he may be wanted for a robbery where he didn't even have the loot. What a fool. What a fucking fool.

He pulled rank and sent Dan to get some food, cigarettes and beers. They may be here for a while and he didn't want to be dry or hungry whilst they waited. It was entirely plausible that Joseph was having to hide out from the police somewhere between London and here. He was going to give him 24 hours.

A little time later as they finished off a cool (but not cold enough) beer each and nibbled on a selection of cheap crisps and nuts, Dan said he'd had his doubts about Joseph.

"Well you should have said something about those doubts at the time my friend." Charlie told him without a flicker of hesitation and quite a lot of anger "You going mute has probably lost us our share of that cash."

"Hang on a fucking minute now Charlie, I..."

But he was cut off by Carl "Now it's not your fault Charlie or yours Dan or mine, it's whoever has double crossed us. They're the ones who're at fault here." he was bright red in the face and obviously angry as hell but just about holding it together. "And anyway, it may all be fine, they may have just had a problem getting up here. Who knows what could have happened? Could have got stopped by the police or crashed or broken down like us."

"That Audi was too high mileage, I wouldn't be surprised if it blew up on the motorway" Charlie interjected.

"Or maybe Joseph killed those two idiots and ran off with everyone's cash?" Dan offered.

"Whatever it is, we'll either find out or I will get to the bottom of it, rest assured." Carl said ominously. "For now, let's sit tight."

They tried not to but kept going over different scenarios both internally and out loud of what could have happened. None of them were close to the correct version of what happened. It was a fractious time. Carl tried to keep them as positive as he was able. Tried to keep believing himself that they were on their way, but his gut was saying something very different. Usually his gut was right.

. . .

Joseph and Janet walked through the Radisson to the multi story car park. A man was behind them and joined them in the lift. Joseph pressed the button for the top floor and allowed the man to choose his own floor, he didn't touch another button, so they both assumed that he was bound for the same floor. No one said a word during the time in the lift, but Joseph and Janet shared a glance behind the man. It was a smouldering look and Janet found her eyebrow raising slowly. Seductively. At least, she hoped it was seductive and not comical.

The three walked across the dim car park, the man peeled off to the left in front of them and down another alley of cars. Janet was led toward a white sports car. Joseph blipped the locks and then opened the door for her. This was turning out to be a pretty good night she thought to herself.

"Nice car." She said but actually it seemed more ridiculous than 'nice'. The sort of car some bankers went and bought when they'd had a particularly big bonus and went shopping with a champagne hangover.

They almost reached Glasgow in the white sports car before they learned each other's names. Both secretly knew this was going to be a wild night. As the best night's in one's life start out, totally spontaneously. This was not the sort of thing that Janet (or Joseph) did usually, but some spark had been set alight between them in that bar. A connection that neither of them had had many times in their lives, but one that they both wanted to go with, it drew them in like a spark burning down toward a fuse attached to a large stick of dynamite.

Janet had rarely been this carefree. Her life as a banker usually meant she went out with other people who worked in the financial services industries. Usually, this was great and she did date lovely guys who worked for banks (and other types too). Maybe this was more about the situation than this guy who she now knew as Joseph, but this felt so exciting. More intense; he seemed more interesting than anyone else she'd been out with. Actually interesting was not really how you'd describe him, there was something burning in him, some fire in his belly, some sparkle in his eye that most bankers didn't have. It was more than a glint, it wasn't quite danger, but it was as if his eyes dared her. I dare you to accept this champagne I'm sending over, I dare you to come for a meal with me - a guy you've never set eyes on before, I dare you to come halfway across Scotland for that meal. Dare you!

"Wanna put some music on?" Joseph asked pulling out a cable from the centre console and holding it up toward Janet. She took the wire and retrieved her phone from her bag. She unlocked her phone.

"Let me think." she half muttered under her breath. She wasn't that current, but she had quite a decent selection of tracks downloaded to her phone. She swiped through all the playlists from start to finish, mentally noting one or two possibles (and some definite No Nos), then quickly back up. She hit play and found the volume control and adjusted it slightly upwards as a lone guitar began to strum.

> *Morning, it's another pure grey morning*
> *Don't know what the day is holding*
> *When I get uptight*
> *And I walk right into the path of a lightning bolt*

"Good call." he said tapping his leg. It wasn't the most obvious track to play on a night like this, but what was. This wasn't any sort of a night. They were out in the middle of the country now with no street lights and the sky was insanely clear. The high half moon blazed down on them surrounded by a billion stars. They passed a sign that said Glasgow 20 miles. The time was flying, the chat was easy between them and they seemed to pass from one topic to another easily. Janet pushed the button and wound her window down all the way, Joseph did the same. He pushed a little harder on the throttle and she was pushed a little harder into her seat but even though he was going quite fast, she didn't know how fast but definitely well over the speed limit, she felt safe. She turned the music up high and tipped her head back.

Fifteen minutes later, they pulled up in outside a hotel. As they were led to the restaurant, Joseph asked if there was a nice private table. 'Of course sir', he was told. They were seated at a table off to the side of the restaurant in a quiet area behind some large rubber plants.

"What's with you always wanting to hide?" she enquired.

"I think I'm just a shy and retiring type." he joked. He was so far from being being shy and retiring; more larger than life with a cherry on top she thought to herself.

"Red or white?" he asked her. She wanted red as did he so he called the waiter over and asked him to bring a good red. After a few minutes, a bottle of Fleurie arrived. Joseph briefly took the bottle, looked over the label bounced the bottle in his hand gently, as if weighing it. He stuck his thumb into the concave underside, nodded and passed it back to the waiter to open and pour.

As the waiter left them with three quarter full glasses, Joseph half pulled a small packet from his inside jacket pocket. The packet, which was about the size of a book of matches, looked to be made from a magazine.

"Want a cheeky perk up?" he asked.

"I don't do that sort of thing very often. I'm a good girl Joseph. But I'll have a dabble."

"Well I'm going to take myself off to the rest room my dear." Joseph said bringing his voice back up to regular levels. "Have a look at the menu and we'll get some food ordered. Back in a jiffy."

Janet mentally selected the free range chicken with parsnip purée, creamed leek and truffle, then pulled out her phone and sent her friend Jess a message on Facebook.

Hey babe, WUU2?

She saw Jess's chat bubble start to fill to signify she was typing something.

Alright chick? Having a bite to eat at Terrace with the girls from work. Where are you?
Wanna meet up for a drink?

> *I'm in Glasgow on a conference, just eating with a colleague at the Park Square restaurant. Have fun and we'll catch up soon. xxx*

Ok babe xxx

    She flicked her phone back off and stuck it back in her bag. She'd wanted to just have a little contact with *her* world and to let someone know where she was. It was something she tended to do if she was on a date. She was a single woman and you had to be a little cautious. She didn't think Joseph was a scum bag or that he was dodgy at all, but it made her feel more at ease.

    She saw him on his way back from the 'rest room' and got up to flip flop with him. As he passed her, he dropped the package into her hand. He mouthed. "It's strong." As he did, he crossed his eyes. Then back at normal volume. "Oh yes, they're over that way my darling." She sniggered under her breath and sauntered off. In the toilets, she went to the furthest cubicle. She had no idea how to do this. She unwrapped the package and looked at the small amount of cocaine sitting there. Did she take it all or just a little? Usually when she had it before, someone had done all this bit for her. She'd seen it taken out of a false nail by her hero Tanya Turner once, but she didn't have long nails. Did she roll up a ten pound note? She didn't really want to do that, she knew all about cash and she knew it was riddled with bacteria. It was too complicated so she decided that she wouldn't risk it.

    She left the cubicle and went to the mirror. The toilet was empty. She took out her compact to apply a little more eye shadow. She'd never applied this much before, but for some reason, the more she applied, the better it seemed to look. Was it just this lighting? She backed away from the mirror, but it still looked hot. She applied a little more blusher. What the hell, she re-applied mascara and lip gloss too. Was it too much? Hmm. No, not for a girl who'd just driven half way across Scotland with a guy she just met. She made her way back to their table.

"I've never done this… on my own." she said wrinkling her nose, "sorry I don't know what to do." She slipped the packet back across the table and it went smoothly into Jacob's hand and was palmed away into his inside jacket pocket in a flash.

"No need to apologise. We can take ourselves off after we've eaten and have a little if you still like."

The waiter was back and took their orders gracefully before topping their glasses again and bringing a bottle of iced water.

"So tell me more about this robbery then and where have you stashed your million quid?"

"Well I stole a piece of modern art worth £17 million quid. Have you heard of Rothko?"

"You are very funny. What do you actually do?"

He gave her his usual 'dabbling on the stock market' spiel. He was well versed in this by now and it flowed out of him with conviction.

"Oh I work in the finance industry too." She smiled. He hoped not in the markets as she could soon unpick his knowledge. "I work for a bank, but the irony is that I'm really rubbish with my own money. I seem to have no control over my spending. It's like I see something I want, like a new dress or handbag or shoes or furniture or perfume or, well you get the picture, I just have to have it and all thoughts about how much something costs or how much money I have seem to just go out the window. And yet, I advise customers how to conserve and manage their money. Funny old world eh?" she laughed.

I bet you could help me spend two and a half million quid in cash too Joseph thought to himself.

By the time they'd polished off their desserts, they were stuffed and quite drunk. They'd drunk almost two bottles of the Fleurie between them and they were both slurring their words but they hadn't noticed. Joseph suggested they have some champagne and ordered some Perrier et Jouet from the wine list. He used the facilities once more before it arrived, taking a little toot of coke whilst he was in there. As he came out of the toilets feeling on top of the world, he bought condoms from the machine feeling his luck was in. If it wasn't, then he wasn't sure what a guy had to do. He had laid all the moves on her now.

He arrived back at the table to a glass of champagne held up to him. They chinked glasses.

"Bottoms up!" he said casually.

She took him at his word and downed her glass and then succumbed to a huge, un-lady-like burp which cut through the atmosphere of the restaurant. She went bright crimson and he simply buried his head into his hands until people stopped staring around at them. He was embarrassed but laughing so hard he couldn't control himself. His shoulders jumped up and down involuntarily as she kicked him under the table.

"I think I need to get out of this restaurant now." she said under her breath.

"I think you're right, you do." he laughed. "Err, sorry we do." he corrected himself.

"How are we going to get back to Edinburgh?" she asked looking genuinely confused. She had just not thought any of this through. He raised his shoulders un-knowingly. "I think we'd better not drive back in this state," she said stating the obvious, "perhaps we should get a room?"

"Are you definitely ok with that? You're pretty drunk; sorry we're pretty drunk. I could get us separate rooms..." he left it hanging in the air wondering why he'd said that as he definitely wanted to share a room with her.

She thought for a moment and then said "No, no that would be too expensive. Besides I want something that you have." she winked and pointed at his jacket where his inside chest pocket was located.

He reached inside and pulled out the packet of condoms. "Really?"

She smiled, "You got me. And yes, we will need them." She felt dirty and a little slutty. But this didn't feel like a bad thing to her. This was living.

He asked the waiter if there were rooms available in the hotel and if they could take their champagne to their room? He said he'd see to it that it was taken up for them. He showed them to the reception saying he'd have their meal added to their bill.

Compared to Janet's hotel room in Edinburgh, the room Joseph booked was just beautiful. Roomy, plush, expensive drapes, thick carpets. The works. They finished the champagne and Joseph ordered another bottle from room service which made Janet smile even more.

"While we're waiting, do you want to join me?" Joseph asked holding the cocaine wrap between his fingers. He poured some onto the dressing table's glass top and divided it with his credit card into four lines of about 2 inches in length, then took a note from his wallet which had obviously been rolled up and used for this purpose before. He took it between his fingers and created a very tight straw, then hovered up the first of the four lines, then passed the expensive straw to Janet. Previously she was worried about the bacteria. That worry was well and truly gone. She followed what he'd done, sucking up hard and the line disappeared. She pulled back as it stung her nose. She rubbed the top of her nose as if trying to dislodge what she'd sucked up there. But almost immediately she got the hit making her brain woozy and hot and heightening her senses. She suddenly smelled Joseph for the first time, he was musky and yet fresh like some just picked herbs. It was lovely. He took the straw back and did the third line and passed back. She wasted no time. She was ready for the little sting on the back of her nostrils this time.

"You're pretty good at this," he said, "you're like a little Dyson aren't you?"

"I think you're right" she said laughing.

The champagne arrived and Joseph allowed the waiter into the room to open it and serve their first glass. They were still sniggering to each other about the Dyson remark. The waiter asked if they were celebrating something special and Joseph said that they were indeed, but gave no further detail. He pushed a twenty note into the waiter's hand as he left.

"What are we celebrating again?" Joseph asked once he closed the door.

Janet thought for a second and then said "The meeting of two great minds!" and held up her glass to his. "Bottoms up!" They downed the drinks again and looked into one another's eyes. Joseph moved closer, reached around her waist and pulled her toward him and kissed her. She kissed back equally passionately. He enjoyed the taste of her lipstick and lip gloss and the smell of her perfume and her hands on him. They kissed for a long time and as they had been throughout the rest of the evening so far, seemed to be on one another's wavelength; neither seemed to want to rush.

"Can we have another 'toot'?" she asked half muffled by his lips "Or is it too soon? Am I getting too giddy with it?" she asked.

"You can do whatever the hell you want gorgeous." He pulled away and cut up another few lines, just two this time. It was strong stuff this, so he didn't want to end up going mad with it. He handed her the note to roll up. She gave it a pretty good go and he told her as much. She went fuzzy again and sat on the edge of the bed. After that, things went a lot quicker. Where they had been tender before, it became passionate and intense and fiery. Janet straddled Joseph naked on top of him on the bed. She'd ripped her knickers off and thrown them behind her and now they were on the chandelier above her. She rode him rhythmically, massaging his chest with one hand and drinking champagne straight from the bottle with the other. Intermittently, she poured champagne into his mouth from up high and he did his very best to drink it but it was so bubbly most of it foamed up and slid down his cheeks onto the bedding. Janet was quiet but it was very obvious from her face she was enjoying every second, as was he. Their senses heightened by the powder up their noses.

She dropped the champagne bottle. He caught it before it spilled. She threw her head back, squeezed her eyelids closed tight and swam in the moment for a good thirty seconds. Once her eyes re-opened, he gave her the champagne back and she continued to neck it as he eased himself toward climax.

They lay in a collective glow and sniggered at the state of Janet's knickers as they hung from the bedroom's chandelier.

"Ripping them off and flinging them over my head was probably not the most lady like thing I've ever done." They collapsed laughing. It was funny but she had sore marks on her hips where she'd ripped them off.

Joseph rolled over toward the phone, called room service and asked they send up some another bottle of champagne. While they waited, he got them Perrier waters from the mini bar and then held up a selection of spirits and mixers. Janet asked for a vodka and tonic. Neither of them knew what time it was and had no care. It didn't seem even slightly odd to Janet that Joseph was walking around the room totally naked even though she'd only met him less than seven hours ago. She watched him as he goofed around making drinks and wanted his body near hers again. She pulled the sheet to cover herself, but it wasn't that she felt odd being naked, she just had a slight chill. A phone had vibrated a few times as if receiving text messages but they were ignored. They were both in the moment. That moment that happens when two people connect.

They chatted and joked and played games whilst they waited for room service. They laughed about Janet's huge burp at the end of their meal and she covered her face up in embarrassment reliving the moment. Once again, she went bright crimson which Joseph thought was hilarious.

After they'd drunk yet more, Janet said (slurred) she wanted to have a cigarette. Joseph who also didn't smoke, apart from very occasionally, said he'd also like one. They dressed and made their way down to the hotel's bar where they were able to buy cigarettes from the bar staff. Let's go to the car park to smoke Joseph said, adding 'I need to get something from the car'.

At the car park, Joseph lit a cigarette and passed it to her before lighting one for himself. They walked to the car and he lifted up the boot lid (which was at the front of the car) and pulled out a bag which was very obviously Gucci.

"Don't really wanna leave this in here overnight."

"Is it your million pounds?" she asked glancing at the bag.

He nodded, adding "And one or two other necessities." and tipped her one of his winks. "God, I fucking love smoking. Why's it got to be so damned bad for you? *And* make you stink."

"Shit isn't it? I started smoking when I was at school which was pretty stupid, but I don't really smoke more than one or two a week now. How about you?"

"Just when I'm nervous about something." he said.

"What could you be nervous about? You're the most self confident person I've ever met." she said and this was not a lie. " At least you seem it on the outside."

He just smiled, choosing not to comment any further. "At least we'll both stink, so it's not so bad."

They started to walk back toward the hotel's entrance, Joseph with the bag slung over his shoulder. An Audi drove up the ramp and toward them and Joseph stopped in his tracks. It was going faster than it rightly should have been in a multi story car park, but not crazily fast. Then Joseph saw it was a different car to their get away car and anyway, he'd sold that. They would not be in that car if (when) they came for him.

"Are you ok?"

"Yeah, I was just a little shocked by how fast that car was going, that's all." he lied. They took the lift straight up to their floor and walked to room 374. Joseph stuck the bag on the floor next to the bathroom entrance and poured what remained of the champagne into the two glasses. Tonight, they had hollow legs.

"Ring and order some more booze, whatever you want." With that, he disappeared into the bathroom.

"Good idea." she said and picked up the phone. She went to pick up her glass of wine, but knocked the glass to the floor where it smashed. She barely noticed. Janet was definitely not thinking straight. She ordered a bottle of 'good' Scotch, with two glasses and lots of ice. Janet could no longer remember that the last time she'd drunk whiskey with Allan, an old boyfriend, she'd actually quite liked the taste and actually drank way too much of it, passed out unconscious so much so that Allan panicked when he couldn't wake her up and called an ambulance. She awoke up in hospital just slightly before she had her stomach pumped. This was neatly swept under the carpet of Janet's memory in her current drug, champagne and wine fuelled state.

Joseph turned on the taps to mask the sounds he would be making in the bathroom. He could hear her slightly muffled on the phone to room service. The odd words came through - '...Scotch... ...ice... ...how long?'

He pulled the side panel from the bath. It came away easily. He only had to hide it from her and she was pissed beyond belief anyway. He stuffed the bag into the cavity and pushed the panel back. He peaked out of the gap in the door and saw Janet was having yet another line and he decided he wanted one too.

Barely noticing the smell of smoke on one another, they had sex again. Their third showing. Though the other times had all blurred into a mash up of sex, drink, giggles and drugs now. Definition to the evenings proceedings was fading. The sex this time it was less sensual. The finer edges worn away. Almost animal now.

...

A sharp double rap at the lock up door rattled through the space inside and awoke Carl. He went to open it with a feeling of relief spreading through his mind. Checking his watch, it could only be the rest of them. No one else would be about at 6:30am. Nevertheless he asked who it was. 'Kyle and Jim' was the answer. He pushed the door open.

He was shaking his head as soon as he saw the two of them. The looks on their faces told him everything he needed to know. His face and head was going bright red again.

They came in looking sheepish as the others woke up. The five of them were a sorry sight. All the risk, all the work and nothing to show for it. None of them were thinking straight now. Talk about having the rug pulled out from under you.

After they were ditched at the services. They'd wanted to hot wire a car from the car park, but finding nothing suitable, they'd had to hitch a ride with a lorry. They'd got as far up the M6 as they could, then gone across country to find a car eventually getting an old Ford Fiesta which served its purpose.

"I don't fucking believe this." said Charlie.

"I'm sorry, but how do we know this isn't some plot that you're in with that fucker?" Dan asked. "Do you really expect us to believe that he just walked away when you went to the bog? You two throw us off his tracks and then two weeks down the line and you go meet up with him and get your share of the cash..."

"How the fuck we know *you're* not in it with him?" Jim came back. "Right now, I don't know who or what to trust. My fucking head's comin' off... What I *do* know is that he is one devious fuck."

Carl looked directly at Kyle and Jim "You wouldn't do that to me would you lads?" the years they'd know one another writ heavily over his face.

"You know the answer to that Carl. I don't even like that smug, fucking twat..." Kyle trailed off, hurt that his honour had been questioned in this way.

Carl turned from Kyle and Jim to Charlie "Ok, can't believe we didn't start this earlier, we need to put that insurance policy we took out into action."

The others looked warily at one another.

"Ok, gonna need to get my hands on a computer?"

Carl raised his hands slightly to show he was in charge and he had a plan. "Ok, Dan and Kyle, get to Edinburgh train station. There will be plenty of people with laptops in their bags on trains. Go and get one. Jim and Charlie, you guys go and get breakfast and supplies for everyone. I'll wait here, just in case he turns up. Oh and get some newspapers."

Carl sat down in the quiet of the empty lockup. He tipped his head back and thought about how stupidly trusting he had been and how he wanted to just kill someone. Anyone. Just to release some tension. Just stab and stab and stab.

. . .

Joseph had stopped moving and was simply laid on his back. Dead of heart failure. Janet was atop him unknowingly having sex with a dead Joseph. Her eyes were shut, her head tipped back, she ground her hips against him and had another orgasm. She vaguely noticed he'd stopped moving and thought to herself with a smile on her face 'I've worn him out'.

Janet briefly traced a finger over herself from her neck, over her nipples and down her stomach. She shuddered, then collapsed onto him, rolled to the side and let out a quiet giggle. She didn't want to wake him. Her body dipped quickly into half deep sleep and half unconsciousness.

Room service had finally made a decision on what counted for a 'good Scotch' and brought up a bottle of Laphroaig with two heavy crystal tumblers and an ice bucket. After knocking several times, firmly but not so loud as to disturb other, frankly more respectable, guests, the Scotch was taken back to the bar.

'Which woman orders a bottle of Scotch at 5am?' Josh the young waiter muttered to himself as he walked away. 'Someone with a death wish?'

FOUR

The day after

At 11:00am precisely, she sat up in bed. Wide eyed, sweaty and confused; taking in her surroundings. Yet more unfamiliarity. Then, it came back to her. Hotel. Edinburgh. Alone. The dead guy... Joseph... he was in Glasgow. What else? She had inherited a crazy car and stolen a bag full of money. She wasn't sure how well it sat with her conscience. 'You stole off a dead guy Janet', she told herself. A little shocked when it was put that way. 'You used to be such a nice girl.'

She walked to her window and looked out at Edinburgh. She could see the castle and the gardens below, then further in the distance the train station and then a bridge and something clicked. She realised that she could see the hotel where she was actually staying. For her banking conference. And she had bags and clothes there.

The conference would be finished now she seemed to remember. She probably should have checked out from her room. She rang and explained that she had been ill and would need to keep her room another day. They were fine and asked no questions thankfully. She couldn't face bumping into conference stragglers today.

A large gurgle erupted from deep within her stomach. She was hungry. Very hungry. She had barely eaten yesterday. Had she missed breakfast? She dialled reception and asked if she could have breakfast brought up. 'Of course Madam' was the reply. She asked for a continental breakfast with coffee and sure enough within minutes there was a knock at the door and a young man had a tray with her breakfast. Her papers sat on the carpet outside her suite and he brought them in and placed them on her dining table. She took her mind off recent incidents for a while tucking into warm croissants and drinking strong coffee. She scanned the Scotsman for any news of a death at a hotel in Glasgow but there was nothing. In The Times, it was all the same stuff. Political scandal. Upcoming elections in the US. Shock horror, a TV star had snorted cocaine at a party and someone had filmed it on a phone. 'So what?' she asked the paper. Again, she was mainly looking for news of a dead man being found in Glasgow. There was no such a story.

She kept scanning. On page 10 of the Times though, a headline above a small article grabbed her interest. **£17 MILLION ROTHKO NABBED UNDER THE NOSES OF TOP LONDON AUCTION HOUSE.** A Rothko had been stolen from an auction house in London by thieves posing as the secure courier company who was supposed to deliver it to its new owner. The painting had recently sold for over £16.7 million. Didn't Joseph say something like - 'he'd stolen a painting worth millions'?

Massive co-incidence? If he was behind this, it would explain that bag of cash. He'd just sold the painting on more than likely. He seemed very smug with himself - as you would be if you'd successfully lifted a painting worth millions and then sold it on. No, it had to be. Surely. It had happened the morning that she met Joseph. It couldn't be a co-incidence.

It made up her mind. If it had been someone's hard earned cash, that might be different, but there was a strong possibility that this was the money from this stolen painting. If she didn't have it, someone else would. Who had lost out after all? The person who had bought this. But surely, they would have some sort of insurance. If not, they would take the auction house to court for the money and they would probably have insurance. She needed to check more of the news and see what was going on. Had any other gang members been caught? Or were they likely trying to find Joseph and that bag of cash too? They were going to feed him to... someone or something. Those particular details escaped her right now. She greedily finished the rest of her breakfast plate.

She needed to get out of her dress and into something less flash. She had no toiletries or spare clothes, she smelled. A lot. She couldn't rely on the concierge to bring her deodorant. Could she? She needed to charge her phone and had no charger with her. No, plus she needed to get out and get some fresh air. She'd been in hotel bedrooms for days it seemed.

She went out in her black dress and high heels. She looked pretty odd she knew, but this was a necessity. She simply avoided eye contact with anyone. She put on her 'fuck everyone face.' It was similar to Lamborghini girl but with less panache. She found a nearby chemist and half filled a basket with everything she would need if she was to spend the next week in a hotel room. Hotel toiletries were all well and good and nice as a little treat occasionally, but not like having your own toiletry bag filled with your own toiletries. Next she got a few changes of clothing and some very needed new and spare underwear. This was not the usual clothes shopping trip, there was no trying clothes on, she took a pile of clothes to the counter and handed over a wad of cash. Then finally, she found a mobile phone shop and pulled out the dead mobile she had been carrying around. A young sales man found her the correct charger.

Safely back in her suite, she charged the phones and each had several new messages awaiting. She was trying as hard as she could to ignore that window back to her 'usual' life, but it was not going away. She was missing from a financial conference and she'd missed two business meetings. Her boss was annoyed as hell. Finally, she sent a message to say she had food poisoning. It did the job, her boss gingerly replied asking if she needed a doctor? She said she was over the worst of it now and would keep him up to date.

Ignoring text messages on Joseph's phone, she examined it to see if there was anything else in there that might be of interest. There wasn't. Apart from the text messages that had come in since they'd met, there wasn't anything of note. It seemed Joseph either didn't have any friends or just deleted messages after he'd read them. No Facebook. No chat. Very unsocial.

...

"Why would he come to Edinburgh?" Carl asked Charlie and Dan.

"Surely, you'd go to the opposite end of the country if you screwed over your mates? I don't get it." Dan said in a hushed tone.

"Guys, guys, we don't know for sure he's here, all we can tell is that his phone is located here currently. He could have had it stolen. Or he could have left it here to throw us off his trail. That's much more likely knowing that slime ball." Charlie pointed out.

Carl had driven the three of them in the bigger Merc from the lock up. They had a bag with two guns, knuckle dusters and baseball bats in the boot. Not that they thought they'd need it for Joseph. To them Joseph was a posh public school boy with a criminal mind, but he was not able to handle himself. Carl was worried about the fact that there had been no response whatsoever to his texts, calls and answer phone messages he'd left. Maybe he had just left the phone here as a decoy to put them off his trail? Theoretically, he could be half way around the world by now. Laid on a beach somewhere hot and exotic. Or was he just being his superior smug self, lording it up in a posh Edinburgh hotel thinking he'd got one over on the muscled up thickos of the gang?

They sat in a huddle in the corner of the bar, keeping an eye on reception and trying their hardest to look like they fitted in here. They were doing an okay job of it. They didn't have the air of business men about them, but they could pass for staying in Edinburgh for a lads weekend, just about. Charlie had asked reception if there was a Joseph Nicholson staying here. There was not. Charlie had said they were meeting him in the hotel bar but weren't sure if he was staying in the hotel. Now they were going to play the waiting game. Sooner or later, he'd have to pass through the reception *if* he was in the hotel.

With the thinking that the woman from Glasgow might be with Joseph, Carl set out what was to happen. Scenario One. If they saw Joseph. Grab him and bundle him into the car and get him to the lockup. It didn't matter who saw or how much noise or disruption this made. Scenario Two. If it saw Joseph and the woman. Exactly the same as scenario

One. Except with the pair of them. Scenario Three. If they saw the woman from Glasgow without Joseph, they would need to show caution. She had seen Dan and had a good look at his face and probably at Carl's from following her car. Plus she was potentially the key to finding Joseph. She had not seen Charlie, so he would follow her and try to get her isolated. Charlie seemed very comfortable with this. He said had a trick up his sleeve.

. . .

 She ate Croque-Madame from room service, slept for an hour then awoke a little restless and decided to go to the spa for a massage. After all, her life was going to be changing and she was going to be doing a lot more Janet pampering. May as well make a start on that now. No time like the present.

 Feeling relaxed and fresh (she had decided to have a facial whilst she was in the spa), she resolved to venture out into Edinburgh. It was a warm Friday evening. Go for a drink. She stuck a cheap blouse and jeans on she'd picked up on her mini clothes shop and covered her black eye as best she could with several heavy dabs of Touche Éclat. As her blackened eye was mainly in her eyelid, she found if she went quite dark with eye shadow on the other side it evened things out.

 She wound her way around to the bar where all this madness started. She scanned the cocktail menu, ordered a Singapore Sling and went over to sit at the table where he'd been. The bar was quiet and she could relax and catch up with friends online. She'd stayed away from Facebook, but she knew she had a lot of messages awaiting her on there as she'd been off the radar for a while. A few friends wondered when she'd be back in London.

After finishing up three drinks, she set off for a stroll. Once again, she had a taste for drink tonight. She was going to take it easy though. Last time she got a taste for it, she ended up losing her memory and waking up next to dead Joseph. One or two more couldn't be too bad though. She walked across Princes Street and up the hill to George Street and took a left. Window shopping as she went. The shops were closed now, but she was making mental notes of things she liked. She found herself in a dimly lit bar not dissimilar to the bar she'd just left. Dim lighting was good. She didn't feel like she needed to hide, but it felt good to be able to dissolve a into bar without standing out. A blackened eye did that to you. At the bar, she ordered a large Bombay Sapphire & tonic with a good squeeze of lime. It was still quiet and the bar man said he'd bring her drink over for her. There was only a handful of people in. She sat at a small table in the corner and sipped her drink slowly, savouring the delicate, herby fragrance.

Positive and happy now, she'd put the tough day and memory loss behind her. She evaluated her life and found herself at a cross roads. Except it wasn't a cross roads, it was more like a roundabout with ten or twenty exits all going different directions. She had a good career but was utterly bored with it. It only went one direction and that was further into finance, which was fine, but good god it was boring. She didn't want to be bored anymore. Life was too short to be bored. Now, she had the opportunity to make a new start and do something she really wanted. Not just something she'd drifted into because she'd happened to be good at mathematics from a young age. She knew of women her age who'd been able to set up in business as they had the backing of their rich, city husbands who invested in them. She sneered at the frivolity of their cake making businesses and dog grooming bars their husbands bankrolled for them. But given the choice, now that she had it, what would she do? Her possibilities were limitless. Well almost, she still needed to see exactly how much cash was in the bag, but she guessed definitely upwards of two million. Maybe she needed to do nothing for a while. Just go and travel; enjoy herself. A little time on the French Riviera or perhaps Thailand or maybe the West Coast of America; it was quite a boyish thing, but she wanted to drive the West Coast from LA, through San Fran where a friend from university now lived, on to Seattle and finally up to Vancouver where she had a Aunt she was fond of. It would have to be during the summer (this summer?) and in a convertible, but not an American one, too big for her. Maybe a Lambo. If they did convertibles. And with someone at her side. She'd be no good doing this alone. It'd need to be with a nice guy. She wasn't sure why this need was so strong. She just wasn't particularly good at being single. As independent and successful as she was, she liked a man around. Not to look after her. She definitely didn't need looking after. She just didn't like being on her own. Her own company.

She looked up from the trip that was unfolding at the bottom of her large gin and tonic glass and straight into the eyes of a guy sat at the bar. He smiled and looked into his pint, like he was a little shy. He was cute. Very cute. And damn, he already had the upper hand on her as she'd held the look for a fraction longer than him. She should have looked away straight away. She was getting cocky lately, but she supposed she quite liked it. The new, more confident Janet. She played it cool and continued to sip her drink. She was wondering if he would make a move. She doubted it from the way he looked away and back into his drink, but it was amazing what a pint could do to someone's bravado. She gently reminded herself of what had happened to her over the last few days and told herself - 'No!' The last thing she needed right now was to meet a man. She was not out for that, she was out for a few drinks to help herself shake off last few days. That was what she told herself. The reality was that she found herself watching him after a few minutes. Looking up from busying herself on her phone. Being careful to not make eye contact again, she kept her eye on him and a minute later, he looked up from his drink to her again, but this time she avoided his eyes. He was tall, probably six foot, with a mop of dark hair and light blue or green eyes, she couldn't quite see in this light.

The doors opened wide, letting in the noise of traffic and a lot of woman. A hen do started to pour rowdily in. Not the usual pink sequinned cowboy hats or printed T-shirts. They were actually just dressed regularly, but their vibe still very much said hen do (or out for a good time / off the leash / bring it on boys / I don't usually drink but I'm sloshed now). Perhaps they didn't really know where they were going or where the most appropriate bars were, but this was not one. They congregated on mass at the bar. Surrounding the cute guy. They ordered drinks (mainly vodka) and shots and then the cooing and giggling started and it was all aimed squarely at the cute guy. He must be used to this sort of attention she though.

    He lasted about two minutes before ducking out of the crowd and made for Janet's table in the corner. He wore dark, slim jeans, a white polo shirt with orange stripes on the collar and loafers. He had his jeans rolled up slightly showing tanned ankles. His wispy hair style was the sort that was supposed to look 'just out of bed' but had actually cost a pretty penny at a decent hair salon.

    "That was getting a little uncomfortable." he told her

puffing his cheeks out in relief. "Are you expecting someone or do you mind if I sit with you a while until I'm safe again?"

"Not expecting anyone, so help yourself. If you wish." Green eyes and he looked a little like a mod she noted to herself. "Thought you were going to get eaten alive just then. They seemed to have a taste for you." she said with a smirk.

"I think you're right. If I stayed, I may have ended up on a hen do for the rest of the night. I think they wanted me as a good luck charm or something."

"Believe me, that's not what they wanted you for," she said ominously, "more like sex slave I reckon."

He spat some of his beer out almost choking causing some of the younger hens to turn around and semi glare at Janet. She held her glass up to them as if wishing them a good night and under her breath whispered "Lucky escape."

"I'm Janet by the way. Would you like another drink? You seem to have drunk or spat most of yours away."

Just about able to speak again after his choking episode, "I'm Charlie, nice to meet you and yes I'd love another beer thanks. Becks."

'What are you doing?' she asked herself as she set off for the bar with the eyes of some of the hen's burning into her. She had ruffled some feathers of some younger, more 'made up' girls who were on the hen do, but her growing confidence meant she was right up there in their grill ordering drinks for the two of them. Previously, she'd have shrunk away but not any more. She was now a woman who got the better of people. This time she refused the large G&T in favour of a regular; she needed to retain a certain amount of control.

"So what do you do Charlie?" she asked sitting back down and sliding his beer over to him.

"I do IT stuff. I'm up here working for a firm of solicitors. Setting up networks and systems for a new office. How about you? Actually, let me guess... You do something to do with marketing?"

"No."

"Ok, you're a scientist?"

"Oh dear Charlie you're not very good at this are you? I'll let you have one more try."

"Mmmm, this is tough. Something career ish, I can definitely see you power dressing for a meeting... Accountant?"

"My God! Do I really look so dull? I'm in... Well actually something that's not much more exciting to be honest. I'm in banking but I don't work in a bank, I work for consumer banking at a head office. So actually, I guess it's similar to an accountant in that I work in money." Ironic, she thought once again, I certainly am in MONEY.

"What does that involve then?" Charlie asked looking genuinely interested like it was something he'd never heard of.

"Good question. Mmm, what do I do? Well I work on a team who come up with financial products for consumers." My god it sounded so dull she thought to herself. Then added "I used to work as a fund manager where I was very good at moving large amounts of cash around." She finished feeling very pleased with herself and her own little in joke.

"Cool, sounds interesting. And do you work here? In Edinburgh?"

"No, I'm just here on a financial conference. Actually, the conference has finished now, but I'm taking a few days off work to explore Edinburgh." she said galvanising something in her own mind. "It's my first time here. Such a lovely city." Although, I've hardly seen that much of it she thought slightly guiltily. Must get out and see some more of it tomorrow. "How long have you been in Edinburgh then Charlie?"

"Ooh, about a week now. It's my first time here too. We're Edinburgh virgins." he took a swig of his beer. "Cheers!"

"So have you found any cool places you can recommend to me?" she asked hopefully.

"I was going to ask you the same question. I've barely had any time off since I got here, lots of waiting around and not being able to go out."

"I heard the Candy Lounge is fun, it's not far from here... Want to try it?"

He did. They walked slowly along George Street in the warm evening. 'This feels a little too much like deja vu of the other night don't you think?' A little Angel on one of her shoulders asked her. 'Don't listen to that crap', said a voice from the other side. 'He's cute, he's fun, go with the flow. What you going to do? Lock yourself in the wardrobe in your hotel room and never come out again?'

Candy Lounge was a little busier than where they'd come from, but still not rowdy.

"My turn. What do you want?"

"Ooh, Hendricks and Tonic please." She excused herself to go to the loo.

She found herself in front of the mirror. Touching up. Staring at herself. At her face. Drifting away on her romantic road trip with Charlie. Top down. Wind in her hair. The coast flying by to her side. Charlie taking care of the driving. Of her. Heading for a beautiful hotel in LA. Blissful. Content. Then just blank. Staring. Staring. The door opened as a women came in and Janet came back to herself.

"Wake up you idiot!" she whispered at herself. "You just met him an hour ago." Her mind finished off with 'What you doing you shallow fool?' She exhaled heavily realising she was tense and holding her breath. Shaking her head at herself, she applied some lip gloss which worked out quite well. The side to side movement of her head as she berated herself mean't the lip gloss went along the full length of her lips.

She leaned into the mirror and pointed a finger at herself. "Don't you think you've had enough adventure in the last few days for a while?" With that, a toilet flushed in a cubicle and she exited back to the bar.

As she returned, Charlie was sat at a booth awaiting her. A booth always felt so much better than a table for some reason. More intimate and cosy and sociable. Charlie was holding her G&T up. "Can I just express my shock at you ordering a drink which comes with cucumber in it? That's blown my mind."

"This is the twenty first century you know." she replied sarcastically. "I see you've pushed the boat out with a..." she swooshed her hands around his drink as if displaying it on a game show, "pint of beer. How imaginative."

"Well I am but a simple IT worker me lady."

They talked about where they were from. Holidays. Bosses. As Janet neared the bottom of her glass. She suddenly felt incredibly sluggish. It hit her like a wet slap around the face. Her eye lids heavy and her head had become leaden to the point where she could barely hold it upright. Her eyes were struggling to focus on him now. She blinked several times but they stubbornly would not do as she wished. Several times, he swam between semi focus to just blurred blobs of colours and back in front of her.

She was aware of Charlie saying they'd better get some fresh air as they were drunk and he helped her out of the booth and out of the Candy Lounge. Outside they walked down the street a little. By now, she was really struggling and had her arm around his shoulder. He had his arm around her and under her arm. She thought she heard him say 'Come on you thieving whore' and asked him what he said.

"I said, 'Come on you big bore.'" She looked at him, confused and still wasn't really sure what he was saying. She squinted and shook her head, but that just made her vision go worse. A thousand lights shooting across her vision. It felt like her brain was loose and wobbling around inside her skull. Swimming about in a gin rinse.

"Where are you staying?" He asked her, but she just continued walking. It was too much to talk and walk. Her body was just telling her walk and keep walking. If you want to stay conscious and not puke, then keep walking. She was aware he was on his phone speaking to someone arranging to pick them up from somewhere. Good, she thought, he was getting some help as she couldn't walk much further. He was soothing her and telling her she would be fine. She'd simply had a little too much to drink. She started to say that she hadn't had much, but her mouth was no longer connected to her brain. He asked if she'd eaten and had maybe got food poisoning. Finally, a car pulled up beside them. It looked like a taxi. A big black car. He opened the door for her and she fell in across the back seat. Another car door opened and she was vaguely aware that Charlie got in and slammed the door. The car sped off pushing her back against the back of the seat and then hit the brakes hard rolling her forward and almost went into the footwell. The last thought her mushy brain could manage was 'this is no taxi Janet'.

FIVE

Two days after

There was that feeling again. Deja vu. Was this dream? Nightmare? She wasn't really sure what the feeling was, just that it was familiar. She was struggling to open her eye lids. Her body felt poisoned and pained, like she'd run a marathon and just crossed the finishing line. She could hear people talking but she wasn't sure who. Her head was spinning; she put it down and shut her eye lids as tight as she could and the conscious world swam away to blankness.

She slept for another two hours. Not a peaceful sleep. She twitched and flinched. Her muscles tensed and spasmed and locked. In the midst of a fog of a dream, she was being chased around a hotel with very long corridors. Someone or maybe something was following her, it wanted her, for what, she didn't know but she couldn't seem to make her legs work as they should. It was as if they were tied together and she could only take very small baby steps. Dripping in sweat, her hair was stuck to her face and in her eyes. She couldn't find the room she needed. It was further along the corridor. Aware that she was counting up as she passed each room 360, 361, 362… She wasn't at all sure what number she was trying to find, but it wasn't any of the ones she passed. Each time she looked back over her shoulder, she could see the shadow just out of sight. Menacing her. Growing as it gained on her. A hand reached for her and dark fingers crept over her shoulder.

She awoke with a start. Out of breath. Trying to pull her shoulder forward, but it wouldn't move. She was in a large leather chair. Peach leather. Stuck to her skin. There was a car in front of her, but she was indoors. It was confusing. The lights were overhead strips and bright. Way too bright for her sore eyes. The strip lights reflected brightly in the cars black paintwork. She couldn't move and was bound to the chair. Rolls and rolls of brown plastic tape wrapped around her and the chair. Stuck fast. Her forearms loose but her upper arms and body were tight to the chair. Her legs were loose too, but completely useless. All she could do was kick them in the air.

She racked her mind to try to figure out what happened. Was this something to do with Joseph? No, that was all sorted, she'd remembered all that now. He was dead, he'd died in the hotel room they'd shared and she'd taken his bag and his car. She'd left there and gone to Edinburgh. Then what? She seemed to remember going out and having some drinks in a bar. Her brain once again was just not working properly.

She could hear men talking, but not in Scottish accents. She couldn't place them but they definitely weren't Scotch. There was another car in front of the one directly in front of her. Was she in a car auction? The men were not all together, she could hear some to her left and another group to her right, each with roughly two or three men. No women's voices. These men must definitely have done this to her. There was no other explanation of how this could have happened.

"About fucking time Goldie Locks. She's up Carl!" a man to her left signalled the news to Carl.

The two groups of men came around the two ends of the cars and converged in front of her. She looked up at them. They looked at her like people might look at a caged animal at the zoo. A new species which they had not come across before. The man on the far left she recognised. She blinked hard, forcing her memory to come back. It was Charlie. Cute, handsome Charlie from the bar. And he was just allowing this to continue. She saw now. He was with them and he had done this to her. And next to him was another guy she recognised… The car park in Glasgow.

"Ooh Charlie, I think she just recognised you. Maybe you'd better get her some water as a peace offering otherwise, she might not speak to you again. You may have a little headache from a fairly hefty dose of Rohypnol you slugged down in some gin last night darling."

"I think she remembers now." Another of them said.

"She looks rough."

Charlie came back with a large glass of water and offered it to her. She opened her mouth slightly for him to give her some. She was incredibly thirsty. Off the scale thirst. She drunk half the glass but rather than feeling better, immediately felt worse. Her stomach somersaulted. The water had awoken a monster. She felt water begin to fill her mouth.

Without warning, she projected vomit in the direction of Charlie and covered his jeans as well as herself in clear bile. She caught her breath for a short second and then felt more was coming. Charlie was jumped back and slipped in her vomit and then the men were laughing so loud at her and him and it made her head hurt even more. She vomited again. Her body involuntarily heaving even more powerfully this time. Her vision blurry as her eyes watered. The laughing filled her ears and made her head pound. She retched again but the volume was much less this time. Her stomach empty. She hated being sick, but things seemed better now it was out. That strange twilight feeling between wretched and knowing that you've purged yourself of all the poison.

"Want more water? You probably need to rehydrate yourself Janet." the large bald man they called Carl said to her. "You've been sleeping for a long time."

"How long?"

"Since last night. About eighteen hours. I think you have most of it out of your system now which is good 'cos that means you should be about ready to answer some questions for us. You see, we seem to have mislaid two point five million quid somewhere." He paused and raised his eyebrows as if awaiting an answer. "I think you have it. But first we'll get you something to eat, you'll need to get some strength back. Charlie, would you do the honours?"

One by one, they walked away from her. One of the other men came back with a towel and mopped her face. She instinctively pulled away and then thought to herself why am I doing that? Idiot. He mopped her and walked away. You are a fucking idiot she told herself. How could you allow this to happen? She was oddly thinking pretty clearly now. Must be the adrenaline or something but she remembered now that Charlie went to get her a drink and he must have spiked her then. It's the oldest trick in the book. She started going through in her mind how this was going to play out. They wanted the money pure and simple. Surely, they have her handbag and would just find her keycard for her room. It clearly says which hotel is it, so they'd just find it and go and help themselves. Unless... She had an idea what may have happened.

She was going through all this and they were watching day time game shows. Trivia questions about Sport, Film, Politics and Geography. She took everything in to try to see some way or means of escape from this.

Charlie came back to her with a cold bacon roll slavered in ketchup. He offered a very small smile. She did not offer one back and neither of them spoke. There was nothing to say. Nothing that he could say that could patch things up for her. Nothing that she could say that could express how utterly pissed off she was at him. So they remained silent. He put the bread roll into her hand. She took it and stretched it to her mouth with her free forearm. It felt good to put something other than booze into her stomach.

They left her for a good half hour seemingly until the quiz show they were watching had finished and the theme tune was playing. There was some hushed talk among the group, then the leader, Carl came over on his own. He had a cup of either tea or coffee, she couldn't tell which.

"Could I have some more water please?"

"Of course you can Janet." he said holding up the glass of water to her lips. "Maybe just sip it instead of gulping it, hopefully you'll be able to keep it down then." She did as he said.

"Now, Janet, I'm going to ask you a few questions. I'm going to need honest answers and I'll warn you now. I am low on patience." She simply stared at him.

"Where is Joseph Janet? He was a bad lad and he double crossed the five of us. He was supposed to meet us. Here." He motioned to the space they were in. "But he never turned up. We were supposed to share the two point five million that he got from the art dealer, but he did a runner. I think he did a runner to meet you Janet."

She was quiet for a few seconds as if waiting to see if he had finished talking.

"If I know Joseph or know where he is, whatever your *boy* slipped into my drink last night has removed it from my brain." she croaked. She felt rough, but she needed to lay it on thick. "I hope that is a temporary thing, but I'm not sure."

Carl thought for a second. "What do you do for a living Janet?"

"I work in banking." She decided it was best to omit the details.

"So you remember that at least?" he mocked.

"I remember most stuff, I know who I am. I don't have complete amnesia, but the last few days now seem blank."

"And yet you seemed to recognise Charlie when you saw him. Why would that be if you're blank do you think?"

"I'm not sure." she said trying to look forlorn at the blankness of her mind. The expression was supposed to say - 'I want to help you Carl, I really do, but at the moment, I just can't seem to remember.'

"Do many of your colleagues have Lamborghinis Janet? When you turn up to work, do all your work mates drive up in super cars? What does your manager drive Janet? A Bugatti?"

"I don't know what you mean."

"I mean you were driving a Lamborghini when we saw you in Glasgow two days ago and I have to say that's the first time I've seen a girl your age driving a hundred grands worth of Italian sports car. It says to me that you're in cahoots with our old friend Joseph."

"Really? OK, well I'll have to take your word for it until some more of my memory comes back to me."

He put his cup down and folded his arms. "I think you're working with Joseph and that he saw us in Glasgow and asked you to get the money away from us. Sound familiar?"

"Not so far." She shook her head. "Nothing sounds familiar. Your little boy there nearly poisoned me and made my head feel like it's full of mush. I think I have short term memory loss."

"It had better be short term. It's going to start wearing pretty thin this memory loss soon Janet. Have a little more sleep and then we'll have another chat later. The next time we chat, I'd like to walk away from you with the whereabouts of Joseph and more importantly, our money. If I don't, then there is very little point for me to keep you here." he was bright red and seemed out of breath. He walked around the back of her and grabbed onto the sides of her chair. He pulled the chair back onto its two rear casters and then pushed her forward toward the others who were gathered around the other side of the cars. They parted to let her though. This was odd she thought. She was tipped so far back, so she could see his face upside down. He pushed her in between the two cars and back to where she started off. His breath was bad. Coffee and cigarettes and a distinct lack of brushing. It was making her stomach want to wretch again. He leaned close and spoke into her upside down ear. "You're surprisingly mobile. I'll bet if I wheeled you outside this lockup in your arm chair, I could have you to the dock side in half a minute. In fact, let's give it a try! Dan, get the doors!"

Dan ran around the car and pulled back the big doors as Carl wheeled her in the chair through them and across a dimly lit dockside. Until the front of her chair was butted right up to the waterfront.

"I think if you went into the water in your *current* situation, unable to flap your skinny little arms about, I think you would sink very quickly." He pushed her slightly further until the front wheels dropped over the side and tipped her forward until she was leaning tightly against the tape and that was all that held her from dropping into the inky, icy water. There was a lot of commotion around her with the other men whooping. She heard one say 'I'm not gonna' fish 'er out'.

"How does it look Janet?" Carl snarled into her ear. "I don't know about you Janet but the thought of drowning makes me feel a little bit ill. Think you'd like it? Think you'd float?"

As much as the tape held her firm, she still gripped the ends of the arm rests until her knuckles were white. 'He needs me, he's not going to drop me in. I'm his only hope of finding his money.' she told herself. 'Be strong Janet!' She shut her eyes tight. Carl pulled her back and dropped her chair back onto its four wheels and her head jolted backward. She was vaguely aware he asked one of the others to move her back inside. He walked back in front of her. Red faced and panting slightly.

"You didn't answer Janet, do you think you'd like to go in?" Carl asked, his shoulders hunched and his eyebrows raised.

"No I wouldn't like to drown."

"Well, all that is standing in the way of you and the water Janet is what's in your little head... I don't believe that you can't remember Joseph and how you came about that Gucci bag and that Lamborghini. I do believe you can't remember what happened last night, that's what rohypnol does, it blanks your short term memory out. But it doesn't affect your memory of what happened days before. All your plans with Joseph. About how you're helping him get that big bag of cash to safety. Away from us. That I believe is still very much in your mind. So have a little sleep and have a think about your future. And whether or not you want one."

He reached out and grabbed her neck and pushed her back into the chair so she was looking directly into his eyes. Her airway was cut off. "We understand each other?"

She nodded her chin as much as she could though it was difficult in his grip. "Clever girl. Clever Janet." He released her neck and gave her cheek a friendly clap on the cheek. Then he smiled and walked away.

He had been gentle with her, but there was some real power in those meat slabs of hands. She shut her eyes, she was desperately tired, but she needed to think. Think how she was going to get her stupid self out of this mess. She traced herself backward from this point, back to the bar where he bought her *that* drink. He didn't give a thing away. He was so subtle. What a scum bag. So smooth as he handed her a double gin & rohypnol with lots of lime. Her deadly apple in a glass. Ready to put her to sleep and render her defenceless.

She didn't have any pockets and everything she had with her was in her bag. She could probably cut herself out if she could get her nail file from her bag, but that wasn't going to happen, they wouldn't be handing that over anytime soon. What else did she have that was sharp? Her nails, but they wouldn't penetrate the tape. Earrings. Sharp but no match for the tape which was probably 10 layers thick at some points. If they hadn't used so much, she might just be able to break it by pushing her arms out, but it was gripping her like a vice. No give whatsoever. She looked down at herself. Scanning for something sharp. Belt buckle. That would be able to pierce the plastic. If she could perforate a line from top to bottom, she might be able to rip through it. She wasn't sure if she had the strength to do it. She'd probably only have one chance, if they saw what she was up to before she escaped, she'd be in trouble.

So far she'd been pretty lucky, they'd not managed to get what they wanted off her, but if they had that key card, they'd be gone and who knows they may just discard her. She assumed that card had slipped down through a hidden hole in the lining of her bag. She'd lost credit cards in there before. They wouldn't find the gap if they didn't know about it. She'd forgotten about it several times and eventually found all sorts down in there. Lipsticks, nail files, cash.

Making sure no one was around, she could just get the belt off as a start. The problem was the tape was quite noisy whenever she moved. She didn't want to disturb the men. The belt was a simple grey suede belt with a steel buckle. It would punch through the tape pushed hard enough.

At the other side of the cars the TV was turned up. Sounded like they were all in front of the TV once again. A happy little family of thugs and thieves. Watching a boxing match she thought, from the sounds of the cheering crowd, a dinging bell and some overly excited commentators.

She freed the belt and unbuckled it and slowly fed it through the belt loops. She got it off and tucked it into her side. She wanted to make sure she could hide it if necessary. It needed folding in half but then it would slip neatly next to her leg. If they really looked, they'd see it but more than likely they wouldn't she thought. She pulled it back out and pushed the loop of the buckle back leaving the point which she grasped between her thumb and forefinger. She reached across with her free forearm and was able to reach all the way to the top of the strapping which ran the length of her upper arms. The point gradually punched through the tape into the space between her arm and body. It needed a firm giggling push to break through. She then pulled it back through and pierced again about thumb width lower. She repeated this again and again until she'd perforated a line of ten holes up the full width of the webbing. She tried to push her arms away from her body to pull the webbing apart but it wouldn't budge. Yet.

She continued punching holes in between the first set of holes until she reached the top of the tape holding her upper arms. She couldn't do the very top part as the tape was over her shoulder and to punch through the tape would mean plunging the point into her skin. Once again, she tried to push her arms outwards, the tape seemed to give a little more than it had before, she could see the perforations stretching but it still would not tear. She was determined though. It was amazing the determination a threat to your life could give you. Taking a deep but quiet breath and she started punching more holes again one in between each of the existing holes. Ten minutes later, she'd punched another set of holes through the tape. This time she pushed her arms outwards but it still held fast. But she could just about get her hands to meet in the middle so that she could push outward against them. The tape started to tear but it made a loud squeak. She stopped moving and heard movement. She shut her eyes and lolled her head to the side. She could just about see one of the men stand up and look over the top of the cars, he soon dismissed the noise and sat back down.

    She needed to plan her escape route before she released herself from the tape. There was a door to her left, but it was too near to where the men were gathered around the TV. If she got to it before them and out, they would soon catch her, she was a good runner, but one of them would no doubt be faster. There could be a back door but she couldn't see it. There was a door to her right which led to the back, it could possibly have a back door or a window but she couldn't see from where she was. She seemed to remember hearing a toilet flush back there. That would probably mean there would be a window but probably a small one. There was no other exit she could see. She would have to take her chance. Or she could just tell him where Joseph was and what happened to him and return the money. She could but somehow she thought that would not be the last of it. *Oh thanks so much for giving us our money back Janet dear. On your way and have a nice life!*

    No, she had got to this point, she now needed to see this through. Something in her had changed in the last few days. She would have been a crying, screaming, gibbering wreck at this point if this was her previous life. To be fair, she could have a good old cry now, but she would not allow herself to do that. She was stronger and would remain strong. If caught, she would then 'fess up as to Joseph's whereabouts and what happened to him. She still had the money as a bargaining tool. She could take them to it and then scream blue murder and take her chances with the police. What would they do about it? Probably she had broken some laws along the way and would spend a little time in prison, but a little time in prison was better than being fish food.

    She placed her hands back together and with as much control as possible, pushed hard. Gradually straightening her wrists out as the perforation down her left side opened up one hole at a time. The temptation to rush was overwhelming as they may decide at any moment to come over and interrogate her again, but she knew if she went too fast it would make noise. They still seemed to be engrossed in their boxing match. There was a lot of boxing chat and encouragement of their preferred fighter.

She tore all the way through the perforation. Now she needed to peel back either side. This was taking too long. She shut her eyes tight again to force her brain to speed up. *Take the blouse off.* Of course, it was obvious, the tape was stuck fast to her top, but now she was no longer secured to the chair and had freedom to move, she could slip down and out of the top. She'd then be just in her bra, but that was the price to pay for her escape. Slowly and silently, she slid downwards and out of the floral cotton shirt. She was free. Well of her tape bond at least. She had to work fast. She went low and toward the door at the right of the room. A quick look revealed it was a disgusting toilet with a tiny frosted glass window. She'd never get out of it. Fuck.

She went back to the car and as she suspected the keys were in. She sat down on the floor and leaned back against the car. She thought through her plan. She would need to be fast and time it exactly right. She crept round the car as low as possible to the car nearest the men. As quiet as a mouse, she reached through the half lowered window and grabbed the key from the ignition. Single thankfully, no bunch of keys to make noise. She saw the backs of the heads of the men, they drank beers and were eating pizza. A regular little party. Whilst they left her to fester in her own vomit. Mother fuckers. She ducked back down and tracked back around the car furthest from them. She gently lifted the handle and slowly pulled open the door. This might have alerted them, but it didn't. She slunk low into the drivers seat. The window was down on their side. When she turned the key, she'd need to work quick to wind up the window and lock the doors. That should keep them at bay for a short while. Electric window switches. Check. Central locking button. Check.

She held the window buttons down, grabbed the key and turned. She pumped her foot on the gas and revved the engine. It fired up and she saw the rev counter hit the red line. It was deafening in such as small space. She saw the men moving from the corner of her eye, they were jumping around manically. She slammed the door shut, then realised that the windows weren't going up. Damn where they broken? She released the buttons and pushed again and they started to lift. She hit the lock button with her other hand. Now, they were all around the car. They were all shouting crazily at her, baying her name. Knocking loudly on the window at the side of her head.

"Janet, what the fuck are you doing?!" Carl demanded.

She heard one shout 'smash the fuckin' windows' and another 'with what?' It was time to go. She pulled the gear lever to reverse. Took the handbrake off and pushed the accelerator. She went backwards and hit the doors and they made a big dull bang, but held firm. She pushed the gear lever to drive and went forwards, men were jumping out of the way. There were a variety of expressions ranging from surprise to anger. She braked and placed the gear in reverse again and hit the accelerator. Hard this time. She went flying forwards onto the steering wheel as the car went flying backwards. It hit the wooden doors and blasted through like a ten pin ball.

She pushed the brake peddle and the car came to a stop. The engine purred as she sat for a moment looking at the men. The courtyard lit up red from the brake lights. They looked stunned and confused. Two of them jumped into the other car, a Mercedes, which seemed smaller than the one she was in and then they were shouting at each other, no doubt about the whereabouts of the keys. She held the key up to them and pointed to it with her free hand. She was focused on Carl.

The expression of anger on his face actually changed from outright anger to a small smile and his head shook slightly as if to say 'We weren't good enough. Well done. You got one over on us'. But there was still menace in his face, this was her throwing down the gauntlet and him saying you got us this time, but you won't be getting us again. Once we catch up with you again, that will be the last chance you get to turn over Joseph and the money.

It was time to go. She turned the lights on and pulled the gear lever back to drive once again, turned the steering wheel and set off. As she flew off, she dropped one of her now signature winks at no one in particular. It was only going to aggravate them, but to be honest, they were about as mad as they were going to get. She looked down and remembered that she was just in her bra and felt her face flush hot. All cocky and yet only half dressed. That cockiness might just turn out to be my downfall she thought. How the hell was she going to get something to wear. She couldn't very well walk into a shop in her bra and ask where the blouses were. No shops would be open at this time anyway. She didn't really want to be doing too much driving around in just a bra as she'd probably get stopped and sectioned. Where could she find something to wear? On a clothes line? That's how it would happen in a film, but more than likely clothes wouldn't be out over night. How about a clothes bank. That's where she sent her clothes that had sadly passed out of fashion. Where would she find a clothes bank? The one she used in London was at a shopping centre. Maybe she would see a shopping centre if she looked out.

She continued driving in no particular direction and saw a pub with a Scottish flag hanging outside. An idea popped into her head. A long shot. She pulled over, had a look around. No cars about, no people about. She got out of the car, bold as brass climbed up on the wall and yanked the flag which tore off its pole, walked back to the car and drove off at speed. She pulled up a side street, got out, folded the flag so it was in a triangle and then wrapped it around herself in a sort of boob tube style, looped the ends around again and tied them at the front. It was probably the oddest thing she'd ever seen someone wear. 'Style it out' she told herself firmly, 'carry it off with confidence and you'll get away with it.'

Now she needed to get back to the hotel as soon as possible as they had probably followed her back there from Glasgow. Although they didn't have transport currently. They clearly didn't know her hotel room or they would have taken her from her hotel room. The reason they'd done what they'd done was because she'd got out of the hotel and into the public and it was difficult to just nab someone in public view. Unless they looked blind drunk and like they needed a helping hand to get home. If she went straight away, she'd definitely beat them there. Then what? Well she needed some stuff, she'd lost her phone and bank cards in that bag they have. She needed to get back to the hotel room and either get the money and get out of town or lay low while she figured out what to do next.

She drove to the side of the hotel and parked up on a double yellow line. Got out with both sets of the key clutched in her hands. Just in case. She walked toward the hotel and asked for a replacement key card from reception. They were very cool about the lost card. 'These things happen Madam.' 'They certainly seemed to with me' she thought standing in the reception in her patriotic boob tube. She felt pretty silly in it but looked outwardly as if she was super confident. She was a Lamborghini driving millionaire for christ's sake, why wouldn't she be confident.

Back in her room, she laid back on the bed. Finally able to relax a little after yet another horrific night. Her headache still screamed from the rohypnol. She took a few painkillers and shut her eyes. Losing her phone was not good, but it was locked at least and she could buy another and back it up from her computer. Actually, there was Joseph's phone, she could just use that, put a new sim card in.

Joseph's phone started to vibrate again. Someone still thought he was alive. She sat up. Actually, she thought, how had they tracked her to Edinburgh? She had lost them in the car driving away from Glasgow. Definitely. She'd pulled over several times and they were not following her. But yet, Charlie had just managed to rock up in a bar she was having a drink in. So how did that happen? He can't have just happened to be in that bar. It would be a miracle if they'd managed to find themselves in that same bar just out of chance. So if it wasn't chance, then they must have some means of tracking Joseph. Did they have something in the bag? She went to the bag, there were no pockets, just the main compartment. She stuck her hand down the sides of all the cash, but couldn't feel any gadgets. The phone dinged again, Joseph had another message. Lucky man. Was it the phone? She'd seen something on her computer about 'Finding my phone' or 'Track my phone'. Was it an app? Or something in settings or something. There was definitely something she'd seen.

They probably just tracked the phone here, as they had more than likely tracked it to the hotel in Glasgow. So if the phone wasn't here, more than likely they would track it and follow it where it went. She could post it to London and they would probably follow it there. But how could she get out of the hotel to post it in the first place? They'd more than likely be at the hotel by now, in the lobby waiting for her to come down. Or the little one would be wandering around the corridors looking for her.

One thing was for sure and that was she needed to be rid of Joseph's phone. There was no reason to keep hold of it now. They might still not be at the hotel yet, so perhaps she could get out. But she was so tired. She put her head back to rest for a moment. 'Come on Janet!' She forced herself to get up and grab Joseph's phone. There was a message from Carl.

U just sined your death warrent janet

She shouldn't reply, but she couldn't help herself.

Original Carl x

She peered around the door into the corridor. She could see no one there. She meandered down toward the lifts area. A porter's trolley stood alone in the corridor. The porter was in the room and she heard a man telling a women they were going to miss their train if they were much longer. She sensed an opportunity and quickly opened a pocket up on a wheel-able suitcase, pushed Joseph's phone deep into it, closed it back up and continued walking. She got to the lifts and did a loop and walked back to her room. She walked past the couple and the porter, their bags (and Joseph's phone) now on their way to the lifts. Good riddance. The phone was charged, hopefully, the men would track it and follow it.

Shortly after Joseph's phone started its journey on the 12:30 from Edinburgh Waverley station to London King's

Cross, followed by Carl and Jim, she'd sneaked out one of the hotel's rear fire exits. Her very helpful concierge had ordered her a taxi and met her there. He protested but eventually accepted a thick wad of cash in an envelope as payment accepting the story that 'some bad people were after her.' The wad would cover her stay at the hotel and give the Concierge a very nice tip. She got back to her old hotel. Her plan now was to lay low. Super low for a good few days. She caught up with friends and family and let them know she was fine but was taking a short break from work. That was her story, but the reality was she did not plan to return to work. At least not to her previous work. In fact, she wasn't sure she could go back to her previous life at all.

. . .

The Glasgow hotel made several oversights in the discovery of Joseph Bainbridge's body. The cleaner should have alerted the cleaning co-ordinator that the room had not been cleaned for several days. The duty manager was supposed to find out what was happening with the room, but after one call to the room phone and one to Joseph's phone where a message was left, he forgot to make any further calls amidst a pile of other jobs and duties. All their systems failed. In the end, the hotel staff were alerted that there may be a problem by one of the window cleaners. He saw Joseph on the bed and even from a distance, immediately knew there was a major problem.

The manager poked his head around the door and the smell hit him like a smack to the face. He swiftly retracted to the safety of the corridor where he immediately called 999 from his mobile phone.

Thirty minutes later, an ambulance crew decided they didn't want to touch anything and that the police should be involved. Caution was the best approach now. Shortly after that, Inspector Casey arrived. He spoke with the manager on the way from reception to the room and on the basis of what he heard, he called in the crime scene team. If the guy had just been on his own and had died, then fair enough, these thing happen. But this guy wasn't on his own, he'd been with a woman and now she was gone. It had foul play written in large print all over it.

With his handkerchief over his nose and mouth, he stood calmly in the corner of the room watching the crime scene officers do their work. They dusted for prints, photographed the room and the corpse and tagged evidence. So far, nothing much to go on. No phone. No car keys. No bag. Just a wallet and a suit. He tried to take in the whole room and get a sense of what had happened. There were two empty and knocked over bottles of champagne, along with an empty bottle of red, evidence of cocaine use, there was a used condom floating in the toilet.

When Janet had fled the room, she had left a good looking corpse. Now, after a week of Joseph's body consuming itself from the inside out along with all the chemical processes and reactions that entailed; his body was a shade of sage green with purplish patches. His eyes bulged out of their sockets and his lips were parted by his tongue which protruded slightly. A reaction to the pressure increase in his diaphragm from a build up of gases. Where he previously had a flat and defined stomach, it now bloated to the point he looked several months pregnant.

Casey left the room for the corridor and closed the door behind him. "Tell me everything you know once more please." He asked the manager. "The time they arrived. What they ate in your restaurant. How much they spent. What they ordered on room service. How much they tipped."

"Okay. The problem here is that they checked in a week ago. So I'll tell you what I know and if you have questions which I don't have answers for, I'll do my best to find answers." Casey nodded understandably. "They arrived mid evening, around 8pm and ate in the restaurant. They had booked by telephone. Ate two courses and drank two full bottles of red wine. Mr Bainbridge was a very generous tipper from what my staff have told me." He handed over a receipt for the restaurant bill. "Then after the meal, they booked into a room. That is the last dealing we have had with them. With him."

"So you just left them for a week? What about room service? Meals? Cleaners?"

The manager was bright red now. "Yes, there have been several breakdowns in our systems which we will be working to ensure don't happen again."

Casey raised his eyebrows. They said everything that needed to be said about this.

"A cleaner saw the girl on the day after they checked in. She was attempting to clean the room but the woman asked her to come back another time. Apparently, she had a blackened eye and she acted strange."

"Strange in what way."

"Shifty and nervous. She first asked the cleaner to come back later and then she said no much much later. My staff did not see her again after that."

"CCTV?" Casey enquired expectantly.

"I have my duty manager going through it now and he will report to me shortly what footage we have. I'm sure we'll have some of the pair of them passing through reception."

"I'm especially interested in getting a face shot of the dead man's companion."

"Yes, of course. Anything else I can help with?"

"Not for now." Casey dismissed him and returned to the dead man's room. He would need to speak to the woman. There was no doubt. He okayed the coroner to take the body away for autopsy. He'd be glad to get the body out of the room. After the body had been zipped into a body bag and removed, Casey pushed the windows as wide as they'd go to allow some air into the room. The stench was distracting. The thing that struck him as being odd in this room was there was no bag or suitcase. They had checked in on the spur of the moment it seemed, but no bag at all seemed wrong.

"Sir." A call came from the bathroom.

Casey walked to the door to see who was calling. It was Diane, the oldest woman on the team and the most experienced.

"This panel was loose on the side of the bath and I found this inside." She held up a black gun with a pencil though the trigger.

Casey would spend the next two weeks on and off the investigation. He managed to get the CCTV into some local TV news and the stills of the woman into Scottish papers. Unfortunately, none of this made the national media. It infuriated him. This lack of interest south of the border was what held the investigation back to his mind. It was typical.

His commanding officer told him to bring the investigation to a conclusion, one way or another. And yet, something niggled at him about what he found in that room.

Something was really wrong with it all. The fact that there was no bag. Who travels without a bag? Even just a small overnight bag. Or work bag. Something.

He filed his report. Secretly however, he vowed to keep the investigation going.

PART 2

SIX

Two hundred and twelve days after
Janet was awoken by the sunlight streaming through the light cream curtains in her bedroom. Another sunny day. 'You could never get too much sun' was her first thought of the day. It was pleasantly warm and she had slept with just a sheet and a throw. She was in her new house. After renting for five months, it was good to be more settled.

Her place in London was now rented out. Furnished with her stuff. It felt pretty odd to have other people sitting on her sofa, sleeping in her bed and using her pots and pans but it had been the simplest way to do it. Fleeing Edinburgh, she had been worried they may still track her somehow, so she'd allowed herself just one day in London to tie up all her loose ends. She met an estate agent at her Clapham flat and gave them the keys. She handed the whole thing over to them and so far they'd done a pretty good job. It was rented out within 2 weeks and since then, she'd not heard a peep. Just seen the rent money going into her UK bank account each month minus their fees of 13%. Well worth it she thought.

She'd then booked a suite at the Mercer in Barcelona and called ahead to explain she would be expecting a large parcel. She wrapped the bag full of money in several layers of bubble wrap, then placed it in a cardboard box and repeated the process twice. She parcel taped all the edges and googled 'courier a parcel London to Barcelona'.

She'd packed her large wheel-able suitcase (to the brim) and taken a taxi to St Pancreas. A ticket to Perpignan was purchased and she took the next Eurostar via Paris. As she sped first class across France, she set about stamping out the digital footprints that would eventually lead the unwanted to her. She logged into Facebook on her iPad, went to her account settings and eventually after a little searching found the button - PERMANENTLY DELETE ACCOUNT and without much of a thought, she killed it. Dead. Yes she had photos and messages she'd have preferred to keep but she had to take steps now to make sure no one was able to trace where she was. She also deleted her Twitter account. She only had 41 tweets, so it wasn't the end of the world. The twitter-sphere would not implode on itself with the lack of her content. There was also accounts on MySpace, LastFM and Pinterest (no pins). Her phone, which the gang had, was locked but with a little help from a tutorial she found on Google, she was able to figure out how to completely wipe all her information from the phone. She couldn't resist sending a message just before she wiped it saying 'bye bye boys'. She had no idea whether they would see it not, but still it felt good. She would have to get phone numbers for friends by emailing them. Just like the social media accounts she had which were barely used, she had more than two hundred contacts in her phone, but she probably only really wanted to contact a handful, twenty at most. It would be a pain, but she'd get their details back. She'd got to the point where she had people in her contacts who she didn't really know. Possibly business contacts or friends or acquaintances who's details she had swapped on drunken nights out.

Did she need to change her name? She seemed to recall telling Charlie what her name was. Definitely her first name, she wasn't sure about her surname. Would that be normal to tell someone you were having a drink with what your full name was? Probably not. Janet was not a very common name among women her age. That was not a good thing. What else did they know that they could use to track her? Profession. She had said roughly what she did for a living although, based on what she usually told people, she would not have mentioned her employer. Charlie knew she lived in London. What else? Did she mention her age? Probably, she seemed to know how old Charlie was, so it figured they had discussed her age and it wasn't something she was concerned about, so why would she not tell him. That was quite a bit to go on, but so long as she didn't blast her whereabouts to all and sundry online, she would more than likely be ok. She'd worked out she was putting 1,300 miles between them. As well as the whole of France. Surely that had to be enough.

From Perpignan, she'd taken a cab to Coulliere. This was pretty much the last town on the French Riviera before reaching the Spanish border. The plan had been to go all the way through to Barcelona, but it was just too much in one go. Ten or so hours on trains. Plus the Edinburgh to London journey with a short stop over. It had been better than a plane (she hated flying), but the whole point was you could jump on and off trains.

Coulliere just looked so beautiful. It was the first time she'd seen the sea on this journey and it just seemed so incredibly blue and welcoming. The terracotta tiled roofs glowed in the late afternoon sun and the tiny town seemed so comforting. The taxi driver had taken her to what he said was the best hotel. In Coulliere, she was able to relax for a night or so and get over her ordeals that had happened in Glasgow and Edinburgh. She researched apartments to rent in Barcelona. She considered staying in Coulliere but it didn't give her the camouflage she required. With Barcelona, she would have the madness that is Barcelona going on all around her.

By the time she arrived in Barcelona by taxi, she had three apartments to view. She viewed all three apartments and took the last one. A fourth story apartment in the Gothic Quarter or Barri Gòtic as the locals called it. Two small bedrooms, a large grand bathroom which was inexplicably the largest room in the apartment, a kitchen, slash dining area and a compact but bright living room. The living room had double doors which opened to a small balcony overlooking Via Laietana. A busy street where there was usually a lot of noise most of the day and night. Car horns. Screeching tyres. Men and women shrieking at one another. Consumed with the heat. She loved it. Very... Spanish.

It was the way it was furnished which made the apartment though. Antique pieces mixed and matched with contemporary furniture. A strange mixture of reproduction Spanish art from Valasquez to Dali via Goya, Miro and Prado.

Far too much bull fighting paraphernalia dotted about the apartment but hey this was Catalan Spain. They loved it here. A brightly decorated bull fighting spear stood up in one corner of her bedroom which appeared to have dried blood on the white fluffy decorated stem. Was it bull blood or man blood she wondered. It was hooked on the spear end. This hook was probably how it stayed attached to the bull she thought but wasn't sure. Her opinion was that it was a barbaric way of entertaining people. It creeped her out as did all the other bull fighting ornaments, paintings and photos - usually of proud looking bull fighters just dodging huge bulls whilst dressed as if for a lead role in a ballet. She quite liked it when the bull got his man but she decided that was probably best kept to herself around here.

Right on time, the Hotel Mercer called letting her know her parcel was awaiting her. She had to get rid of all this cash into a bank security box as soon as possible. As much as she'd grown used to having this lump of pure cash around her without any security, it just didn't make any sense to keep it in her apartment.

After finding the Spanish for security deposit box (caja de seguridad) and asking around at one or two banks, she found a small bank that had exactly what she needed. She created an account and was made aware of the costs for the box which would be taken by direct debit. The bank was in a beautiful old building not far from her flat. The next day, she took half the cash in and asked for access to her box. She was shown upstairs by a young lady who introduced herself as Sandra. Sandra made no small talk at all. This was not *that* type of a bank. It was a bank of discretion. They wanted to know nothing of your personal life. The safety deposit boxes were on the fourth floor. Sandra showed her into one of several similar looking rooms. She pulled out Janet's security box which was quite large and unlocked it but did not open it. She explained that once she was finished, she just needed to ring the bell by the door and Sandra would come back to get her. Sandra spoke very good English. Once Janet was alone, she opened the box lid and unzipped her bag. She took her time counting the money. She was fairly sure she'd got about half the cash, certainly in weight. She carefully counted two of the bundles of notes. Each bundle contained two hundred twenty pound notes. All brand new, making up four thousand per bundle and there were three hundred and four bundles in this bag. According the calculator on her phone, this was

£1,216,000.

So there'd be roughly two and a half million across both bags minus the bits she'd spent which didn't amount to very much. Just wait until she'd had a real shopping spree. No, Jesus this wasn't a joke. Two point five million pounds was a really scary amount, but there was no going back at this point. She had pissed off the people who wanted this cash quite royally now. She'd made her (very expensive) bed and now she'd have to lay in it. The next day, she took the Gucci bag in with the other half of the cash. Again she was shown to the room, this time by Marcos. Again, he explained the routine for calling him back and with that, he left her to her privacy. She couldn't be bothered to do counting again. What did ten or even a hundred thousand matter at this point. She knew roughly what the contents came to. Once she had all the cash out and into the security box, she closed the lid. The bag lay empty apart from one or two notes lying about in the bottom loose. She scooped them up and stuck them into her handbag. It was time to stick this incriminating bag into a bin. She stuck her hand in and found the base was open on one side. It was the hard piece across the bottom of the bag which gave it shape and solidity. There was something under it. An envelope. Beautifully handwritten across were the words Mr J. Nicholson. Was that Joseph? Had to be really she guessed. She placed it into the bottom of her handbag along with one bundle of notes and then zipped it up the Gucci bag. She wanted to get out of the room and back home. As soon as she was out of the bank, the Gucci bag was dropped at the nearest charity shop. Once home, she read the letter.

Dearest J,

I do apologise that I couldn't come to meet you personally recently, but you know how discrete we need to be in our line of business. Once things die down a little, I would like you to help me with a little project around the Sea of Galilee.

An acquaintance of a friend of a friend has recently acquired a piece and needs some help with transportation logistics from some calm, Still Waters and I know you are well versed in such matters. If you could help, that would be Nice. You have my details when you are ready to get in touch.

With Best Regards, MPW

What the hell was all that about? Talk about cryptic. She was sure it was meant for Joseph, who would not be reading it anytime soon. It may have made perfect sense to him, but she doubted it. There seemed to be a code in it, but if there was, it was not making itself clear to her. Did Galilee still exist, she thought that might be an old biblical name. There were other things in there which were capitalised which seemed to stand out. Still Waters and Nice should not be capitalised. Unless they were names of things. Or places. She read it again. Sea of Galilee and calmer, Still Waters. Hmm. So the project was that MPW wanted to get something from the Sea of Galilee to Still Waters and that would be Nice. She decided she'd let this percolate for a little while. She was a clever girl she reminded herself and she would crack this one way or another.

During five months renting in the heart of Barcelona, she enjoyed not working. She took Spanish classes. She had taken Spanish at school, enjoyed speaking Spanish whenever she was in Spain and it came back to her quickly. Her new life was simpler than before, less complicated and stress free. It was a life where she didn't draw attention to herself. She blended in to her surroundings and the people around her. She visited the safety deposit box weekly and squirrelled away about a tenth of the cash into other bank accounts. She was buying a house and couldn't very well turn up with a bag of cash. Plus it made sense to 'diversify her investment'.

Over the course of the next few months, Janet travelled. She did her tour of the Americas. Planes, trains and automobiles. Starting off flying to Vancouver, through Amsterdam with Royal Dutch. A week of exploring Vancouver and spending time with her favourite long lost aunt before setting off toward Los Angeles via Seattle, San Francisco, San Jose and Las Vegas. She travelled business class or first class wherever she went for no other reason than because she could now. When you had the money, why would you not travel with table service. She mainly took the train with one stint on a

Greyhound between San Francisco and Las Vegas but decided the train was a much preferable means of getting around. The Greyhound didn't turn out to be as romantic as the song America would have her believe. She was in no rush and took her time to explore as she went. She took photos but didn't put anything online as she had nowhere to put them. She would get them printed once she got home. And put them in an album. Just like people used to do. Her life was analogue now.

She stayed for a month in LA soaking up the atmosphere, the culture, and the just plain out-there weirdness of the place. LA was one of those places that split opinion. You loved it or loathed it. Janet fell into the love camp. She mainly enjoyed the showy craziness. She had stints at the Four Seasons and the Bel-Air hotels before renting a one bed apartment near Santa Monica. Didn't have a sea view, but was just a five minute walk to the beach.

She had sat next to a red-head called Tess on the train from Las Vegas to LA. They exchanged email addresses and Janet got a mail from her a few days into her LA stint. She really didn't think she would do. Tess was 27, from Sydney and a free spirit. She'd been traveling for the last eleven months and had no plans to stop traveling and head home anytime soon. Janet was drawn to the adventurous aura that surrounded Tess. Tess was drawn to Janet's hedonism. They hung out together occasionally meeting in The Beverly Hills Hotel on Sunset Boulevard, drinking Mai Tais and Frozen Mojitos and going to gigs at the Viper Room and the Bootleg Theatre.

Tess was tall and elegant and had her own distinct style. 'High class hippy hooker' was the look she was aiming for she so she said. Janet's blond hair combined with Tess's red locks attracted the boys like boozy drunken bees. They buzzed around and were occasionally allowed to get them a cocktail and if they had some good chatter, they'd be allowed to stick around for a while longer. Now and then, the boozy bees would get lucky. But mostly, they were having too good a night to let it get spoilt by men.

Tess had her own money. She inherited a large chunk of it from an older cousin she'd known until she was four. She'd never seen her since that fourth birthday and it had been a total shock. Some people just had this sort of luck Janet thought, before reminding herself she'd had a little break recently too. Tess certainly didn't have an aversion to spending her way through it.

After the west coast of America, Janet wanted to go to Cuba and South America. Firstly Havana, then Rio before heading onto Buenos Aires. Then finally, she would go to Barbados and find a beach hut and relax for a month. She convinced Tess to go with. Tess had wanted to explore South America too but was a little unsure about doing it alone. The arrangement worked well for the pair of them. They'd stay ten days in each place, give or take, and share accommodation. Neither of them needed to stay places long enough to find jobs and work to earn their keep or conserve their finances.

They stayed in Havana's most exclusive hotel; Janet took a suite. It was grand but fabulously old fashioned and dilapidated; stubbornly remaining in a different era. They sought out the very best bars the place had to offer and drank copious numbers of Mojitos nightly. Mojitos were a drink that hit you hard in the morning and the best way to combat the thud in the back your head was to take an afternoon cocktail and get back on the wagon. A week into their stay, a Saturday, they found one of the local's drinking dens and were very pleased with themselves. The whole point of traveling was to get away from the tourists. Away from the beaten track. No tourists found this place. It was a dark hole of a bar. Hot, sweaty, sticky, smokey. No well turned-out visitors wearing designer brands in this bar; just local Havanans with few worldly cares. Drinking their way through simpler lives. A motley Latino jazz crew played between drinks and smokes providing an irresistible foot tapping backing track. The Mojitos and Caipirinhas were delicious and lethal in equal measures. Two guys ended up chatting to them, one of them said he owned the bar. A striking pairing with slicked hair, sparkling brown black eyes and big collars. Their English was broken but it didn't dilute their swaggering double act. The pair were amazed that these two had found the bar and quizzed them on how they managed it. They bought them drinks and kept them flowing. Janet watched the pair like a hawk even though she was getting drunk and giddy. They didn't seem like the sort that would spike their drinks, but this was Havana and Charlie hadn't seemed like the sort that would spike drinks either. Janet was so concerned with ensuring they were straight up with the drinks that she missed the real problem. The drinks didn't need spiking, they had the kick of a vexed donkey without any additional chemicals. From about 11pm, the night speeded up as those nights tend to. Before they knew it, they were dancing on the bar with the men, getting whooped by customers. Then they were at the friend's flat which was above another bar with the two men. Drinking again. Beers, shots of tequila, but this was not the salt and lemon type, it was more refined, you could drink it straight and it was smooth and tasty. A joint was passed around. It made Janet feel loose limbed and giggly.

Tess danced with the bar owner's friend to a vinyl record they'd put on which was perfect follow on music to what had been playing in the bar. Janet was slouched on the sofa chatting and flirting and laughing with the bar owner. Discussing their collective thoughts on America. Then he was talking about her hands and how beautiful they were and then before she knew it, her finger was in his mouth. Sucking on it. It shouldn't have but it made her giggle even more.

Then he was pulling her up some stairs which he seemed to have pulled from the ceiling out of nowhere. As they climbed them, the stairs waddled side to side under their weight. And then they were on the roof of the building under a billion stars. He had deck chairs into which they collapsed. It was the perfect stargazing spot. Occasionally Janet called out to Tess to ensure she was all good. Tess would call back 'all good hun'. She wanted to make sure all was well but at the same time it was nice to have this privacy. She liked the bar owner. He was cheeky, charming, handsome and funny. He produced another joint from his chest pocket. Then from a tin box which sat between the deck chairs he pulled another bottle of rum. He poured them a small glass each and downed his straight off. She decided that was a sign all was ok. It was delicious. She took the bottle to see the make, but there was no English words on this bottle. She reminded herself that she'd need to take it easy from now on. She could easily imagine herself ending up here at the end of her remaining night in Havana. She felt incredibly content.

Suddenly, from downstairs, she heard the atmosphere change. Something happened between Tess and the bar owners friend and she heard a slap above the sound of the music. She jumped up and got down the rickety steps as quickly as she could. Before Janet knew it, they were in a full on shouting match with the bar owners friend. Janet grabbed Tess to make for the door. The bar owner pulled out a knife from a sock and jumped in front of them as if to stop them leaving holding the knife up toward them. He'd stopped speaking in his broken English and was now just shouting in Spanish at both the girls and his friend. The knife was a particularly nasty looking job which was really quite dirty. Hunting knife Janet guessed. She was panicked and trying to find out from Tess what had happened but all she could get from her was 'we are leaving!' Tess ignored her and went as if to slap the bar owners friend and then kicked him as hard as she could in his crotch in a single sharp action. It was the most amazing thing she'd ever seen. He dropped like a stone to his knees. The knife dropped onto a chair allowing his hands to cover and protect the source of the pain. He had stopped shouting and was whispering quietly to himself in Spanish. Janet grabbed the knife and Tess once more and pulled her toward the door. She was shouting something back at the man she'd slapped about rape and being presumptuous. They got onto the street without talking and started down it as fast as their feet would take them without actually breaking into a run. A loud crash exploded behind them. They looked behind briefly and there was a plant pot strewn across the road. She guessed the bar owner's friend had slung it. At the end of the street, Janet clattered the knife into a bin and the pair of them burst into nervy laughter at exactly the same time. Probably from their massive bursts of adrenalin starting to subside. They ended up with cans of beer sitting on the beach watching the sun coming up, chatting the pointless chatter of people who've drunk a skin-full. Tess confided that she had wanted to have sex with the guy, but he said that they wanted a foursome, then he had just started in on groping her roughly. 'Fucking men!'

Tess was a lot of fun, but Janet soon discovered she was hard work to live with at close quarters. Janet believed her life to be manic, messy and generally a little on the sporadic side. Tess was all this to the power of ten. They lasted 4 nights staying in the same suite. Had a rum drunk row about politics and decided the morning after that they'd both prefer a bit more space. The crazy thing was Janet had absolutely no interest in politics. They stuck together though and went on to visit Rio and Buenos Aires before locating side by side beach huts in Barbados. As beach huts went, these were the finest money could rent. Tess stayed in Barbados for a week, lazing around on the beach like an exotic Aussie lizard before heading off to find some more culture in Europe. She said she would 'start in Naples and work her way north until she could see the northern lights'. Janet said she would visit her next year, either in Australia or wherever she happened to be.

This paradise was too perfect for Janet to give only a week to. She stuck around and learned to scuba dive with a handsome, blue eyed instructor by the name of Erik who was Danish. They ended up chatting after her morning lesson and Erik asked her if she'd like to get a drink later. A drink turned into several drinks. Drinks turned into a meal and the meal turned into a night in her hut. That night turned into the next two and a half weeks. Erik was physically extremely fit. At 46 years old, his stamina would have shamed most 18 year olds. They both shed a tear as Janet left to return to Barcelona. Erik said he would keep in touch and may visit her in Barcelona. Janet was happy to have spent the two weeks with him, but was now ready to get back to her life in Barcelona where she had her home comforts. Oddly, she was homesick for the place.

On her return, Janet picked up the keys to her new home from the estate agent's office. It was a world away from the beeps, shouts and screeching tyres of Via Laietana. It was actually 2.1km as the crow flew, but that made all the difference. It was also clear of the humidity that sometimes descended upon the dark streets of Spanish cities helped by a cool, salty breeze coming up off the Mediterranean. The breeze was warm, but somehow refreshing. It drifted over the city, up the hills and finally reached into her terrace and through her open doors and windows. Combined with the marble floors and thick walls, it meant the temperature was always just right. Cool in the summer and warm in the winter. Well that's what the estate agent had assured her at least.

It was a town house built above a ground floor garage. She'd selected this house in the same way someone would have selected a plot of land on which to build a castle in centuries gone by. It was atop a hill which meant she had good views around and could see people approaching. Secondly, it was extremely secure. The ground floor was basically just garage and a door with no windows. If someone did manage to get into the garage, there was another locked door before reaching the house. She had had a new door fitted on the day she moved in as she thought the original one looked a little flimsy. That could not be said of her new door which was solid oak, with two latches and a dead bolt. Even though so much time had passed, she knew she would always have to be a little wary. The amount of money she stole from Carl and Charlie and their crew, she knew there was always a chance they would still try to track her down. A small downside really, but one unfortunately that would always be present.

She was furnishing the place gradually. So far, she had furnished her bedroom and the lounge. She had bought an amazing Italian corner sofa from eBay for a few hundred euros that had cost about five thousand new. It was super low slung and she'd ensured everything else in the lounge from the coffee table to the stand for the TV was equally low. She accessorised the sofa with mix and match cushions and it looked amazing, even if she did think so herself. The bedroom, like a French courtesan's boudoir, she told herself. Grand and yet feminine with a Queen size antique Louis XVI bed and matching wardrobe. She'd contrasted it was a white leather Barcelona chair in the corner and tucked behind the chair was a blood stained bull fighting spear that had somehow made its way from her rented apartment to her new house. Her last line of defence.

She knew soon her mother would want to come visit and several friends had expressed an interest in coming to see her. She'd been formulating her house 'back story'.

'How can you afford this house Janet? This lifestyle?'

'Oh, I can't, I'm long term house sitting for Nancy, my old friend from Uni / School / my old job / insert as appropriate / who married a Spanish guy. He's very wealthy and they decided to take a few years off and go travelling around the world. I think they're in Easter Island at the moment...'

Her red Vespa stood outside her front door; she knew the salty sea air would eventually be the death of it. Unfortunately, her garage was now filled with a sort of replacement for the Lambo and there was no room for the bike. She'd splashed out on a '95 Porsche 911 cabriolet in powder blue metallic with light grey checked cloth seats. She'd thought about something older, more classic like a 60's Mercedes Sports, but then she remembered she'd heard some stories from friends who had old classic cars that they broke down all the time. The idea of a classic was great but she needed something that was reliable and the Porsche was just that. She had bought it from a classic car garage in Barcelona and was particularly proud as she had spoken only in Spanish during the purchase process. The car had come highly recommended as it had full service history and had seemingly been maintained without cutting corners. The salesman had shown her several examples of this maintenance such as the tyres which were all matching and (almost) new, Michelins; a gleaming engine and new Porsche car mats. They had said another good reason to buy this car was that there was a good independent Porsche garage nearby in Barcelona who would be able to continue to maintain the car to the highest standards.

Her car was the two wheel drive model and it had a considerable list of extras such as an electronically retractable roof, heated, electrically adjustable 'comfort' seats and dual airbags. When she picked up the keys having paid the outstanding balance, she was so excited. She started up the engine, which though on a different plane to the Lambo still had a throaty exhaust note, hit the roof button to lower the roof in about thirty seconds and off she went. It was so slow compared to the Lambo but it stuck a much larger grin on her face. Something about the top being down and endless blue sky overhead.

She'd spent a lot of time exploring around Sitges further down the coast from Barcelona and she liked it very much there. She would go north up the coast today though towards Blanes and see if there was anywhere that took her fancy. She blipped the garage door remote control she kept in her glove box and it slowly raised up. She eased the car out and hit the close button. The roof lowered as she waited for the garage door to finish closing. All set, her hair still wet from her shower, she set off. Driving coastal roads in a topless

Porsche was a great way to dry your hair and give it a natural Latin tousle.

After lunch on the beach. Her phone pinged and she grabbed it to read the mail that had just arrived. Oddly, now that she rarely got emails, they were exciting to receive. It was from her mother.

Hi Janet, thanks for sorting my flight ticket darling.
Business class on British Airways... what a treat. Just let me know if I can give you something toward it. I do have money you know! I'll see you at the airport on Friday. It'll probably be 2 o'clock by the time I get through the customs. Do you want me to bring you anything out from the UK?
Your dad keeps asking why he can't come out, but I've told him we're having a girly weekend and he would be bored. Perhaps he can come out in a few months? It would be nice for him to see you if you are not planning on coming back to the UK this year.
See you Friday! Mum xxx
PS. Alex sends his love and he wants a trip too.
PPS. Can we go see flamenco?

She felt a warm glow inside at the thought of seeing her mum soon. If she was really honest with herself, she had been a little lonely. Apart from meeting and spending time with Tess, there was a slightly solemn loneliness. She picked her book up again and the bookmark fell out and blew off a few meters before she had chance to weigh it down. She grabbed it and took it out to have another read. She'd been doing odd bits of research about the Sea of Galilee and had thought she might be onto something. It turns out the Sea of Galilee still exists and there had been several reports of findings including a 6,000 year old burial site that was now underwater. Part of Christ's cross was apparently found there. There were tons of news reports and articles on Google about this type of stuff. Could it be that they had part of this cross? If so, it would be worth a fortune to the right buyer or collector or museum. What was the film where they were hunting down the Holy Grail? Could have been one of the Indiana Jones films, but that was supposed to be worth a fortune, if it existed.

What did the letter refer to exactly? Once again she took her phone out and typed *Sea of Galilee* into Google. This time however she scrolled lower down through the results that showed up and one in particular jumped out at her:

'The Storm on the Sea of Galilee'.

She clicked on the link which took her to a Wikipedia page and very quickly she read '...*biggest art theft in US history and remains unsolved*'. This looked a whole lot more interesting and it sparked a memory she'd forgotten all about. On the night she met Joseph, he made a joke about a stealing a piece of art. He joked that he'd stolen a painting worth millions of pounds then she'd seen the article about the stolen modern art painting. A Rothko she seemed to remember. Could this person who wrote the letter - MPW - be part of Joseph's gang? No, he'd said he couldn't meet him in person. It seemed that MPW had paid Joseph the money for something. Perhaps for stealing the Rothko and now MPW had the whereabouts of another piece of art that he wanted Joseph to steal. It seemed like a piece of a puzzle might have clicked in.

. . .

"She's in Barcelona." Charlie said over the phone to Carl.

"Fucking bitch, really? How do you know?" Carl asked sounding anxious. "Do you have an address?"

"No, not yet. I just know she's there."

"Come round." and with that, Carl hung up.

Following Janet's escape with their hard earned cash, Carl and his cohorts had searched tirelessly for her. Once they tracked down the phone to a semi detached house in Brighton owned by a self employed couple, they knew the trail had gone cold. They decided to spend a night in a low grade hotel in Brighton during which they could look at their options for getting the cash back. There seemed to be fewer and fewer options. Things got very heated. The 'conversation' ended with a scuffle which left Jim with a broken nose from Dan. Jim left shortly after followed by Kyle. For them the trail was dead, they accepted that they had been outdone by this woman. Kyle's advice to the group was 'know when you're beaten'. That advice only strengthened Carl's resolve to get that 'fucking woman and *their* cash'.

Carl asked Charlie to track her down using his knowledge and experience of the internet. He promised him the whole of Kyle's share of the money if he managed it. They would then share Jim's. So Charlie had started the process of tracking Janet down, he had the best knowledge of her, but even with his tech skills, the trail really had gone cold. He didn't know enough about her to dig sufficiently. His understanding was that she would be interrogated once he'd spiked her, otherwise, he would have asked more questions in the short time he spent drinking with her. As it turned out, she was no use once she came around and then they fucked up and allowed her to escape like a set of idiots.

He knew Joseph had been found the week after Janet had fled Edinburgh. There had been an investigation into his death and possible murder led by Lothian and Borders Police. Charlie had been hopeful that some clue would come out that would help him to track Janet down. There was CCTV footage of Joseph and Janet arriving at the hotel, entering the restaurant and getting into the lift. It was possible to see her face, but it was just not clear enough. The footage was not up close enough and consequently when they zoomed in, it became too grainy. If it had made national news, then perhaps someone in London might have recognised Janet and come forward. For those who knew her well, they might have put together that she had been in Scotland at that time and that it looked sort of like Janet. Even then, her friends would have called her first rather than call the police. However, it barely made an impact south of the Scottish border. An autopsy was carried out on Joseph's body which found that he died of acute opiate intoxication resulting in sudden cardiac death. When their leads to his *date* for the night also dried up, they concluded he probably died during sex and his girlfriend or date had panicked and fled the scene. The police appealed to her to come forward for help and therapy to get over her ordeal.

Carl's house was huge (but ugly Charlie thought). When he arrived Carl showed him into what he referred to as his den, it was downstairs and was the size of a large lounge. It had an extremely large corner sofa and an even more extreme TV on the wall. Dan was there, slumped on the sofa. He was living with Carl at the moment, so Charlie was expecting this.

He could hear dogs barking somewhere in the house and Carl shouted 'ZIP IT YOU STUPID MUTS!' And they promptly zipped it. Impressive Charlie thought to himself.

"Ok, so I'm ninety nine percent sure she's in Barcelona, but I want to do some more checking before I fully confirm it."

"Ok, that's cool. So how did you track her down?" Dan asked.

"Well we only had a few key bits of information, her first name, age, profession and where she lived. But we also knew she had been on some type of conference in Edinburgh and that's what took her there. I tried to get her full name from the conference organisers, but 'cos I was not a delegate, they wouldn't give me the information. But I found her anyway on the delegate list on the website along with the bank she worked for. Turns out her surname is this odd Ukrainian name that's pretty rare. Karpenko. Janet Karpenko."

"Can you get to the point Charlie?" Dan said, an edge in his voice, "How did you find her?"

"Ok, stay with me. Keep calm. So I remember on the night in the bar she showed me a funny video on her phone that was on her facebook page. Her cover photo, the bit at the top, was of Barcelona. I didn't realise it at the time but I saw a picture recently of all this crazy wavy architecture and it's only in Barcelona. Some old dude called Gaudi, from like the sixties or seventies or maybe earlier. So then I started looking for a British woman called Janet in Barcelona, but I still couldn't find anything. I think she basically deleted her Facebook profile and all her other social networks. Twitter and what have you." Charlie continued, giving them far too much detail. "So then I started looking for a woman called Janet Karpenko who worked in consumer banking and eventually, I found her on her company website along with a photo. So then I find her mum in London. There's not many, even in a city of ten million. There were fifteen. Took me a few days, but I managed to find the contact details for all of them. Then I called them all. I rang each and asked to speak to Janet. And Bingo! the last one I got through to told me her daughter Janet was currently living in Barcelona. So, then I managed to hack her. Turns out her mother is called Yana Karpenko. Came here in the sixties. Janet has been emailing her letting her know how lovely it is in Barcelona. Apparently, she's house sitting out there. No doubt spending all our cash."

"Brilliant Charlie! But did you get her address?" Dan asked with an ironic edge.

"No not yet... But"

"Well can't you email as her mother and ask for the address?" Dan interjected once again.

"Let me finish man... Her mother is going out to see her in a few days. I'm planning to follow her out there. I've even got her flight time and number."

Carl went behind a large, dark wood desk and unlocked a low drawer and counted out some cash, then held out a wad toward Charlie. "Here's some cash for a flight and hotel. Get out there and get her located?" Carl asked. "Then let us know and we'll come out. It'll probably get messy. I don't just want the cash back. I want to make her pay. She thinks she's so fucking clever but she won't when I'm cutting her thieving fingers off. She's messed with the wrong guy with me."

Charlie just nodded. Feeling a little shocked and queasy at the thought. He really wasn't into all the violence and needed to get out of this world sooner rather than later. Bloody thugs.

There looked to be about a grand to Charlie. It went into his back pocket. Charlie knew Carl gave him cash as a way of staying in control. He wanted to play the big boss. That was fine, he could do that. Charlie actually had plenty of money himself that he could use. Carl didn't know that he earned upwards of £700 per day as an IT security consultant. But hey if someone wants to give you a grand, you take it. Right?

Once Carl had shown Charlie out, he went back down to the den.

"What do you think? Good news eh?" he asked Dan.

"Who knows, hopefully it's not a wild goose chase like Brighton. That was a fucking dog's dinner. I think we underestimated that woman all along and look where it's got us. Hopefully, this isn't another false trail. We need that money." Dan's voice was raised.

"I know babe, I know." Carl said placing his huge arms around Dan's boyish frame. He kissed him gently on the forehead.

"We still gonna ditch him when we get the money right?" Dan asked hopefully.

"Yes, we're not sharing the cash." Carl said shaking his head gently. "We've done the most work for it. We're gonna move to somewhere warm and have an amazing life together." Carl kissed Dan passionately on the lips.

Twelve years earlier Carl had made one simple mistake that led him to meet Dan in prison. Five full weeks after a robbery in Cardiff, he had been picked up by Police in Leeds. He had thought he was home and dry and enjoying the spoils of his riches. He was speeding. Not even going crazy, just 12 miles per hour over the speed limit and got stopped by an unmarked police car on the M62. Driving the five year old Bee

Em 750i L (fully loaded) he'd bought a few weeks before. His Sat Nav' was guiding him back to his new city centre apartment he'd just moved into with his, then girlfriend, Kirsty. The young police officer that came to his window was very good, he clearly clocked his face straight away but gave away nothing. Spoke very calmly to Carl about the speed he was going and asked the usual sort of stuff - was he aware of the speed limit, was he the registered keeper of the car, etc, etc. He even told Carl he wouldn't keep him long before returning to his unmarked police car.

As he went back to his car to do some 'checks on the car and get the paperwork', he was straight onto the radio. As Carl daydreamed about his upcoming holiday to the Maldives with Kirsty and whether or not to buy her a new car (was three months in too soon to buy your girlfriend an open top sports car?) two more unmarked police cars, this time with armed officers were flying up the M62 behind him.

Carl was still thinking he was home and dry, waiting for a ticket and a slapped wrist. Little did he know, even in Leeds he was clearly a big target for them, they blocked him from behind first and by the time he was blocked at the side by another unmarked car in the slow lane, he was in the sights of two semi automatics. Surprisingly, it wasn't the unmarked police car which was stopped at an angle in the slow lane that caused the fatal pile up, but the people on the other side looking over to see what was happening. One driver turned his head briefly to sneak a quick nosey, unaware the driver in front had slowed for a sly look too. As he turned his attention back and saw the car he was going to hit, the driver behind swerved at the last minute and fish tailed into another two cars then back across the three lanes and into the path of an articulated car transporter. The transporter jack knifed and shed a car from its top deck which wound its way onto the top of a green Ford Fiesta. It stopped it in its tracks and almost flattened it. The young couple inside were crushed to death. Blissfully unaware of what was about to hit them. They died instantly. Another ten were seriously injured.

He didn't see Kirsty again. She didn't know about Carl's chequered past, she thought he was a bit of a wheeler dealer, cars and what have you, but she certainly didn't know he was an armed robber. He'd take Kirsty back in a blink if he ever got the chance, but he was a realist and knew that was never going to happen. She was a catch, blond with the most sparkling blue, green eyes you'd ever seen. She'd be with someone else now, settled with a family no doubt. She had her own business as a physiotherapist. He could never quite imagine what she would have said, had he been able to get hold of her after the arrest. He couldn't waste his one call in the police station on her, he had to get his solicitor. There were chances to get in touch with her after that, but it just didn't happen. Probably best all round to be honest. He'd been punching way above his station with Kirsty as it was. She was pretty, middle class and he was. . . well he wasn't really sure what class he was from, but he was pretty certain it wasn't the same as hers.

As he was taken down and stuffed into the back of an armoured transit van, he decided he was not going to be a victim during his time in prison. The next 10 years (hopefully significantly fewer) were going to be tough. A Category B prison and that meant lifers who could handle themselves and lots of people who would want to get one over on Carl. He didn't have much experience of fighting and violence (yet), but he was strong and on the odd occasion he'd had to, he'd been able to handle himself.

He was sharing a cell with someone else who was in for violent robbery - Dan Witt. They got on well and Dan, who would end up doing the robbery with Carl in Manchester, gave him the lowdown on prison existence and how things went down on their wing. Apparently, the hard men of the prison were Wilf Lamb and a man called Reaper by inmates or Terry Reaps by screws. Both were in for murder. Lamb and Reaper surrounded themselves with three other murderers. Together they looked like a bunch of rabid, whipped dogs. All gaunt faces, tattoos, dark eyes and stubble. Hungry for fresh inmate meat. They liked to target lads that were new to prison and especially those that were new to prison life such as Carl. They played mind games with them for their amusement.

"Nice group of lads." Dan joked ironically. "It's best to keep your head down around that lot. I seen one of em kick the shit out of a lad in here. Literally." he gestured subtly to the right of the group. "Think he's called Dean, the one on the right. Greasy hair, tattoo of a knife through a heart on his cheek. Charmer. Dunno what had gone on, but I heard something going down in the cell next to ours. I knew not to get involved, you just don't, you don't see anything, you don't say anything, but I got up and walked past the cell door which was closed but I could see in the window. Clarky, my neighbour back then, was on the floor, he was unconscious but he was still getting his head kicked. Was horrid. He was in his undies and he'd shit and pissed himself, I think in his unconscious state, but it carried on. I walked away 'cos I couldn't just stand there." he held up his right hand and stuck his thumb out. "A. 'Cos I'd get seen by them. Not good." then stuck his forefinger out. "B. 'Cos I'd alert a screw to what was going on and that would be much worse. I walked past again slow and looked in and they'd stopped and were going through his stuff. Was probably about drugs. Usually is in 'ere. As it happened, he was alright. His face took about 6 months to get back to normal, but he changed after that. He wouldn't speak to a soul. He looked terrible 'cos they had to take his eyebrows off to stitch em up. Poor bastard. I'm no threat to anyone in here, apart from I might help myself to someone's cigs if they're careless and leave 'em knocking about, but he wouldn't speak to me after that. Went into his own little world."

"Unlucky." Carl said shaking his head.

"No, not unlucky mate, he wasn't smart enough. He somehow got involved with 'em. Just don't do or say anything that would involve you in any way into their fucked up lives." Carl listened and nodded. Thankful for the advice.

"You do drugs?" Dan asked, but Carl shook his head. "Good, keep it that way in 'ere 'cos it'll end in tears. Have a smoke. Enjoy a smoke, but keep it at that. I loved a smoke and I used to do drugs. Whatever I could get my hands on. Speed, charlie, Es, Skunk. But I'm smart. I left that behind once I came in here. Drugs in here is bad news man."

Dan had come through the 'care system' and the care system had well and truly let Dan down. His parents had been serial physical abusers. They also threw a fair bit of verbal and psychological abuse Dan's way, and for the rest of the time they compounded it with neglect. This was all before Dan was school age.

It was a neighbour who blew the whistle for him. The family was paid several visits by social services. He remained true to his parents and would not speak out against them. He knew they were very bad to him on a regular basis, but he loved them all the same, he had no one else to cling to in his lonely young life. No siblings, few friends. It was unsurprising therefore, he attempted to protect them. But even as he kept his mouth shut, the bruising and scratches told their own story. Especially the circular bruising which gave away the biting which was his mother's particular specialty. Usually if Dan broke anything. Another favourite was the cupboard. Where parents might normally send their children to bed early, Dan was pushed into a cupboard under the stairs. There were three cupboards under their stairs and they pushed him into the smallest that was nearest the foot of the stairs. He would spend the night there. When the door opened in the morning, he would crawl tentatively out. He had no choice but to crawl slowly as he would have no feeling in his legs. He would usually be exhausted. The times he went into the cupboard always coincided with his parents drinking and that meant arguing. Arguments were generally about money they owed each other. Money one had stolen off the other. About his lazy father not providing for them. Their arguments could last until 3 or 4 in the morning. Sometimes the police knocked on the door, sometimes their neighbours would bang on the wall. Generally, it was a grim, exhausting environment for a child. On the occasions he ended up in the cupboard, Dan would be upset and cry for a while. Crying was not too bad. The first few times, it had been screaming. Screaming meant the shouting at him continued and that things were thrown at the cupboard door. Once he had cried himself out of tears, Dan would carefully push the door a few millimetres outwards, it would just give him a tiny amount of diffused light, but it was enough so that he could occupy himself. He had some trinkets in the cupboard. A pocket guide to cars and a pack of superheroes Top Trumps. He knew them almost off by heart. He'd test himself on his knowledge of them. It was a simple game, but it took him off into other worlds. Worlds without screeching and screaming and banging doors and smashing glasses. A world where he could fly. Soaring through the sky, he could look down on his town and be free. His other world was his driving world. He was obsessed with cars and driving. Especially fast cars. Ferraris, Porsches, Aston Martins, Lamborghinis and Bugattis. Anything from Germany or Italy with an exotic name and a high top speed. The fastest cars in his book were a Ferrari F40 and a Porsche 959. They could both do 200mph or damn close to it. He would flip flop between which he would have. It usually came down to the Porsche. He would imagine being behind the wheel and accelerating so fast he was pinned to the driving seat. Then he would just keep going red lining the cars engine in each gear until he closed in on 200mph. Other cars and trees and buildings flashing past him faster and faster. Leaving everything behind him. He'd get himself almost into a trance. It would help him to drift off and snatch a little sleep. Come the morning, he'd hide his trinkets away under the junk that was in the cupboard and creep out. His sore eyes blinking and watering.

 Dan was placed in a children's home which was better to him than his young, uneducated parents had been, but not by much. He had food and warmth and no one shouted at him or pushed him into a cupboard, but there was little in the way of guidance and certainly none of the love he craved. Just to have someone to hug him. Read him a story before the lights went out. He was taken under the wing of others within the care system, but this only resulted in him learning how to smoke, drink and steal from a very young age. Unsurprisingly, it was usually booze and cigarettes that he would steal. His education suffered. No one set him any targets or gave him any goals to try and achieve. After he turned ten, he was fostered with several families but by this time, he was a challenging boy and it never lasted longer than four or five months. Then he'd be back in the home. It was a familiar routine.

The system's biggest failure however came when Dan was 16, there was no longer a place for him in a home. In the system. He was seen as an adult and therefore spat rudely out into society. It was time to stand up on his own two feet. Sink or swim. He managed to just about tread water. Living in squalor initially with some others who had outgrown the system, crashing on sofas for months at a time until he had a little money. He had no qualifications and finding work was something he couldn't seem to do and no one around him seemed able to help with. As with many in his situation, he found ways to put a little money in his pocket, but it was all illegal. Petty theft was what he mainly seemed cut out for. Something, finally, in which he excelled. His life as a petty criminal gave him the other thing he craved in his previously lonely life besides money; it gave him friends. Good friends. Friends that would ultimately lead him down the wrong path, to prison (and an early death), but for now good friends. And now Dan's new friend was Carl. A spark lit between them. They became the brother for each other that neither had previously had.

Dan had been in prison twice before, so he knew the ropes. Carl had come to a life of crime late and consequently only went to prison for the first time at thirty two. Up until he was thirty, he'd held down pretty average office jobs for a few different companies. He found he was pretty good at holding down a job. The only problem was there seemed to be a ceiling to his salary and he had hit it. Pay rises still happened, but a pay rise of two or three percent per year made so little difference to your monthly take home pay that they may as well not bother. He wanted more. It started quite innocuously with just taking the odd bit here and there from the warehouse at the import company he worked for. They imported designer accessories like bags and shoes, usually stuff that was out of season. He found that he could top up his monthly salary by a few hundred quid by selling stuff on Ebay or at the pub. Selling stuff at the pub made him very popular and led him to hang out with the wrong crowd. They were the ones who eventually talked him into the bank robbery that got him into prison. As much as he hated prison, he knew this was his path now. He would not be going back to his office jobs with their management hierarchies and glass salary ceilings.

As happens in prison, there was little guidance for Carl from the officials of the prison apart from being told where he would eat, sleep and shower, but lucky for him, he had Dan to put him right, tell him how things worked. Within that first year, Dan would become a life saver for Carl and cement their lifelong friendship.

Both Carl and Dan had thought they were straight until they met in prison. Or was it just that they had convinced themselves of that? Carl had always gone out with girls, but once he ended up in a cell with Dan. He started to have feelings that he'd not had before. Perhaps it was just Dan or perhaps it would have happened with any bloke he'd ended up locked away with. As they talked, he would look at Dan's lips and want to reach out and touch them and kiss them. Their first few months were July and August and it was unusually hot. There was no air conditioning and Dan would sit in the cell without his top on and sometimes just in his boxer shorts. Carl would look at Dan's scrawny, lean body and yearn to hold him in his arms. Through their conversations, it transpired that Dan was pretty confused about his sexuality, he'd rarely been with girls and when he had, he'd not seemed to enjoy it. He didn't talk about girls in the same misogynistic way that most blokes inside did.

They went for months in this way; their friendship getting closer. They opened up more and more about their lives. It was the best therapy for Dan. It was the only therapy he'd ever had. He'd never really spoken properly to people about his childhood. About how let down he felt by his mother. He had almost expected it from his father who was a drunken, foul tempered rat through and through. His mother wasn't like that all along but gradually acted more and more like him. One night in the dark as Dan talked; recounting a particular incident in which he had been beaten by his father on his childhood's solitary family holiday, Carl went to hold him. Their embrace turned to a kiss. Their kiss turned to a caress. The caress turned into a fumble. Very quiet fumbling. Even though they were in their own cell, the walls were known to tell their secrets. It was a first for both of them. They had both fumbled a little at school but nothing serious and nothing since.

After that night, there was no turning back. There was no embarrassment, it was mutual and they both said as much to one another. It turned into a very mature relationship. A relationship with a hint of daddy / son role play occasionally. Not for kinky reasons but because those were the roles they found themselves in. Dan was very much the emotionally immature one of the two. Considering it was the first gay relationship for both of them, it was very stable. They had been extremely close ever since. During their time in prison, they rarely spoke outside the walls of their cell. If they had given away what was going on to other inmates, they'd be made to suffer. On the outside, none of the other members of the gang had known about them. And they wanted to keep it that way with their one remaining member - Charlie.

Their relationship was strengthened when Carl found himself in a prison fight over some disputed rules in a game of pool. His opponent had fouled and left Carl snookered. Carl said he should have a free shot. His opponent disagreed. Then Reaper got involved in the argument. Carl should have just backed down, but he got stubborn instead. Carl said he was going to hit his opponent's ball and then he would have another shot. When he went to take his second shot, he was hit around the head with a pool cue by his opponent. As Carl hit the deck, stunned and semi conscious, Reaper jumped in and started in on him. Swinging punches that threw Carl's head from one side to the other. That was until Reaper found three of four inches of a pen knife plunged into his left buttock by Dan. The blade sank right in the middle of a tattoo of the Grim Reaper which he had had since he was twenty one.

It put Dan in a huge amount of danger because he did it in front of Reaper's buddies but he panicked and felt Carl was going to die if he had not acted. He ended up in solitary for a week and his parole was probably delayed by about six months. The act would mean that the two would be life long friends as well as lovers. Reaper was discharged from the prison's hospital after one night and tended to sleep on his front after that. He also walked with a slight limp from pain the deep scar tissue caused him. Carl spent two nights in hospital. He had concussion, a broken nose and a huge bump on the back of his head. He looked a sight when the nurse discharged him. He had two deep purple bruises under his eyes. It was more painful than it looked. The pain was much more focussed on the back of his head which throbbed for about a week. It made him dizzy and sometimes he had to just go and lie down with a cold towel on the back of his head. It wasn't just physically that Carl suffered. He seemed to be quite sensitive emotionally during his recovery and could easily burst into tears for little or no reason. Luckily this didn't happen outside of the cell he shared with Dan, but several times, he found himself sobbing quietly at night into his pillow. On the times that Dan heard him, he went to Carl to comfort him, rubbing his back and soothing him back to sleep.

Carl and Dan steered well clear of Reaper after that. They also steered well clear of all his buddies who were liable to take a pop at them. Reaper blamed the pair of them. This was a problem. It made prison life much more stressful having to look out for yourself in the common areas and even in your own cell. They both knew it wasn't uncommon for inmates to have 'falls' in their own cells. Their defence was to stay close to one another wherever possible. Not that Dan would have been much use against Reaper, he was all of nine and a half stone and Reaper was a muscular fifteen stone. He worked out in his cell for an hour or more every day without fail and his body was rock solid. Carl didn't work out, but physically, he liked to think he would be able to handle himself in a fair fight. Reaper had told his buddies those fags would come to regret what they had done. 'Maybe not while they were in prison, but some day.'

SEVEN

Two hundred and seventeen days after

As they reached the drop off area at Heathrow airport, Yana's taxi driver helped get her bags out of the boot of the car and placed them on a baggage trolley for her. Going the extra mile for her meant she gave him a five pound tip which went into his top pocket; separate from his fare which went in his back pocket. He confirmed the time he would be here for her return and wished her a pleasant flight. She found her check in desk and joined the short queue. Almost immediately, a man joined the queue behind her and she gave him a friendly co-passenger smile, which he returned.

She was well travelled and knew the drill at the security area, she was wearing slip on shoes in case they needed to come off, she had no belt to remove and all her documents and passport were in a clear plastic travel wallet. Yana had given herself plenty of time before her flight. She bought copies of The Daily Mail and Telegraph, a bag of wine gums, sparkling water and some chewing gum and then found the British Airways business class lounge with the help of a pretty young British Airways uniformed girl. Plenty of time to get a gin and tonic to sip while she read the papers. She had disliked the last few times she'd travelled as she'd been rushed. Both times flying with a budget airline and subsequently didn't have use of a lounge with complimentary drinks and food. She saw the man who had been behind her in the queue sitting not far from her. He was looking in his duty free bag and ordering a pint of beer. She kept her eye on the departure boards, but there was no gate as yet. She was very early.

Once on the plane, which was barely half full, she was pleasantly surprised at just how much nicer this was than the last time she had flown. More complimentary food and drink. Very attentive staff. Lots of space. She was a little tipsy as the captain announced that they were starting their descent into Barcelona. By contrast, on her last flight, the only choice had been a tuna sandwich as everything else had sold out. She didn't eat tuna as she didn't agree with the way they were fished, so she went hungry. She had been unimpressed to say the very least.

At the baggage pickup and passport control in Barcelona Airport, she saw the young man again. They were efficient and she was through in no time at all and saw Janet waiting for her. She speeded up her luggage trolley toward her and gave her a big hug.

"Oh, so nice to see you mum!"

"You look so well sweetheart. I hope you're taking care of your skin in the sun." said Yana holding Janet's face gently. "You don't want to end up all wrinkly like Auntie Pat."

"Don't worry, I use a good sun screen mum. C'mon, we're over here."

She looked around to smile a co-passenger farewell smile at the young man but he had disappeared.

. . .

"Thanks Yana." Charlie said. "You've been a very helpful lady today." He sat outside what he assumed was now Janet's house in the hills above Barcelona. Janet's house that she had no doubt bought with cash that belonged to Charlie. He'd been met at the airport by a friend who'd gone out the day before and rented him a car. Charlie had paid him a hundred quid and his flights. As they had reached the house, the garage door had opened up, probably from a remote in the car, but possibly from someone in the house and Janet had driven her Porsche cabrio inside.

He accepted to himself at least that he had a little thing for her. She was cute. He got the look now, she was obviously of Russian heritage. The high cheek bone structure and the deep thoughtful eyes that probably came from a tougher than Western existence. As he'd followed her in his nondescript grey metallic Fiat Punto, he'd been intrigued by the back of her head. The wind rushing through the short, slightly curly locks. She occasionally turned to her mother and laughed. She looked so vibrant and alive and funny and pretty. But he had to remember she'd screwed him over. She was the enemy. He waited outside for an hour but there was no further movement.

He found a hotel nearby which wasn't too expensive and checked in with his one bag. He had a sleep for the afternoon and set his alarm for 8pm. He wanted to go back when it was dark and have a good look around. It had crossed his mind that this might be a friend's house, but then who would have the automatic garage door remote control for their friends house? No this was more than likely where Janet was living now. He knew he needed to alert Carl as soon as possible. He would take a dim view of Charlie messing around when there was so much at stake, but he needed to make sure he was giving him accurate information. He set back out at nine o'clock. It was getting dark now by the time he got to Janet's house, it would be dark enough to get a good look at the set up.

He assessed the neighbourhood. It was a quiet little street. Detached houses which was quite unusual. No one was around but he could hear conversations in houses. Some had Spanish TV programmes on loud enough for him to hear and some Spanish music. As he approached Janet's house, he realised it was going to be difficult to get a good look in. On the street side, there were no windows at ground level just the garage door. He went around the side of the house which dropped away over the hill down toward Barcelona. The window at his level was a large patio which was open. He could hear them talking. Ice cubes clinking in glasses. There were seats on the terrace and some stuff on a table; a mobile phone, ashtray and a magazine. He guessed they would be getting more drinks and would no doubt be coming back out shortly. He shifted himself down past the side of the terrace where there was a little cut out in the rock.

They came back out and were chatting non stop. He didn't really know what he was expecting to hear them saying. If they had said anything interesting, then they'd got it all out. All they were speaking about now was Janet's sisters and brother. Her Auntie Natalia was also a big topic of conversation, apparently she had been having an affair with her personal trainer and it had all come out when her Uncle Alan had found some 'sexts' that she had sent him. All very interesting but this was not getting him anything useful. He guessed they'd already chatted about how she ended up with this house and a Porsche before he got here. It was time to call in Carl. This was going to get messy no doubt. The house was pretty secure apart from the fact that she obviously liked to sit out on the terrace overlooking the city. This would probably be how Carl and Dan would go in. He would leave them to do the nasty work. They would probably enjoy it.

Once away from the house, he called Carl and let him know he had indeed found her. She was currently with her mother but she was going back to London on Tuesday. So in terms of keeping this as clean as possible, Carl said he would come out on the Wednesday or Thursday depending upon when there were flights they could get on. He gave Carl her house number and street name and spoke about how the house was very secure, that the most viable entry point would be the terrace when she was in. Carl wrote it all down on his desktop pad. Charlie also gave him his hotel name and room number. Then they discussed the money and Charlie informed him he'd not seen any sign of the cash bag. There were signs she'd spent some of the money on the house and the old Porsche. Charlie guessed it totalled about a quarter of a million. Carl said that was a relief considering she was blasting about in a Lamborghini in the past and guessed it left probably just upwards of two mill. They would have to write off anything she'd spent to far. He scribbled **£¼M SPENT** over **£2.5M LEAVES £2¼M**. Still more than worth chasing the bitch for. He wrote **BITCH** underneath the figures.

Once they were off the phone, Charlie reflected on Carl's tone on the phone. It bothered him. It was just a little short. A little too... he couldn't quite put his finger on it. Like he was working *for* Carl rather than *with* Carl. It had also bothered him when he'd seen him at Carl's house too. When he'd been there with Dan. He knew they had been friends for a long time and something had happened in prison which had bonded them together. A fight where Dan had saved his bacon or some shit. Either way, it just didn't feel right. He maybe just needed to keep an eye on the two of them and make sure they didn't take a chance to do one with the cash once they got it. Assuming they would get it. That was still unclear where the actual cash was. It was still not 100% guaranteed that she had the cash. It could be some crazy co-incidence where she was in that same hotel and with that same bag. A long shot, but crazy shit happened in this world sometimes.

EIGHT

Two hundred and eighteen days after

Reaper, dressed in grey jeans and black jumper, stood behind Carl's desk and read with interest the notes scrawled across it. An address and a hotel, both in Barcelona and some figures. One which was particularly interesting to him. **£2¼M**. Reaper had followed Carl and Dan out of the house, they were currently drinking in town with some other guys. All about Carl's age, all quite a bit older than the scrawny little runt - Dan - AKA, the pain in Reaper's backside, literally, since he'd stuck that penknife deep into it. He'd said he wouldn't forgive or forget and that he'd eventually get his revenge and tonight was that night. But this might just throw a different light on the situation. What was this money? Who was at this address in Barcelona and what was this hotel? His initial thoughts were that this amount of cash could be at this location, probably something to do with drugs. But then **BITCH** was scrawled beneath the figure. Women as a general rule weren't stupid enough to get into dealing drugs. Who was this BITCH? Seemed she'd got Carl's back up something bad.

He'd been staking out Carl and Dan for a few days now and he knew the layout of the house. He also knew that Carl had some old school security. Two dobermans. Fucking cliché. Well if Carl liked clichés, then Reaper would use one to disable them. He'd chucked them both half a steak which they'd greedily gobbled up. Unfortunately for them, both steaks had pockets cut into them which contained crushed sleeping tablets. They would either sleep for a long time or forever, he wasn't sure which and hadn't really cared. They were either breathing very shallowly. Or not at all. He still didn't want to take any chances, so their collars were now fastened together with a washing line and the washing line was looped to fasten them to the door handle of the utility room Reaper had gained access through. The last thing he wanted was to get attacked by two dogs.

He decided to have a look around the house, they'd be a while going by their usual routine of three or four pints at the local boozer. Might even be quiz night. Woo hoo. He hated the style of the house, all a bit too showroom. A little too pristine. Totally characterless. It could easily have been one of those furnished show homes that you just buy and move into. Which men would put up dado rails and curtain pelmets? It just didn't seem right to Reaper. Walking around the house, he was filled with more hate for Carl and Dan that they would live in a house like this. This wasn't the house of two ex cons. There were IKEA picture frames on the shelves which still had the IKEA pictures in. That was weird. He'd planned how he would get into the house, but not really much further ahead than that. He wasn't sure whether he would jump them as they arrived back or wait until they were asleep. Asleep would be better, but, no he couldn't do that because of the dogs. They would find the dogs on their return unless they awoke before they got back. If they did, they'd be woozy and they would probably think they were ill and whisk them off to the vet. It would have to be as they arrived back. He had a gun with him. It would be unlikely they would have a gun on them as they came back from a pub. But he would need to be very strong with them so that things remained in his control. Dan wasn't much to deal with physically and he'd taken Carl before albeit with the aid of a pool cue.

. . .

Yana had just loved her first full day with her daughter in over a year. She didn't get this kind of 'access' any more. Janet was so busy with her work, so this was a real treat. It was usually a snatched phone call here or there or she'd pop in unannounced. When she did, it was never for very long as she always had some place she *had* to get to after; a party, a meal or the gym. But they had really talked last night and today. She felt they'd 'connected' as young people say.

Today her daughter had taken her on an open top tour of Barcelona in her car. It had been hot but so long as the car was moving, there was a lovely breeze. If they did get stuck in any traffic, Janet blasted them with air conditioning. They had seen the Olympic stadium and the Nou Camp football ground, the cathedral (still unfinished) and a few of the buildings designed by Gaudi, then they had gone to the port and then driven to the beach out of Barcelona where they had a picnic and sunbathed in the afternoon sun. She'd even taken a dip in the sea and it was a long time since that had happened. The sea wasn't warm but it was a temperature that once you were in, it became very pleasant. They'd paddled together although Yana couldn't stop worrying about her daughter's car which she'd insisted upon leaving with the top down. She'd asked her about work and how it was possible for her to take such a long break from her job. Janet had explained that she'd saved up enough to take a year out and that her boss was keen to keep her on, so would save her job for her for when she was ready to go back. Yana had asked outright if she had had depression and if this was why she needed time off but Janet insisted she didn't *need* to take time off but she *wanted* to. Lots of people took a year out and travelled the world, but she just wanted to take a year out to live in the sun and explore a city she'd visited once and fallen in love with. She may stay longer she hinted. If she was to get her Spanish going well, she may stay and get a job out here. Although Yana couldn't really understand the reasons why this could or should be, she consoled herself rather selfishly by thinking it would be rather lovely to have a daughter who lived in Barcelona who she could visit every few months.

That evening as they ate on Janet's balcony high above Barcelona, Yana asked if she was seeing anyone.

"Not at the moment mum."

"It's been a while since you've had a boyfriend." Yana commented.

"Yes, it has mum." she said looking up from her grilled chicken salad and patatas bravas, "not sure what you want me to say here mum."

"I don't know, just I thought you would have lots of men after you. You're a catch for any man. With your career and you're young and attractive."

"Yes, I'd like to think I am and will be for the foreseeable future. I'm just not too bothered at the moment. There's plenty of time for men." she raised her eyebrows as if in preparation for more inquisition. No more came. Then she felt like she'd told her off a little. "Besides I did meet someone recently who I really thought I liked but they turned out to be a total shit. Well more than that really, they were really bad to me but let's not talk about it. I'm happy as I am and I want you to be happy with me as I am."

"Oh I am, of course, I am." she said. "Who was this total shit anyway?"

"MUM, you're a nightmare. There's nothing to talk about really. I met him and he tried to take advantage of me, but I got the better of him. Full stop." she stuck another fork full of potatoes into her mouth. "Now eat up and don't be so nosey."

"Janet! How can you say that, I'm just looking out for my daughter," after a short pause, "just remember there are plenty more fish in the sea and lots of them are very nice and not out to get one over on you."

"What is this mother's obsession with getting their daughters and sons married off? Is it just that you want grand kids?" she asked raising her eyebrows. "It is isn't it?"

"Well maybe a little..." she conceded and they laughed at the stupidness of their conversation. "So this boy is totally off the scene now?" she asked knowing this was the last question she'd get in.

"He is totally OFF the scene. He doesn't even know I'm in Barcelona," she said a little smugly, "that off the scene enough for you?"

. . .

Reaper had scoured the house and apart from a big stash of cash in Carl's drawer, he couldn't find any more. There was a safe in the bedroom behind a picture. Yet another cliché. He was no safe cracker so he'd discounted that. He had, he guessed, ten grand from the desk drawer, which was a decent nights work in itself. Did he want to be content with that or did he want more? He did but he just wasn't sure if wanted the hassle. Those fags could bring some other people back and then he'd definitely have a problem. Might it be better to cut out now with ten grand and no hassle? He also had an address in Barcelona which seemed to have a very large amount of cash attached to it. The Barcelona address was a risk, he could stake it out and figure the deal with it, but equally, he could get the lowdown from Carl in an hour if he decided to stick around. This was tough.

Reaper sat and rocked side to side in the executive leather office chair. A fancy one with a head rest. The rocking helped him to relax and clear his mind. He thought on it for another five minutes. The quick and dirty way to get his revenge with these two would be to lay in wait and take them down when they got back from the pub. They'd probably be slightly drunk. He'd be clear headed. It would be easy. A few years ago, that would definitely be the route he would take. He had mellowed though, he was a little wiser now and the best revenge he could take would be to use the information he'd found here to grab whatever that money was out from under their noses. He covered his tracks. He took a snap of the address with his phone. He exited out the back door. They'd have no idea that it had been him. They'd just think any old thief had been in and relieved them of their cash. Dumb asses.

Reaper was a thug. He knew that as did everyone else who'd come across him in his life. His name had been his self fulfilling prophecy since school. But he was also clever. He was well versed in technology. He actually enjoyed reading and read quite a bit, not that he'd let any of his acquaintances know that. He'd grown up a lot as well. He actually wanted to move along with his life. He knew he needed to leave Reaper behind in order to do that. He knew that would be difficult. It would probably mean he would have to drop the people who knew him as that, but he was fine with that. He was a loner at heart. Perhaps whatever it was that was that awaited him at the address in Barcelona was his new start. He may have to be ruthless. That wasn't a problem. Within ten minutes of leaving Carl's house, he'd figured out how he could be in Barcelona for the 11:30 am the next morning. He'd also viewed the house on Google Maps with the satellite view and had a good idea of its exterior layout.

NINE

Two hundred and nineteen days after

Janet woke up late. 10:30am was really late for her. But she'd been up late drinking Rioja with her mum last night and boy, she could put it away these days. Earlier in the night, they'd been to watch Flamenco and had had a fair few G&Ts. They'd loved the flamenco. Janet had booked them seats near the front which was brilliant even though her mother mentioned how loud it was at least eight times. She thought it would be all about the dancing which was amazing to see. The feet were like blurs most of the time. But they both found that the music and particularly the singing was what did it for them. The hurt and the passion and sorrow in the voice.

At the end of the night, her mum had been bouncing off the walls down the corridor to her bedroom. Like a teenager who'd been at their parent's booze cabinet. Janet giggled as she watched.

It seemed she was still in bed as there was no noise coming from anywhere in the house. She'd leave her mum to sleep for now. Sleep the booze off. She reached for her book and inevitably, the letter dropped out. It was by design. As a bookmark, it reminded her to read it and think about it every so often. It was scrawled with ideas and theories. She was now fairly sure that the Sea of Galilee referred to the picture **STORM ON THE** Sea of Galilee. But had so far made little headway with the other parts to the puzzle. Still Waters. Research had brought up information about the proverb or fable of 'still waters run deep'. Meaning that a calm exterior hides an impassioned nature. Or that quiet people can be dangerous. There were pages and pages of this on Google. But it didn't add up to anything in terms of a breakthrough on the painting. Certainly not to her. She searched again and skipped a few pages and went to search page 4. This brought up more diverse results, pop songs, TV show episodes and design agencies named Still Waters. She tapped the tab at the top to images. Not surprisingly, lots of shots of water, women in water with their tops wet, yachts, book covers and the Four Tops album cover which seemed to show the band's reflection in some still waters. Videos? News? She tapped the News tab. This was more interesting. Several stories about a boat or rather a super yacht called the Still Waters which was owned by a Russian billionaire called Nicolay Zhestakova.

She looked up, pondering the ceiling for a second before reading on out aloud. "Zhestakova crashed his yacht whilst docking it into, what a surprise, another Russian billionaires super yacht," and the bill for this little fender bender was nearly $20m. This happened two years ago. They'd probably be patched up by now she thought. "Zhestakova had made his vast amounts of money by owning mines first in Russia but then had expanded to Australia and Africa. As the metal markets had shot up, so had his value of hundreds of millions into tens of billions." The news article said his current fortune stood at "$35 billion". She whistled to herself. Owned a football club in Spain. Houses in London, Nice, LA and Moscow. Outspoken against the Putin government.

"So original," Janet said to herself, "bloody oligarchs." Reading further down the article. He had also been fined €25,000 by the Port de Nice for dangerous sailing.

Was this the other part of the puzzle? A **BOAT** named Still Waters which was **DOCKED IN** Nice? Joseph's contact seemed to suggest that this picture was something to do with this yacht. **COULD THE PAINTING BE ON THE YACHT?**

She dug out her iPad, tapped on Safari and Googled Nicolay Zhestakova. There was a Wikipedia page about him. Tons of news articles about him; mainly about his crash in his yacht, but some about him buying a rare Ferrari at auction for some offensive price and then a lot of articles about the football club he owned and players they were buying. She clicked on the Wikipedia page.

Nicolay Rustam Zhestakova was born on June 30th 1967 in Novgorod in Western Russia, between Moscow and St. Petersburg. He looked just like any average guy to be honest, nothing stood out in his looks. He was stylish but when you had that sort of money, that wasn't necessarily his style; you could pay someone to put your wardrobe together each season. He had started at the bottom, literally. As a miner in one of the mines he would come to own. He worked his way up through the unions and then into management. The first part of this rise, he managed to do with charisma, intelligence and hard work. The second, he managed get a lot of people to back him financially for a management buyout of the company during the time of Perestroika in the late eighties and then he turned around and screwed them all over. He'd been in court a lot. Most of the people he screwed over tried to sue him, pretty much all unsuccessfully. Much of the page was about allegations of bribery, theft and fraud. Boring, boring, boring, not to mention very predictable oligarch behaviour.

"Oh, here we go - 'has one of the largest private collections of baroque and renaissance art in the world'. Does that happen to include a stolen Rembrandt Nicolay?"

Behind her, her bedroom door swung open.

"Who are you talking to?"

"Haha no one, just myself mum."

"Okay, well, I have coffee and toast for you out on the terrace darling."

"Ok. Thanks. I'll be out in two ticks."

She folded the letter back up and stuck it into her book. Her mum had been a very busy bee. The table was all set up with as many preserves as she could find, plus coffee, milk and sugar.

"This is lovely mum. Thanks."

"Well if I can't look after my little girl once in a while." She said with an expression that said, it's been too long.

Janet smiled her best I'm a good daughter smile. Inside, other things were on her mind. She could feel a trip to Nice in her very near future.

...

Nicolay kissed Julianne on her lipstick free lips one final, final time. He gently bit her bottom lip and felt the plumpness of it against his tongue as he pulled it toward him. Her eyes looked deep into his. He shouldn't have stayed last night but he couldn't help himself. She was so exquisite. She did PR or something like that. Maybe PR in fashion. They didn't talk about it much. The great thing was that she didn't want him for his money, she saw him for his personality not the gifts he gave her. Her incredible cheek bones, plump lips and beautiful hair were all too much for him and he would find himself day dreaming of her at family meals and whilst on business calls. Dreaming of the next time he could see her. She didn't pester him about anything. She was just so much cooler than anyone else in his life to date; others by comparison that seemed to cling to him and his money like barnacles to the underside of a boat.

"I will see you when you are back from Paris, my beauty." he said with his mixed up accent which still bore a strong Russian inflection mixed with hints of French and American. Like an aging MTV Europe presenter.

"You will indeed my little Nicky." she said cheekily and blipped him on his nose with her forefinger. "Now go on or you'll never get back and you'll be in big trouble with you know who."

He pulled the door gently behind him until it clicked and started across the small graveled driveway to the double car port. His car sat alongside Julianne's TT. He'd not been at the auction at Ferrari's racing track when his car had been bought, but he had sent Sasha, one of his staff. Sasha had specific instructions on how much he could bid up to to get the car. In the end, the bidding didn't get quite to Nicolay's limit of €15million. Sasha had it taken straight to Ferrari's classic car restoration workshop once the auction was won. It needed a small repair to the drivers seat leather and Nicolay wanted the engine stripped and tuned. Just to be sure he would get the very best out of it. What would be the point to spend that money on a car and then have it running at 90% of it's capacity? Then he would keep the car at his home in Nice. Well, it was a topless car. There was no roof, so it would be useless in Moscow or London and he didn't spend enough of his time in LA to appreciate it. He also thought people in LA wouldn't give it the respect or admiration it deserved. Americans would probably think it was an old Corvette.

He dropped the '58 Ferrari 250 Testa Rossa into 2nd for the tight left hander, saw it was clear ahead, straightened the corner out across the apex and floored the accelerator once again at he allowed the steering to right itself. The 12 cylinder engine growling for all its worth. Many said this car should not be driven at all so many years after it was manufactured, let alone at speed but Nicolay hated that attitude, this was a racing car, several of the 30 or so other cars built in the 50s and 60s won the Le Mans 24 Hours Endurance Race. Racing was at its heart. Of course, even with the overhaul he had had done at Ferrari, this wasn't a hugely fast car by todays standards. Compared to most of his other cars, it was slow but that was missing the point, none of them gave you this feeling or made this particular sound. This car did the thing that Julianne did to him, it reached deep into him and stirred his soul. It made his heart beat faster and the hair stand up on the back of his neck.

Much more important than any of that was knowing that none of his contemporaries could get their hands on one. They saw themselves as equals, as their yachts were almost as big as his. As they pulled up in their Mercedes, Bugattis and Rolls. But all of them paled into insignificance next to the 250. Ultimately, the Bugatti was just made by Volkswagen anyway and the Rolls by BMW. None of them had the breeding of the 250 and it showed on their faces when they saw him. The Ferrari said '*fuck you all to hell and back*'. Doesn't matter what you own, you don't own one of these and the chances of another one coming up for auction are microscopic.

The drive from Julianne's hill top house down into Nice, especially at 6:00 am when the road was all but deserted was about the most sublime drive you could take. He had a huge smile on his face for most of the drive and especially as he pulled into the Ports car park. He skipped around the port practically to his yacht. He had a little business call to take care of and he liked to do his calls from his private study on his yacht. He especially like to schedule them at this time to keep his people in Moscow on their toes. It would now be about 8:30am there.

His assistant - Alex had made an Americano with an extra shot and cold skimmed milk ready for Nicolay. Nothing to eat. Nicolay never ate breakfast. Alex was on the inner, inner circle. Only very few people knew of the secret study. Alex knew he was never, *ever*, to disclose the existence of this study or for that matter any of Nicolay's secrets to anyone. He knew that his predecessor had been indiscreet about some of Nicolay's secrets and paid a heavy price. A price Alex would never wish to pay. He took the coffee in to the main study and pulled on the hard back copy of The Brothers Karamazov by Dostoyevsky on one of the shelves. It was a thick book which was hollowed out and contained a mechanism to unlatch a small secret door into the inner study. This room also acted as a panic room should the need ever arise. He placed the coffee on the desk a few minutes before Nicolay was due and went back to the main deck to greet his boss. Alex lived wherever his boss lived. He was at his boss's beck and call whenever he needed him apart from his bosses 'downtime' such as last night when his boss went off to the 'casino'.

Alex busied himself on the deck. There were always jobs to be done on such a large vessel. He liked to ensure he always looked busy. He was paid a healthy salary and on top of that lived in beautiful villas and yachts. He always knew he was expendable though, so he liked to give the impression that his boss was getting good value for money.

"Dobroye utro Ser."

"Dobroye utro Alexandre." came the reply as he walked across the gang plank.

Alex went about his business. No one else was up or around on the yacht at that time. Nicolay took his sunglasses off, went through the doors at the rear of the yacht to the main living area, through there to a door to the study and then to the back wall of the study and accessed the secret door to his private study. He closed the door behind him. The door always remained closed. It was never left open. He sat down behind his desk, took a sip of the coffee and looked back at the wall in front of him. At his pride and joy. Rembrandt's 'Storm on the Sea of Galilee' from 1633. It depicted Jesus calming the storm as set out in the Gospel of Mark from the New Testament. As with many of Rembrandt's paintings, he painted himself into the painting. He held his salmon coloured cap to his head with one hand and onto a rope attached to the main mast with the other. Nicolay was a religious man and this image of the calming Jesus filled him with a special tranquility. Of course, the painting was a little out of proportion in his secret study, but who cared when you were looking at a painting which only around ten people had seen since its theft in 1990. The value was immense at the time it was taken and had risen since due to its notoriety. It was probably worth $40 - $50 million or more now. Nicolay didn't have it for its value. He didn't need it. The painting was in many ways similar to the Ferrari 250. It was his way of sticking two fingers up at the world and saying I did it. On my own. Against the odds. But unlike the very public racing red Ferrari that sat not far away in the Port's car park, this was his secret two fingers. A large smile spread across his face. He dialed the Moscow office number.

...

Charlie pulled up to the curb at the foot of Janet's road. It was already baking hot. He had the sunroof and windows open. A man was walking up past his car on the opposite side. He briefly glanced over. This was a man who looked totally out of place in this suburban Spanish street. He wore the wrong clothes (a dark long sleeved shirt and dark jeans). He had a compact backpack and he was so pale, he stood out like a sore thumb. He also had an air of someone who didn't quite know where he was going. Charlie pulled on the handbrake gently and sat for a moment. The guy was homing in on Janet's house. No doubt about it. He was on the right side of the road and he looked at the number on each house door. As he reached her house, he slowed slightly and veered off toward the side of the house. In the blink of an eye, he was gone. If this was a friend coming to see her, he would surely knock on the door, not go down the narrow gap between her house and the next house. It was very clear which was the door you should go to as a visitor. Charlie sat for a while waiting to see if the guy came back out. One minute. Five minutes. There was no sign of him. Was this someone Carl had sent? Surely, he'd have told him.

He sat unblinking. Examining particularly the sides of the house for the stranger to come back out. The stranger would surely figure out he was on the wrong street or at the wrong house. There was no movement for half an hour. The next movement was the garage door started to lift. Charlie found he was holding his breath and had to consciously tell himself to breathe. This was not the guy, it was Janet and her mum. They were on the move again. He sat low in the seat as if sleeping. His baseball cap pulled low so there was no gap between it and his sunglasses. He watched in his drivers side door mirror for them to pass. This was a silly life for an IT bloke he thought, but it beat tapping keys and it hopefully would mean that he'd get his hands back on the cash that was rightfully his. Janet's car backed out with the roof down. Her mum in the passenger seat with a scarf around her hair. She reversed out the drive and slightly up the hill. He watched as she set off toward him, but kept his eye on the house. The garage door started to come back down. Ten seconds later, Janet's Porsche drove past slowly with its now familiar burbling exhaust note. He watched the house for a moment longer. When the garage door was almost fully shut, the stranger sneaked back around and rolled under the door. WTF? What did he do now? What if the money was in the house? He was supposed to be watching her, but there was a stranger in her house.

   He had to make a call. She would most likely not be taking the money with her. If she'd stashed it somewhere, it would be done by now. If it was just in the house, then he had to stick around to see if this guy was trying to steal it. He got out the car and walked slowly up the road, trying as hard as he could to look like he fitted in. At least he had a tan and wore shorts. He went down the side of the house and jumped over the wall onto the terrace. He stuck his head around and covered the glare with his hand so he could see in. He couldn't see him. He craned his neck around further to get a wider view but there was no movement. He panicked and wondered if he was sneaking out the garage door. Either way, that would probably be the way he would come back out. Charlie quickly tracked back down the side of the house to the garage side. He tiptoed past. It would probably look odd to neighbours, but he was beyond worrying about that now. The garage door was closed down still. He wondered back down to his car and got back in. He would have to wait it out in the car.

With this new development, Charlie began to think a little more about what was actually going to happen when Carl and Dan came. Strangely, he'd grown to be quite fond of Janet in this odd and detached way as he followed her around. He'd noticed he looked forward to seeing her face each day. It wasn't surprising as they had seemed to have a spark when he 'met' her in Edinburgh. It was going to be tough to hand this whole thing over to Carl. One hour passed and Charlie had to get out of the car, it was just too hot to keep sitting there without the air con on. He figured that the stranger would have made his exit by now if he was going to. Perhaps he was either waiting there for her to arrive back or he was just stuck. He took a walk down the street and found a grass verge under a palm tree where there was some mottled shade. Bliss. His phone pinged with a text. It was from Dan.

We are going to be delayed cos Carls houseGot fuckin rubbed and someone killed his dogs. hes distraut.

"Rubbed? Oh robbed. Fucking idiot." Charlie wondered if Dan saw the irony in this occurrence but doubted that would be the case.

OK, keep me posted. Tell him sorry from me. To hear about the dogs

"I ain't goin' nowhere my big, bald friend." he said pulling out a long, stray piece of grass to chew on. He was sufficiently back from the street and out of the way to be able to watch cars heading up the street but they wouldn't catch sight of him. He could also see the house, but there was still no movement around it.

He put his head back and shut his eyes for a moment to relax. He let out a long, heavy breath. He'd been holding it in again. It was coming up to midday and the locals didn't do much around this time as it was just too hot. Charlie drifted off in the relative quiet. Aware of some insect noises; crickets or was it cicadas? They were loud but strangely restful, almost hypnotic. He blinked a few times and saw the palm leaves moving gently above him in the almost there breeze. He knew he was drifting off, but he was just too tired. He just needed a nap for twenty minutes.

He was back in Edinburgh and in a bar with Janet drinking and chatting. Having a fun time and they were enjoying each other's company. They were quite drunk, both of them drinking refreshing white wine. Then they were in Janet's hotel room on the bed and Charlie was kissing her mouth and she tasted amazing, like strawberries. She undid his fly and pushed her hand into the gap at the front of his boxer shorts. He wanted to have sex with her so much. She was just so beautiful. Everything about her, the way she tasted, smelled. He was undressing her and her body was beautifully curvy. He kissed her nipples and her stomach and then she pushed him further down. He was so hungry for her. There was a knock at the door and she got up and answered the door with a sheet around her. Her face all flustered, red and hot. She blew hair out of her eyes as a stranger came in and placed a tray of drinks on the table. Charlie was on the bed, aroused and embarrassed as the stranger walked back out; smirking. He shouldn't be able to see charlie naked like that. It was wrong. And then Janet was sipping the drink but it was an odd colour; like it had been tampered with. He wanted to tell her not to drink that drink as it was going to make her ill, but he couldn't speak loud enough or she was too far away across the other side of the room. It was like he was being restrained. Held down and still by some invisible force.

"Estás bien?" An old lady in a heavy dark blue dress with a bag of shopping in each hand was talking to Charlie. He sat up. She momentarily put the bags down and was talking again and gesticulating up the road and down the road, but too fast for him to get what she was saying. Then he realised he'd been sleeping in a state of arousal and he really wished that she would go away, but she continued to talk to him. She kept pointing up to the sun and then down at him but he wasn't getting any of it. He just just held his hands out to his sides.

"Inglés, pardon." he said to her looking confused to express how little he understood of what she was saying.

She shook her head and started to walk away but carried on talking as she had been, still gesturing toward the sky and back down but just to herself now.

Charlie laid back down and shut his eyes. Then checked his watch. 2:15. She would probably be another few hours if she was at the beach. He decided to have a wander back up to the house to see if he could see anything of the stranger. He gingerly peered around the kitchen window from the terrace. He was there looking through drawers. Shit, the balls of this guy. He felt violated on her behalf. Well he knew the guy was in the house still, all he could really do was keep an eye on things and be ready for when Janet and her mum got back.

He took himself back down the street to his spot under the palm tree. How could it be that he could feel protective toward her on the one hand and yet he was going to lead Carl to her who would probably torture her into giving up the cash? He was confused. This feeling was only going to get more and more intense as Carl and Dan's arrival got closer. At that moment, he heard the familiar exhaust note of Janet's Porsche coming up the street. He scooted slightly to the left so he was a little more hidden. She drove past with the top down and her mum in the passenger seat. Her mum was asleep with her head back against the headrest and her mouth slightly open. Up ahead, the garage door started to open. The brake lights came on and then they went off and then the door closed back down behind them. So they were stuck in there with this stranger now. God, he hoped she would be okay. He sat tight in his spot and watched the house for any signs of movement. He waited until dusk. Windows started to glow faintly as lights were switched on. When the darkness offered sufficient cover, Charlie went around the side of the house to the spot where he could listen to them on the terrace. They were out there chatting. There was no sign of the stranger. He must have slipped out at some point unbeknown to Janet and her mum. And to Charlie.

TEN

Two hundred and twenty one days after

Janet needed to drop her mum off at the airport for 10am. After that, she had a little trip to take. She'd packed an overnight bag and thrown it in the back of the Porsche so she could take straight off. She'd considered flying, but then just thought how nice it would be to drive that length of the Cote d'Azur in an open top car and that seemed like the better option. She could take a stop off somewhere pretty along the way or maybe two. It was about a six hour drive. Normally, the thought of a six hour drive would fill her with dread, but she was looking forward this.

As they got in the car, Yana asked "Are you going off to Nice today then?" motioning to the bag in the back seat.

"Yes, I'm going to go after I drop you off."

"Very nice. Who's your friend there?" her mum asked raising her eyebrows subtly as if to suggest it may be a boy.

"No mum, it's just an old friend from university." she shook her head. "Honestly, stop it with the boys will you. You're relentless."

The goodbye at the airport was not sad as she'd thought it might be. She'd told her mum to come back and visit again in a few months. Her mum just seemed very happy to have had so much time with her daughter and to be honest, she was happy to have had four days with her mum. They'd reconnected on a more adult level, it was more of a friendship and less of a mum and daughter thing now. At passport control, she waved her mum off and her mum blew her a kiss which was very touching. She'd called out 'See you soon!' once more. Janet watched for a little longer as her mother headed to security taking out her tickets and passport from her wallet.

She stuck her phone on the passenger seat and pulled up directions, then clicked the start button. She'd got the phone connected to her bluetooth radio, so the directions came through her speakers.

"Keep right at the fork and follow signs for Barcelona/Ronda de Dalt/Tarragona/Lleida/Girona and merge onto Ronda de Dalt/B-20" It sounded a little funny when the well spoken Americanised lady's voice spoke the Spanish road names. She seemed to almost trip over her words, but she'd just get them out. Janet forked right and immediately saw the signs to follow.

She was relishing this. She'd been a little bored over the last few weeks if she was honest with herself. She needed excitement and spontaneity in her life. She needed the high stakes and the uncertainty. The stuff that had been sucked out of her previous job until she became nothing more than a safe pair of hands moving money around for customers. But this little mission she'd set herself gave her a little of that high stakes thrill back. She didn't quite know what this trip might bring, but she had a gut feeling that there was something in that message. And she felt she'd figured exactly what it was. She wasn't telling herself that she was going to waltz onto that ship and walk away with a stolen masterpiece, but she could go and do a little digging around and see what she could see.

A little over an hour into her journey and she was approaching the border with France. A thought suddenly occurred to her. She pulled over to the side of the road. She leaned back and pulled her overnight bag onto the passenger seat. She rooted through frantically. Ragging some clothes out which she threw onto the back seat.

"Damn! You idiot!" She stuck the car into first and set off spinning the wheels and throwing sand and pebbles out from the tyres.

. . .

The cellar door pushed gingerly open. Reaper poked his ear to the gap and listened. They'd been gone for half an hour now. He'd heard most of their conversations for the last day and a bit. Nothing in any of those conversations led him to believe that either of these women had anything to do with this amount of money that had been scribbled on Carl's desk. Was he missing something? From what he understood, she was house sitting for a friend, her mum was from London and was just out for the weekend. Janet was taking her back to the airport just now. There was some mention of a trip to Nice. If she did have anything to do with this two million odd quid, there was no talk of it. There was no talk of any money at all. There was no money in the house. There was very little of anything in the house, it was more like a bachelor pad than the house of a young woman. This was making him really annoyed. He'd come a very long to find very fucking little.

Perhaps if he went through the house again, he'd find something of more interest. His search had been cut slightly short by them coming back previously. He needed to be more thorough. He went methodically through all the places where there may be information. Starting in the garage and ground floor, he would work upwards. Drawers. Cupboards. Shelves. Everything. Everywhere. Janet had been very, very careful. If she had a bank account, there was no information about it in this house. If she had a credit card, there was no paper work. There was nothing about anything in this house. It was like no one lived here. She was the invisible woman.

In most peoples' houses, there was a place where bills and letters and statements were kept. Like a drawer or a desk. There were lots of drawers in this house, but mostly they were empty. He didn't see anything like this. Once he got to the bedroom, he sat on her bed and once again, he looked through her bedside drawer. There was some creams and ointments and a watch. The watch looked expensive to him but it wasn't a brand he'd ever heard of before. Nothing else. On top of the bedside cabinet was a book. She was reading The Girl with the Dragon Tattoo. He'd heard of it. He leafed through briefly fanning the pages in front of his warm face. Her bookmark was a letter. Finally a letter. But this wasn't a letter from a bank or a rent statement or a utilities bill. This was a proper letter. That someone had hand written. It had been folded twice and was beginning to tear at the creased edges. There were several stains on the letter that had blotted the writing ink. These looked like water and coffee. It was scuffed and dirty and also had what looked like grease marks which had the effect of making the paper slightly opaque. The whole thing had the aroma of coconut as if she had been sunbathing and got oil on it. It was like an old pirate treasure map.

Dearest J,

I do apologise that I couldn't come to meet you personally recently, but...

Now this was interesting. This was very interesting indeed. A letter from someone called MPW to someone called J (that must be Janet obviously). There were additional notes possibly made by Janet in a red pen around the blue ink and written all in CAPS. He found her iPad which was on the kitchen table and Googled the *Storm on the Sea of Galilee* and found the first result that Janet had found a few days ago. It was in purple rather than blue which suggested that the link had been visited before. He found this extremely interesting. After a little digging around, he summarised that something had happened prior to this letter, some sort of meeting or liaison. Then the letter seemed to suggest, reading between the lines, literally with the additional notes, that there was a stolen painting which was on a boat which was based in Nice. His heart was beating fast. He went back to the Wikipedia page about the painting and looked at the value of the painting. He went to her wardrobe and looked again. A bag that had been there was now gone. Was she on her way to Nice to find this painting? Who was this woman that she would do something like this?

He clicked on the history tab of her browser and viewed her full history. In the last few days, she had been doing a lot of research by the look of it. Looking at Nice in France and particularly the port, a boat called Still Waters and a man called Nicolay Zhestakova. She'd been reading through lots of news articles and Wikipedia pages about these topics. It looked liked Zhestakova owned this boat. She'd also been looking at the route from Barcelona to Nice. It was 662Km or 5 hours and 55 minutes driving. Was she planning to drive that? Surely not. You'd take a plane.

He made himself coffee and toast with honey. Then sat himself down at the kitchen table to think. It was taking a chance in case she came back but he'd hear the garage door going if she did. Though the more he thought about it, the more he knew she wasn't coming back. At least not until she'd been on her little trip. Once he'd eaten, he took his coffee onto the terrace and sat for a second to feel the sun on his face.

He remembered she had a phone charger at the side of her bed before. He'd used it to charge his phone up. Now it was gone. She wouldn't have taken that if she was just dropping her mum at the airport. She was taking a trip herself. Her mum was going back to London. Janet was going to Nice. He was going to have to move quickly. He was going to Nice. He'd never been before. He could fly there from Barcelona for about €80. Thankfully, this was on Carl.

...

Charlie was following at a safe distance in his Fiat Punto. The car blended into the mountainous background with its dusty grey paint work. His eyes trained on Janet's blue Porsche. So much so, he was giving himself a headache with the concentration. This was similar to the headaches he sometimes got when he was coding websites. Staring at a screen for long periods of time. He started to wonder why he was doing this and why he didn't just go back to his IT work. He was in demand. It paid well. Well it paid well until you compared it to the potential pay-off here. He didn't really need this pay-off. He had a pretty big lump of savings banked.

He had a nice car and a great flat in London. But it wasn't enough. He'd always wanted bigger and better. When he was 14 at school and everyone had Adidas Superstar trainers at fifty quid a pop, he had to get Nike Air Max at a hundred. He had begged his dad for them. He'd sold his soul to get them. A full six months worth of cutting the grass (weekly), polishing the car (monthly) and a second paper round (mornings to add to his after school paper round). It was ingrained in him though. He was a natural born show off. The problem was this feeling had just grown as he had. Now his life wasn't enough. His car wasn't enough. He needed more in order to show off, in order to be the best. Was it greed or was just being overly competitive? He didn't think it was greed as he was a generous person. At the pub, he'd be the first to buy drinks. But was that just part of the desire to show off and be the centre of attention?

He could really do with some water, but he was tied to her now. If he stopped, even for the quickest stop, he would lose her and this would all be in vain. He didn't know where she was going. He might never see her again should they get separated. Whenever she sped up, he sped up, whenever she touched the brakes, he touched the brakes. But now she wasn't just touching the brakes, she'd fully slammed on and thrown the car to the side of the road. A cloud of sandy dust plumed around the car. He couldn't also pull over as that would look too obvious. Had she spotted him perhaps? He took his foot off the brakes and placed it gently back onto the gas and continued, trying hard to look natural and as if he should be right where he was. As he got closer, he could see she was looking down at something on the passenger seat. He went right on by. He drove as slow as he dared to without looking unnatural. He didn't want to be in front of her. He started to think about where he could pull over all the while keeping his eyes on the rear view mirror. But she was off again. Leaving another dust cloud in her wake. Within half a minute, she flew past him. Her tousled hair blowing in the breeze. Once she was a nose in front, he stole a glance over. She looked straight ahead. She had no interest in a little grey Fiat. She was pulling away from him. That was fine, he wanted some space between them, but he kept her in view. Just.

    He wondered where was she going. This was much longer that any of the other trips she took. It was clearly not a beach day today. This was something more purposeful. She had that look in her eyes as she sped past him. A look that said she was on a mission. God knows to do what. For the next three hours, she drove at just below the speed limit. He thought he could see her sipping water occasionally which was making him feel more and more dehydrated. He was tired too as he'd not really slept that well since the stranger had gained access to the house. He lost concentration for a few seconds and when he looked back, he'd lost her. He couldn't see her car and looked around frantically. He stuck his head up higher like an ostrich trying to see over other cars. He couldn't lose her now. Then he saw her blue car to his right hand side circling the exit ramp from the A9 and it looked like she was heading to… Sète. What was in Sète he wondered. She seemed to be heading for the centre of Sète. He followed her as she drove to a hotel. It was around ten minutes from the A9 through the centre of Sète to Le Grand Hotel. He pulled up a block back and watched. She leaned over into the back seat and fumbled about and then a porter approached her. He opened her door and she passed her bag to him. Then the roof of the car slowly closed. She got out, gave him something, probably a tip and disappeared inside with him. This was too odd. He was a little stunned and not really sure what he was going to do now. Clearly she was going to stay here for a short while, probably for the night at least as they'd now taken her car to park it up.

This was going to be tricky as he would need to try to keep an eye on her otherwise, he could lose her in the morning. He couldn't really stay in the hotel as she would probably recognise him if she saw him, but he didn't really want to sleep in the car on the street. He took a walk and tried to see where the hotel's car park was located. He wandered around the back of the hotel and saw a ramp that went down under the hotel. He would have to check into the hotel as he was going to need to get access to this or he was going to end up losing her. He went back to the car and awaited dusk. He called the hotel from his mobile phone and reserved a room. A single was all they had. Depressing.

Once dusk fell gently over Sète and he felt a little more comfortable with the lack of light, he checked in. He paid half his attention to the receptionist who only spoke in French and half to what was going on behind him. He needed to ensure he wasn't spotted by her. If she spotted him, it was all over. Well it was if she recognised him. Would she? Well she did in the lock up after she came around from the Rohypnol and that was with her brain all mushy. She would recognise him if she saw him, but there was no sign of her. She was probably taking a nap after her drive. He was a little jealous, he was absolutely shattered. He was also desperately thirsty.

Once he was checked in, rather than go and check his room out. He didn't have a bag with him even. He went to the bar and ordered a large beer and a glass of sparkling water with ice, then skulked over to the corner where he sat with his back to the room and drank deeply. He needed to figure a way to ensure she didn't leave the hotel without him knowing. The grim reality was dawning on him that he might have to sleep in the car so he could keep an eye on her car all night. The way she was, she was likely to be off at the crack of dawn. He sat and pulled his thoughts together. At least, now they were in France, the stranger who'd gained access to Janet's house was out of the picture. That whole element was still very troubling. Whoever or whatever he was, he was definitely after Janet or something she had. He'd walked up that street and went straight to her house. He might still be in the house for all Charlie knew. Did he know what she'd stolen? Was he her stalker? A previous boyfriend maybe? He looked a little rough for her.

And then he heard her voice ordering a drink. He'd know that voice. A soft southern accent. 80% London / 15% Birmingham / 5% Ukrainian. She was at the bar ordering a gin and tonic. 'Grande s'il vous plait'. Then she was speaking in French asking about... Where there was a good restaurant? He kept facing away from her, picked up the paper from the table and started to read that and then suddenly felt that was too obvious. He placed it at the side of him and took his phone out and started to read his emails. Then he looked at Twitter. Then Facebook. She was talking again in French, so he sneaked a quick look around. She was sat at the bar chattering with the bar man. She sounded to have a good grasp of French. He tried to understand more of the conversation but it just wasn't going in. After fifteen minutes, she disappeared. He figured she'd gone to eat somewhere.

He drove his car into the garage and parked with a good view of her Porsche. He parked across and about five spaces further from the exit. She shouldn't have to walk past his car to get to hers when she came down from the hotel. He sunk down in the drivers seat and shut his eyes for a second and started to drift off. This was stupid. He could afford to go and have a few hours at least in his room, couldn't he? If he spent all night sleeping in this car, he'd be crippled. He considered disabling her car, so she couldn't take off so easily but then he remembered he wasn't that good with cars and besides he'd need the keys to get into the engine. Even then, he wasn't really that sure. Spark plugs maybe?

ELEVEN

Two hundred and twenty two days after

He was uncomfortable in the seat and his back was spasming but there was something else. In his dream there was a large, ugly blue bottle buzzing around his head. He swatted at it. But it came back at him, flying straight at his eyes. He pulled his head away from its path and banged his head on the car window. Shocked, he awoke to the sound of the Porsche's throaty exhaust echoing through the low ceilinged car park as it slowly drove over the lip of the ramp. He just caught sight of the car's rear right hand indicator flashing and then it was gone. Shit. He'd slept right through. It was ten past seven in the morning and he had to get his shit together. He turned the key. But nothing happened. It didn't even turn over. He pulled the key out, stuck it back in and turned it again. This time, it turned over but didn't catch. He turned it back off and then tried again, pushing down the accelerator at the same time. Not fully, he didn't want to flood the engine. Almost. Once more, he turned off and then on and gave the gas a few small jabs. It caught this time. He was off. Unfortunately, as he reached the top of the ramp, she was gone. No blue Porsche anywhere. She'd gone right. So he hung a right. He saw signs for the A9 and slowed down so he could think. She was either on a road trip or Sète was as far as she was coming. If she was on a road trip, she'd probably continue along the A9, if she was just visiting Sète, then she'd probably go to the beach or something similar and be back later on. If that was the case, he could check back later. If the road trip was the case, he needed to put his foot down and get back onto the A9. That was his instinct. He put his foot down.

She'd been traveling at roughly 80km/h for most of her journey. He was doing 100km/h. She had about two or three minutes lead on him. If he didn't get sight of the blue car within say twenty minutes, then he'd either lost her or she was tootling around Sète or at the beach. His calculations worked out perfectly. He had sight of her within ten minutes.

"This is not good Janet. You're getting predictable." he muttered to himself.

She was taking it slightly steadier today. About 70km/h. The sun was shining. It was thirty degrees and she had the top down and her hair blew about in the breeze. It looked slightly damp. All of a sudden he felt comfortable and relaxed again. The view of the back of her head for some reason really put him at ease. He realised he was too close and dropped back to his safe distance. His thirst had come back and was accompanied by a raging hunger now. 'Good skills Charlie' he told himself for allowing himself to once again be in this situation without any provisions. He imagined she probably had a bottle of Fanta Limón and some tasty snacks. Crisps, donuts and sweets. He had nothing. No spare clothing. He was in the same underwear he'd been wearing for a few days now. He had a wad of cash and a car phone charger and that was it.

Four hours later, he was almost in a trance. His mouth, the driest it had ever been. His stomach grumbled and groaned above the level of the radio. He'd not really been taking much notice what was going on. He couldn't remember anything to do with driving for at least an hour or more. Keeping his focus on the back of her car, the back of her head was almost too much. They were off the A9 and in city traffic. On a dual carriageway on the coast. There was a loud whining noise from his right hand side. It built and built into a harsh rumble. Then a blast through his open drivers window. Then he realised an airplane was taking off next to him. He was alongside a runway. It brought him out of his trance. He saw a sign for an airport, but he wasn't really sure what city he was in. It wasn't Marseille. That was hours back. He followed her a few car lengths back. He couldn't be too far back as there were lots of traffic lights to get through. The Promenade Des Anglais, Nice - a street sign told him. She got through some lights but the traffic was so busy, she got stopped again less than half a minute along. They followed the promenade from the airport end which was in the west end to the far east end. It was pose-y. Open top Mercs, Ferraris and Bentleys everywhere. People walked toy dogs whilst trying to look as if they were on a catwalk. The promenade petered out at a headland which she followed around to the right and then the left. Ahead of them was the port. Hundreds of boats from small and cute to huge juggernauts. She drove down the side of it very slowly and then veered off up a side street. Eventually, she parked up in one of few parking spaces and closed the roof. She got out and was off walking with her bag over her shoulder up the tight, shadowy street. Charlie ramped his car up. Stuck his hazard warning lights on and started to follow at a safe distance. She seemed to be looking at her phone for directions. About twenty feet behind her, two men popped out of a side alley and started following her. Their appearance matched the dark thin streets perfectly. Charlie had a bad feeling about this. They were gaining on her but she seemed so engrossed in looking at her phone, she hadn't noticed them. They were about ten feet behind her now. The right hand man reached behind him and pulled what looked like a sheathed knife from a back pocket. It suddenly occurred to Charlie he had no weapon. He was as defenceless as she was. She turned a corner to the left and was out of sight. As the men too turned the corner, Charlie sprinted to it so he could keep an eye on them. This road was narrower and darker. The men were closer now, visibly speeding up to catch her. Ahead of them, Janet looked up to her left and climbed a few steps to enter the doors of the Hôtel Le Geneva. Charlie breathed a sigh of relief and crossed over the road while continuing to look inconspicuous. The two men continued straight past the hotel.

"You're gonna get yourself into a sticky mess if you're not more careful Janet." Charlie shook his head at her naivety. "What we doing in Nice you crazy woman?" Charlie asked her as he walked past the hotels entrance. She was checking in. He'd come round a little now, but he would have to go and eat really soon. It was early afternoon and was very warm and muggy. She was going to be staying tonight for sure. He knew where she was and where her car was. He ran back to his Fiat and eventually found a parking spot. Then he wandered off and found a little restaurant. Most people where sat outside and he wanted to but he couldn't chance her walking by. He went inside and asked for a quiet table near the back. He glanced quickly at the menu, ordered a large beer and a jug of water, mussels to start and a pizza. He closed his eyes and put his head back for a second. Relieved. His long journey was over for now. Hopefully, she'd reached her destination. But who knew? Janet was more mysterious with every day. He typed a message to Dan.

> She has driven to Nice in France. I am following her. I will msg you as soon as I understand what's going on. Charlie

Any sine of the money or the bag?

> Not yet.

He hoped this would be enough to appease him. He really didn't want to field a call from him right now. Maybe once he'd had a good feed and a full night of sleep, he could handle that. He half expected an immediate text back with more questions, but nothing came.

Several hours later, wearing a new rucksack full of drinks and snacks, toiletries, fresh new socks and boxers and five new t-shirts in assorted shades of blue and grey, Charlie checked himself into a nearby hotel. It was basic in comparison to the Hôtel Le Geneva, but considering he didn't even make it to the room of the last hotel, it wasn't worth spending too much. He fell forward dramatically onto his bed and shut his eyes. His head hadn't quite reached the pillow but he couldn't be bothered to adjust himself. He dragged his phone from his pocket and checked on the time. It was now 7pm. He set his timer to give him eight hours, then rethought and made it ten. That would have him up at 5am. Surely she couldn't be up and off before that time.

He recalled Janet driving earlier in the day. Her damp hair drying out as the wind worked through it. She was so intriguing. In his mind, she had taken on the air of a secret agent. On a mission to who knows where and to do who knew what. He had no clue, but maybe that was the point of her as a secret agent. She knew, she had purpose. He had let Carl know where she was but he regretted it. He wished he didn't have Carl to report to. If he had been smart, he could have taken the same tack as Kyle and Jim and said he wanted nothing more to do with them. Then he could have tracked her down on his own.

He wished he was in the car with Janet on her mission. Unfortunately due to the incident with the Rohypnol, that would not be happening anytime soon. Scrap that. Any time ever. He shut his eyes tight and drifted off.

TWELVE

Two hundred and twenty three days after

When Charlie's phone timer went off; even though tired still, he felt oddly thankful for the ten full and undisturbed hours of rest he'd managed. He showered and freshened up in the bathroom. Once dressed, he sat momentarily in the chair in the corner of the room and tucked into a pain au chocolat and gulped at a bottle of orange juice. Unaware he was staring into space, wondering what on earth today would hold. He really hoped that she was not going to drive further. It was fine for her in her open top Porsche. He was in a small and basic Fiat which was not at all comfortable. He packed up the backpack and set off. He wasn't really sure where he was going. But he'd walk past her hotel and then her car to start with.

As he left the hotel, the sky's street lit ambience was succumbing to the sun as it chased down the horizon. Orange was becoming blue. He loved this time of day. Few people were about and you could feel like you owned the day. Wandering down towards where she'd left her car. He was on the opposite side of the road. It was still there. Good. Check. He continued toward the Hôtel Le Geneva. The hotel was in darkness. Even the entrance was very dim. He walked past. There was a single lamp lit on the reception counter. No one around.

He went and found coffee to take out. Of course, it was tiny, but being French coffee, packed the strength of two large coffees. Now he was going to have to wait around for her to see what the hell she would get up to today. This was like babysitting a wayward puppy. You just had no idea what the hell it was going to get up to next. He found a small alley that led up to some steps across and slightly up from the hotel. He could see the hotel. He was within earshot of her car and within easy reach of his car should he need it. He thought he might be in for a long wait.

Hang on though, here she was. Charlie moved slightly to the side so the wall of the alley hid him from her view. She stood on the top step in front of the hotel doors and looked around. As if she was taking the city in. She tilted her head back taking in a deep breath and filling her lungs. Then she was off. Down the street away from the car. He let her get away a little. He needed to be extremely cautious as there was no one else on the streets. He'd stick out like a sore thumb if she was to see him. She was taking it pretty easy so it was fine. She made her way to the port and went right down to the dock side as if she were about to board a yacht. To the right were smaller boats and to the left were bigger ones. In fact, some extremely large ones. She walked along at a snails pace. Admiring the boats?

The boats got bigger toward the end of this row. Huge in fact. The very last one was shockingly huge. Billionaire huge. She stopped here momentarily. Like she was mentally noting something down about the boat. Then she was off again. Looking at the yacht, there was someone on deck. He looked to be sweeping or mopping it down. She moved away from the waters edge now and walked towards a row of cafes. She took up a seat outside. The waiter brought her coffee and a croissant. Her eyes remained steadfastly fixed to the large yacht that she had examined.

"What's with the yacht Janet?"

She stuck it out at the cafe for the rest of the morning. Taking notes and doing something on her phone. Maybe texting or browsing the internet. Charlie did the same as her and kept his eye on her. Relaxing in a cafe, sipping coffee after coffee, watching Janet was not a bad morning. Even though he wasn't really sure why he was in Nice. At just after midday, a man came and sat at a table at the cafe next to the one Janet was at. It only took a second to click. It was the stranger from Barcelona who had broken into her house. Now he was sat not five meters from her. Looking over her shoulder at what she was doing on her phone.

. . .

As much as she'd been thinking long and hard during her drive from Barcelona to Nice, she didn't really have a plan of action as such. Was this just indicative of how little she had going on in her life that she could drive from Barcelona to Nice without any clear plan of action? It probably was, but was that a bad thing? Many would see that as a good state of affairs. She now thought maybe she would see the lay of the land with the Still Waters. See if she could see how secure the boat was. Nice was more cosmopolitan than Barcelona. It would be no hardship to spend a little time here. Plus obviously, there was nothing to get back to Barcelona for. No job awaiting her.

So far, she'd seen one young man who was not Nicolay Zhestakova on the deck of the Still Waters. A good looking young man who had been sweeping or mopping the decks down, wiping surfaces and tidying things away. First thing this morning, the port had been like a ghost town. Now at almost lunchtime, the port was thronging. The roads around the port were busy, the main car park which was in front of her, constantly had a queue of cars waiting to get in and out. She decided she'd watched for long enough for now, she paid up and went for a walk. She'd been studying the layout of Nice on her phone and she seemed to be not far from the old town part of Nice where there were lots of shops and restaurants packed into narrow little alleys. She decided to head over there. On route, she stopped in at the hotel and changed into cut off demin shorts and a light shirt. She might spend a little time on the beach later. Walking around the road that led to the Promenade des Anglais gave a view along the beach front that spread out in front of Nice and went all the way to the airport. She could understand why this was called the Cote d'Azur. The sea was the most vivid blue she remembered ever seeing. It almost made the heart skip a beat.

At the Flower Market, she grabbed a snack and then headed back to the beach. She took a bed for the afternoon and sunned herself whilst she continued to think about her next steps. It felt good to be somewhere new. A little like a holiday. Even though she hadn't been working recently. Being in Barcelona wasn't like a holiday. It was now where she lived, where she studied, where she spent. But this had the feeling of a holiday. She decided her next step was she'd go back to the port tonight and watch the yacht once again. Hopefully she could see Zhestakova even. It did seem like it would be quite easy to board the yacht if she really wanted to. There was a gang plank there this morning. If the opportunity arose, would she dare? Well if she wanted excitement. That would be exciting.

At nine o'clock that evening, she was back at the cafe. The evening was warm, the sky a hazy, orangey pink. Once again, she was sipping a large G&T. She hadn't ordered a large, that was just how it came seemingly all along the south coast of Spain and France. The young man was on deck on the Still Waters once again, but this time he was with two men similar in age to himself. They were drinking. And playing loud music. Although there was music coming from all directions. Bars, topless cars, youths played music from their phones as they walked by and then the yachts competed with it all. She guessed they had the better sound systems. But then you wouldn't spend that amount on a boat and expect it to come with a shitty sound system.

She got the feeling that man from the morning loved being on the boat and was showing off to passers by. Each time girls walked past, they became louder. They laughed more. Became more animated. Cheese balls. On all the other yachts, the decks were empty. She guessed he worked for Zhestakova who was away and he'd invited his friends over to show off to them.

After an hour more drinking and chatting, they left the boat. Janet paid up and left a tip for the very helpful waiter and followed the three men at a distance. The three went to a pose-y restaurant so Janet went to the bar across the street and once again sat outside so she could keep an eye on what was going on. They would be at least an hour if they were eating so she could if she wanted go to the boat and see if she could get on and have a look. They were looking at oversized menus.

Was this a window? She weighed the situation up. Zhestakova didn't appear to be about. This other man was about to eat a meal. She could have a very quick look around if she was brave. So, was she brave? Actually, she was. This was exactly the sort of thing she seemed to enjoy now. Taking a risk in order to make a huge gain. Only this time the gain would be for her not for some nameless faceless organisation or individual. Was this the gin? The large gin? Very possibly.

Down at the port, things were quiet. At the yacht, there was a gang plank for access, but it was gated. She could see no one on the yacht and no one on either of the boats next to the Still Waters. She walked past and it seemed there were very few boats with people on. She went out wider from the waters edge and doubled back. She was wearing dark clothing, so hopefully would be a subtle presence. Where there were people on yachts, they had one thing in common. They looked like they belonged. They looked comfortable. Relaxed. If she was going to do this, she had to look the same. She had to adopt that same comfortable, 'I belong here' look. She thought about arriving in Edinburgh at the hotel in the Lamborghini and the feeling of power and belonging that gave her as people stared at her and 'her' car. She needed to get back into that mind set. She lifted her head, pushed her shoulders back and slowed her pace down so she didn't look like she was on a mission. She walked along the quayside once more and as she reached the Still Waters, she hopped over the small gate looking confident and as if she just couldn't be bothered to unlock the little gate. She walked onto the low deck at the back. There was an open living area here with tables on both sides of the deck with built in seating. She walked straight through past the two tables. There were stairs to go up a deck or down. She went down. Stepping as quietly as possible but trying to not look like she was tip toeing. The hair on the nape of her neck stood on end and she felt hot and sick. Blood was rushing through her head and she could hear it fizzing in her ears. At the bottom of the stairs was a door which she was sure would be closed and locked but it was ajar. Inside the room was dark. She peered through the gap but the room was empty. This was a large living room with two extremely long and low sofas facing each other with equally low coffee tables in the middle. There were other occasional tables and pieces of furniture around the room. In the corner stood a gold grand piano with a gigantic candelabra on top. It proudly read

STEINWAY

across its front panel. Everything was so ostentatious that the gold grand piano did not look at all out of place. She couldn't work out how the grand piano would have got in. It seemed huge. They must have built the boat around it. There were paintings on either wall behind the sofas but both were modern looking. Certainly not Rembrandt style paintings. At the end of the room was another door. She walked quickly to that internally commenting she was not here to do 'Through The Keyhole', she was here to find a piece of art. No actually, she was here to test a theory out. Nothing more.

At the next door, there was a corridor with several doors leading off it. She walked tentatively down the corridor but was pretty sure there were no people in the rooms, certainly not on this level. There were no lights on and the only light was from ambient lighting streaming through the small side windows. The first room on the left was a kind of study. She walked in. It was very dark but she could make out a large heavy looking wooden desk with a high lacquer top. There was an old picture in here. It could have been a Renoir maybe. She wasn't sure. She wasn't an expert but it certainly wasn't the picture she was looking for. She'd been on the boat for about 5 minutes now and was getting nervous, she hadn't planned to be on for too long. She quickly swept the other rooms on this level. There was no sign. She was a little disoriented. Not sure if there was another deck below this one or how many were above it. The yacht towered above her when she was on the dock, so she guessed quite a few. There were more steps at the end of the corridor to access lower and upper levels. She went down and found four bedrooms, all of which had what she classed as modern art paintings above the beds. Sweat beaded on her forehead and she wiped it away with her hand. Gross. That's never happened before she assured herself. She wasn't sure about checking on the upper decks as they were more open with bigger windows. She went back up to the level with the grand piano and went to the study once more. This was the room with the painting that most closely matched the painting she was searching for.

"Is someone there?" someone called out. "Alex? Emma?" Slight Russian accent Janet thought.

She dropped to a crouch momentarily. "Fuck!" She readied herself to run or hide. She waited a moment more and then went to the door to try to listen. It couldn't be the man who was on the boat before as he was just sitting down to a meal unless he'd forgotten something. This sounded like an older man's voice though. She heard ice clinking into glasses, cans opening and bottles pouring. Now two people were speaking in English, one with the Russian undertone. She guessed that was Nicolay. He was with another man. She realised she was breathing very heavily and calmed herself down. Once her breathing slowed a little, she was able to hear them more clearly. It sounded like they were talking about mines in Africa and enriching processes. The man who she guessed as being Nicolay was talking loudly and the other man too quietly for her to hear what he was saying. Just having half the conversation was making it difficult to get fully what they were discussing. Cigar or cigarette smoke drifted into the living area and down towards the study. She told herself she had to be brave and walked down the corridor to the living area, she could just see their silhouettes in the outside seating area. There were indeed two people. Nicolay, the man with the Russian accent was standing and walking around gesticulating and the other man sat at one of the tables. So now they were blocking her planned exit route. She'd need to find another way off this yacht. Then she saw the standing man coming toward the entrance to the inside area and she moved quickly back to the study and dived in. She stood behind the door. No good. She heard footsteps that were at the far end of the living area on the decked wooden floor. They were getting louder. She went to the desk, pulled the chair to the side slightly and dropped into the footwell. The footsteps grew louder and louder until they were at the study and then they changed to soft steps as he entered the carpeted study. She was blind now, staring into the desk's kick panel. Controlling her breathing, so she made no noise. Well if he came to sit at the desk, she was screwed. She could see the silhouette of his feet standing at the other side of the desk now under the kick board and he went through some papers above her head. Then he walked away from the desk to her right and she heard an odd clicking sound and then a brushing noise and then a light came on sweeping into the study. More shuffling of papers. Then steps as he moved back to the door and then hard steps on the decked wood corridor once more.

"Alex!" he shouted, this time with an angry tone.

She poked her head out a fraction to look where the light was coming from and saw the book shelf that had taken up the end of the study was pulled open and a room inside was lit up with another desk's lamp. On the side wall, she could see a very large golden picture frame. She studied it for a second but could not quite see what it framed from this angle. Then peered further around at the book shelf. The right hand section of the shelves was hinged. One book was leaning out at an angle. It was a big thick book with a hard brown cover.

She tucked her head back in. The footsteps came back in. He was back in the other room routing through drawers and the light abruptly went back out and he left muttering something in Russian. The footsteps petered out as he walked away. He was muttering angrily in Russian (she guessed). Alex's name was used several times. She had no idea what he was saying, but there was no doubt he was extremely annoyed with Alex.

After a few seconds, she came out and examined the book which was now back in place on the bookshelf. She felt it and it would not slide outward from the other books but would pivot. Once again, she could hear the two men talking at the other end of the yacht. She pulled on the book and it moved backward to a 45° angle with a subtle click, then she pulled on the shelf and it swung outwards. The space inside was another study with another desk. In fact, the inner study could have been exactly the same as the outer study. She couldn't be sure, but on first glance it was. The difference was on the side wall was hung the Storm on the Sea of Galilee. Huge. Beautiful. She stared in shock trying to take it all in. So what did she do now? Just grab it off the wall and get it off the boat somehow? She flicked her phone onto torch and stared at the painting with the flash. It was bewitching. The detail. The colours, even though much of the painting was dark and it was set at night in a storm (obviously), it was absolutely mesmerising. It was far too big for this small study. It was meant for a museum or gallery or some large space. The people on the boat were all either pre-occupied with the figure in blue (supposedly Jesus) or trying desperately to sail the boat safely through the storm. And then there was the curious man smack bang in the middle of the picture with a pink beret staring back out at Janet. Some said this was Rembrandt who had painted himself into the picture and hung on for dear life. In front of Rembrandt was someone vomiting over the side of the boat. It reminded her how sick she felt in her stomach. Like there was a hot brick in there just curdling everything she had eaten the last day or so.

"I bet you didn't expect your masterpiece to end up in a secret room hidden from public view did you?" she quietly asked Rembrandt. He looked confounded by the news. The painting was signed on the top of the boat's rudder - Rembrandt and dated 1633. Suddenly she was filled with a sense that this was so unjust. This amazing piece of art was stuck here in this room for the benefit of one person when the whole world should be able to see this. And then the boat in the painting started to move toward her and her feet shifted involuntary forward to steady herself. What the hell was happening? She was so mesmerised by Rembrandt's work that she was starting to feel the pitch of the waves in the sea of Gallilee. A sudden loud, guttural roar brought her back into the real world; it was the yacht that was moving. The idiot was the taking the damn thing out. But it was the middle of the night. She left the secret room and closed the book shelf door back in and the large brown book snapped back into place. She moved down the corridor towards the front of the yacht. They were moving gently through the port passing other boats on either side.

"Bloody hell." she whispered at herself. "You should have cut this shorter." She went back down the corridor to the living area and was astonished to see the silhouettes of Nicolay and the other man still there. Just drinking and smoking away. So if they were there, then who the hell was driving the boat? Was driving even the right word? She went toward the front to the other set of steps and crept up there staying as low as she could but she couldn't see anyone. She went up another level and then she could see a young man who was indeed driving. She had not seen this man before. Probably another of his employees. She went back down the stairs. Janet needed to figure out where she could hide if need be. The bedrooms had wardrobes which would be big enough to get into. Hopefully she wouldn't need that. She had pretty much free reign of the boat for the time being.

After half an hour, the boat slowed down until it came to a complete stop. It now gently bobbed up and down on the calm sea. The man who had been driving shouted something in Russian to Nicolay and he shouted something back and then continued to drink and smoke. The moon shone down and reflected off the sea almost blindingly. Well what now? She certainly couldn't get the painting off the boat now. After a few minutes a klaxon sounded from off to the left and a yacht was approaching them. Then not thirty seconds later, another deeper klaxon and another larger yacht approaching from the other direction. Slowly the two boats pulled up alongside so they were almost touching. They seemed to be about two miles out at sea but not from Nice, they were positioned not far from some smaller coastal town. The lights twinkled in the distance in the moon -it night.

From the bedroom, she could see a gang planks being pushed across to join the Still Waters to the flanking boat. Then the deep bass beats kicked in above. Was that Swedish House Mafia? Surely, that wasn't Nicolay's playlist. She scooted across to the other side of the boat where the other boat had pulled up alongside and leggy women were being helped across another gangplank. She pulled back from the growing party to the smallest bedroom. She could hear people walking above her. Heels on hardwood floors. This was no longer a quiet boat. This was now becoming a very busy boat. She decided she had two choices here. Firstly, she could hide somewhere quiet and hope it all goes away or secondly go and join in the party. Letting off steam seemed like a good option at this moment in time. She was hardly dressed for a party though.

She searched through the wardrobes in the lower bedrooms and underwent a five minute makeover grabbing a pair of black satin leggings and a white silky blouse. Then a pair of bright blue high heels from the bottom of the wardrobe. Manolo Blahniks of course. There was some random make up in the en suite shower room, so she topped up with blusher and eye shadow, then slicked her hair with water and gel. By the look of what she had seen, the party would be full of leggy, scantily clad women hoping to bag themselves a millionaire. Well she didn't need to worry about that. She'd already bagged her millionaire and his cash. This was different. She wasn't totally sure what this was. A game. An adventure. Or did she want this? This yacht? This type of money? All of the above? Possibly…

By now, people were coming through the living area to access the bathroom. She realised she'd been holding it in for quite a while and queued outside the loo just as a girl had gone in. Before long another girl was queueing with her and introduced herself as Alva. She was incredible looking and spoke with lazy Scandinavian accent. She told Janet she passed herself off as Swedish nowadays, but she was actually from just over the water in Riga, Latvia. She was supermodel beautiful with huge hair and high cheekbones; straight from a hairspray advert, dressed not dissimilarly to Janet with a silky blouse which she had pulled off the shoulder on one side. Her denim shorts were so skimpy and Janet would have killed for the gold, high heeled pixie boots.

"Which boat were you on?" Alva asked her with an inquisitive but friendly smile.

THIRTEEN

Two hundred and twenty four days after

Slightly startled, "Do you know, I can't remember, they all look the same to me." laughing trying hard to sound comfortable and relaxed but knowing it wasn't happening. She took a second to compose. Think 'Lamborghini girl' she told herself and pushed her shoulders back. "What about you? Are you a yacht type?" she asked Alva deflecting the attention from herself.

"Not really. More of a car girl to be honest. But I'm not your typical girl."

At that point, the door to the bathroom opened and the previous occupant left smiling at the pair of them. "Do you mind if I join?" Alva asked.

Janet thought for half a second, then nodded with a mischievous smirk. She reminded herself that this other woman was probably quite drunk even though she didn't particularly sound it. She would need to play catch up.

"So who you with?" Keep asking questions Janet told herself, that way she won't have as much time to question you.

"I'm with a girlfriend. I'll introduce you to her. Although she's after some rich douche bag like she's on heat. It's painful. I probably won't see her again tonight. She does this a lot. "

"Who is it she's after?"

"Oh, God only knows, but believe me, he's no looker. Just one of the yacht set that she loves to go out with. I'm glad I've met you. I need a dancing partner." She did a little shimmy as she flushed the loo. "You dance?"

"Love to but I'm gonna need to catch up on a few drinks first as I've not had much to drink and it feels kind of like everyone else is drunk already." She had't noticed but Alva had a large glass of white wine in her hand. She poured half into a fresh upturned glass which was standing next to the sink and handed it to Janet.

"Here you go!"

They finished up and washed, then Alva re-applied some makeup.

Alva led to way to where an impromptu drinks table had been set up complete with two bar staff.

"Two large white wines." Janet said to the younger and hotter of the two bar men finishing up her half glass of wine. They turned to face the party which now filled the two outside rear decks of the Still Waters as well as the rear decks of the two yachts which now made up the flotilla bobbing up and down gently alongside one another. It was a little disconcerting but it kind of added to the excitement.

"Cheers!" Janet said chinking her glass against Alva's. "So what makes you say you're a car woman Alva?"

"Oh, I just really enjoy cars. And driving. I have an open top BMW with a big engine and I love it." She said, her eyes growing wide.

"Ooh, that sounds lovely. What type?" Janet asked genuinely interested.

"It's a Z4 with a 3.0 engine. What about you?"

"Well I have an Porsche 911 cabriolet in powder blue metallic at the moment, but I did drive my last boyfriend's white Lamborghini for a while which was *really* good fun."

"A Lambo, I'm surprised he would let you drive that. Sorry, that sounded rude. I just meant that it's an expensive toy to lend out. Most of the guys I go out with are idiots and think women can't drive. They look so shocked when I downshift into second and throw the back end out on a corner." she said laughing to herself.

"Well, he didn't have a choice really!" Janet said clinking glasses with Alva once more. "Shall we try the next boat along? We can give them all the benefit of our presence." she said with a mock posh girl voice.

Alva grabbed Janet's hand and the two of them teetered off with their high heels to tackle the narrow gang plank that joined the two vessels. They had a glass of champagne on the first yacht and a Mojito on the second. Once or twice, they gracefully filtered out advances from inadequate suitors before ending up back on the Still Waters. Usually too old, too unfashionable or too uncool.

"Ready to dance now?" Alva suggested hopefully.

"Oh yes! Bring it on."

They joined another twenty or so who were dancing on the rear deck of the Still Waters and the other two adjoined yachts. The three boats seeming to bob up and down in time with the music. The almost full moon providing brilliance to light up the party. The music was loud, the bass deep, the alcohol ran freely as did the cocaine and ketamine in the bathrooms. This is how the super rich partied when they grew bored of being roped into VIP areas and rooftop terraces. A private party where excess was welcomed. Where everyone was rich and no one had anything to prove. Where the music could be incredibly loud and no one would come to complain about it.

"Who's the DJ?" Janet asked Alva.

"I have no idea but I love this track!" The sonic heartbeat boomed through the girls and off across the dark waters surrounding them.

"I can't see my friend anywhere." Alva said looking a little bemused. "Good job I found you, otherwise I might have jumped overboard. Don't leave me anywhere okay? I don't want to end up in some rich idiot's cabin. Not yet at least!" She winked at Janet.

Nicolay walked from the bar to the seating area making eye contact with Janet. He grinned at her. He was still with the large man from earlier who he had been discussing mining with. She gave him a friendly but brief smile.

"Who's that?" asked Alva. "I saw that little flirtation."

"I have no idea." Janet said shaking her head, knowing full well exactly who it was and in far too much detail.

"Well he's got your number I think."

"I think we need to find some younger men to dance with us and fetch our drinks." Janet replied with little actual interest in speaking to any men this evening.

An hour later, they were sat on the front of the boat alone. High heels were just not designed to be danced in all through the night. Alva offered Janet a cigarette, which she accepted and took a light.

"Oh it's nice to rest my feet. I may have to remove these shoes for the rest of the night, otherwise, I might cripple myself."

"With you on that." said Alva.

"I just borrowed these from a friend, so they don't fit all that well."

They chatted about where they were staying, how long for and who with. Janet made most of her back story up on the spot, but felt she was pretty convincing. Alva was supposed to be flying back to Malmo earlier that night but had canceled after her friend begged her to stay another night and come to this party.

"I'm so glad I met you. I don't really know how I ended up at this..." she paused "yacht party, but I wouldn't be enjoying it if I'd not met you."

"Ladies. I see you've come to find a quieter part of my yacht. It's a little hectic back there isn't it?" he offered a wide smile, "I'm Nicolay by the way."

"Nice to meet you Nicolay." Alva replied.

"Yes, nice to meet you Nicolay." Janet chimed in. "It's a lovely yacht you have. Stunning."

"Oh, thank you. It's nice of you to say. Most of the people I bring on here take it all for granted. They don't realise how hard you have to work to buy something like this." There was a bitterness in his tone and then he seemed to snap himself back. "What is it that you two do for a living?"

They chattered for a while at the gently bobbing bow of the yacht. The sun was heading for the horizon and darkness was retreating across the sky filling in the pinpricks where the stars had been.

...

"What the hell is going on here?" Charlie asked himself as he stared at the back of the stranger's head as the stranger watched the yacht that Janet was on bobbing in the moonlight half a mile out. He had the benefit of a pair of binoculars which really annoyed Charlie. Charlie was the one who was supposed to be tailing her and here was this guy who turns up late to the party and so much better prepped. He could probably see what was actually going on on the boat. All Charlie could see was a cluster of lights bobbing very slightly about. When the yacht Janet is / was on left the Port, the stranger had ran pretty much at full tilt for near on three miles to keep his eye on the yacht. Heading East with the yacht, he'd ran across beaches, through gardens, scaled walls and fences and hill sides to stay in touch. Charlie had also run just about keeping in touch with him. The yacht had gone out and headed down the coast for twenty minutes before dropping anchor. Then other yachts had come out of nowhere to join it and now, Charlie couldn't be 100% sure, but he thought they were having a party out there in the middle of the Mediterranean. Depending upon the direction of the breeze, he kept getting wafts of dance music from one or more of the boats.

He should probably text Carl to let him know the situation with the stranger but he wanted to see if there were any clues as to who he was first. Perhaps Carl might have some clues but he was worried that it would appear that he had lost control of the situation. The fact of the matter was that he totally had lost control of what was going on. He lost that the moment that stranger walked up Janet's road in Barcelona.

Charlie put his hands on his head and turned around. He was breathing deeply with stress although he didn't realise it. He still didn't understand how the stranger was here in Nice. Did he follow me while I was following Janet he wondered? That would have been tricky. He didn't appear to have a car when he'd spotted him on Janet's street. Plus, it was tricky as hell keeping up with her. Surely there couldn't have been a third car keeping up with him. Could there? The stranger was now sat on his backpack on a rock overlooking the sea; seemingly transfixed by the goings on out at sea. Charlie hung back out of view of the stranger but close enough so he could keep his eye on him and the yacht. He had a feeling that the yacht wouldn't be coming back anytime soon. If at all.

Earlier in the evening, he'd had several angry and annoyed texts from Carl asking what the hell was going on? Charlie had asked him and Dan to sit tight for now. They didn't trust him seemingly from their texts and this culminated in several calls from Carl which Charlie had to drop as it wasn't appropriate to answer them whilst he was trying to keep a handle on events as they unfolded in Nice. His last text simply said

> I'll call you later. Nothing to worry about, but Janet is in transit and I'm keeping close to her. She is unaware that I am tailing her.

"Fat, ungrateful tit." Charlie muttered and hit the lock button. He had no idea how tired Charlie was with all this work. It was bloody exhausting. He'd hardly slept for days it felt like. And now he'd missed another night of sleep.

The sky was turning into a purple and orange sheet as the sun came up to hide just under the lip of the sea. The more he thought about Janet on the yacht with God knows who, the more stressed he felt. Had some type of reverse Stockholm syndrome occurred within him? He had been the aggressor back in Edinburgh pretending to meet her by chance and then taking her trust and good nature and ripping it into tiny shreds by drugging her and delivering her to Carl. She must have been terrified and now he really regretted it. He wanted to take that back but what was done was done. He just could not imagine doing that again to anyone. Now it felt like he worried about her night and day. This was all so wrong because nothing could ever come of all this now. One thing he did know for sure was he wanted rid of Carl and Dan for good. However this played out, he needed to be rid of them. That could be tricky. A couple of million pounds meant that they weren't going to go away in a hurry. He still wasn't a 100% sure she ever had the money. What he was certain about was how cool this woman seemed to him as he watched her from afar. An enigma. Whoever or whatever she was, she was switched on and just got on with it. She seemed to grab life by the lapels, rough it around and take what she wanted. Do what she wanted. Whenever she wanted. First, he saw her driving a Lamborghini in Glasgow. She had seemingly stolen that from Joseph. She escaped topless from six blokes in one of their cars after giving them finger. She'd moved to Barcelona and started driving a classic Porsche. Now she'd driven to Nice for who knows what reason and broke onto a yacht that had then gone on to some weird yacht cluster party. Now how did this compare to his previous girlfriends. Not in their wildest dreams would they live their lives like this. And now he had spent all this time observing her, he wondered whether he would ever be able to go back to meeting sensible girls in dreary bars. He wanted to live his life as she did. He wanted to live his life spontaneously. Packing up and moving to new cities. Driving exotic cars. Taking road trips. Spending endless days on beaches. He wasn't too sure he'd want to do the breaking onto yachts part. But he supposed it depended why she'd broken onto the yacht. Was there a greater prize than what she'd already taken from him and the rest of the gang? Or perhaps she was simply invited to a party on a yacht and she turned up early and decided to go onboard before her hosts arrived. That seemed unlikely, surely if that was the case she would have awaited her host on the back of the yacht in the open area, not go straight into the inner rooms or cabins. That would be like turning up at someone's house and then letting yourself in and going upstairs to the bedrooms. What was she after? Was she putting herself in terrible danger? He thought there was a good chance she probably was. He decided he couldn't just sit there all day, he would need to do something. He didn't know what, but sitting and watching from a distance it was not. The stranger looked like he was happy to wait it out, but it wasn't sitting well with Charlie. He set off back toward Nice.

. . .

It was now 10:30 am. Janet was returning from the loo and looked around the rear deck. The party had petered out. The majority of the party goers had returned to the two yachts they had arrived on and were either in cabins or internal rooms sleeping or more likely with the amount of cocaine consumed, having bad sex. One or two people were sleeping across seats on the decks and on the right hand boat, a young man and woman sat at the very low back deck with their feet dipped in the water and their eyes locked on one another. She returned to Alva and Nicolay. He was charming, humble (for a billionaire) and funny. Not at all as she had guessed he would be. He exuded a style that men his age simply didn't have. It was difficult to describe it. Effortlessly relaxed, yet smart. As though he'd been dressed by Tom Ford before the party and still looked absolutely pristine even at this time of day. Yes it was probably some stylists job to dress him but still she couldn't help but feel an odd attraction.

Someone shouted Nicolay's name and something in Russian. He excused himself momentarily. When he came back, the other boats were sailing off. The sound of motors accompanied the initial momentum of the boats. The yacht that had been on their right was heading out to sea with three pale blue sails at half mast. It looked majestic and tranquil. The other one sailing east towards Italy. She wondered what works of stolen art were on those boats? This boat contained a stolen Rembrandt; so perhaps a yacht was the perfect hiding place. It made total sense. With a house, there was always a chance, someone could get in or that an authority figure could see the piece of art. But not out at sea. Who ever went on one of these yachts apart from the fortunate few? She remembered reading about a lot of other paintings that had also been stolen on the night when the Rembrandt was taken. At least another ten paintings or more including Manet, Degas, Vermeer and a second Rembrandt. Were they all just floating about out here at sea viewed only by those on the inner circles of their privileged owners? They had to be somewhere and if you could afford to buy one of them, even on the black market, they'd still cost a hell of a lot, so it's likely they'd all be in the hands of the super rich.

Nicolay suggested that that they could take some comfier seats at the rear deck now that the other boats had left. He made coffee for the three of them and effortlessly pulled together a buffet breakfast of granola, chopped bananas, honey and yoghurt. He grabbed a very well stocked fruit bowl from another table and brought it over.

"We can at least have a healthy breakfast after all the bad things we put in our bodies last night." and he winked at Janet. It was an almost fatherly wink. Not a sexual one. He winked a lot she noticed. It put her very much at ease. Much more so than she should have been to say that she shouldn't really be here in the first place. She had blagged her way into this position, she was not here because she knew anyone. Not really at least. She kind of knew Alva and now she kind of knew Nicolay. Both would be short lived friendships she thought. Especially if they knew why she was on board.

"What plans do you have today ladies?" he asked the pair of them. "You're both more than welcome to stay aboard, but equally I can get you back to Nice if you wish?"

"Well I was supposed to fly back home to Sweden. Malmo. But I stayed to keep my friend company, but I seem to have lost her somewhere along the way. So I currently don't have any plans." She looked expectantly toward Janet.

Janet pulled an expression that said 'thinking' for literally a second, then blurted out. "Don't have any plans. Staying on board would be good." she paused, then added, "If I could freshen up." She wasn't thinking about sunbathing. She was thinking about Nicolay and her attraction. She smiled at the chatter but felt annoyed on the inside with herself. With her shallowness. Her predictable-ness. She couldn't even just enjoy this for what it was. A day on a beautiful yacht in an amazing setting.

"We have everything you could possibly need to shower, sunbathe… freshen up. You are my guest now, you can do as you please. What is mine is yours." He spread his arms out to show he meant everything on the boat.

"Lovely, thanks." said Alva.

"Very sweet of you." added Janet whilst thinking slyly that she intended to take him at his word. Although, how she was actually going to take such a big painting off this yacht was yet to be figured out. Could she take it out of the frame and roll it? Could you roll a Rembrandt? Probably not, it would be canvas stretched on a wooden frame. She would need something large enough to put it in like a suitcase. Would that be big enough? She couldn't remember now that she was away from it whether it was huge or tiny. All she could see was Rembrandt's calm face staring out. Staring out of the painting at her. At Janet. 'Get me out of this Janet. Free me from this place.'

"I'm going to grab a shower if that's ok?" said Janet.

"Of course, it's okay. As I said I want you to make yourself at home. There is a guest bathroom straight down." Nicolay said motioning through to the living area to the corridor beyond. "Third door on the left. There should be everything you need in there. If there isn't, let me know what you need."

Half an hour later, feeling refreshed and wide awake now, even with no sleep whatsoever. She opened the door to the bathroom and looked back down the corridor to the back deck. She could see the two of them sat at the table still chatting and laughing. Across the gangway from her was the study door. The door was askew. She had another look to make sure they were still chatting and flew across the narrow corridor and into the study. She still hadn't figured out what her plan of action was. She just wanted another look at the painting. See how big it was. See how it was attached to the wall. She pulled on the book that unlatched the book shelf and manoeuvred it all back to allow a gap into the inner study. It was big. In fact it was huge. It was way too big for her to do anything with. It probably weighed a ton too. She held onto the sides of the picture and lifted it slightly. It moved up the wall remarkably easily. She had thought the frame might be gold but it wasn't. It must be wood with gold leaf. She lifted it a little further and felt it unhook from the wall. She would certainly be able to carry it, but it was just so big. She tried to hook it back to the wall but now couldn't find the hook.

"So he was right, you are up to no good."

She jumped back from the wall. She was literally caught red handed. The painting in her hands. She stood there holding the painting in front of her. She placed it down on the floor and leaned it slightly against the wall. Her heart was popping out from her chest.

"Have you seen this?" Janet asked Alva in a whispered tone. "This is a stolen Rembrandt you know?"

"Yes, I know."

"You know?" Janet asked incredulously. "How do you know?"

"Yes, it's called the Storm on the sea of Galilee. It was painted in 1633. It depicts Jesus calming the storm with the disciples all around him."

Janet's face contorted as she was at first confused and then she started to realise what might be happening.

"You'll need to wait here for Nicolay." Alva said and with that, she smiled and pushed the door back into place and it sealed with a click.

"What have you done?" She looked around frantically for some kind of release for the false wall but there was nothing on this side that she could see. There had to be some way of getting out though she told herself. She scanned the room. Nothing jumped out at her. There were no books on the inside of the wall.

Then a few moments later she heard a conversation taking place on the other side of the door. It was muffled so she couldn't quite make out anything of meaning. Then the door clicked as the latch unlocked. It moved outwards once again and there stood Alva with Nicolay.

Nicolay smiled at Janet and beckoned her to follow him. She stood for a second without moving and he turned back and once more beckoned her. He nodded his head as if to say 'it's ok'. But it wasn't ok. She knew that it was about as far from ok as it was possible to get. She walked out the study with a heavy heart. In the inside living area, Nicolay asked her take a seat on the low slung sofa.

"Alva knew it as soon as she saw you last night." Nicolay said to Janet.

"It was a bit of a giveaway when you were wearing all my clothes and shoes."

Janet felt her face go hot and red. "So you work for Nicolay or you fuck him or both?" Janet asked looking at Alva.

"I work for Nicolay."

"And you didn't have a friend who went off with a guy last night did you?"

Alva shook her head and sniggered slightly.

"I want to thank you Janet." Nicolay said prompting what must have been a very surprised look on Janet's face. "No, really. This has been very useful to me in terms of security. I now know for example that my contact Matthew Weiss has a very big mouth and cannot be trusted. And that I will have to deal with him in due course. You see, I cannot have people know about this painting. It's too precious to me. I mean, do you know how difficult it is to get hold of a Rembrandt? It's almost impossible. Not one like this anyway. I was offered some sketches but who wants sketches. Would you want sketches? I wanted a real Rembrandt. A Rembrandt painting of Jesus no less."

Janet figured that MPW, the writer of the letter must be Matthew Weiss. Her mind was whirring.

"I mentioned this in passing once to Matthew and wasn't sure if he would take the bait, but he obviously did. What I'm not sure about is how you came by this information from him?"

"What does it matter?" Janet asked indignantly.

"I suppose it doesn't really. Matthew will be dealt with accordingly. Unfortunately my dear, this does not bode well for you." he said with a regretful tone.

"Really? Why's that?"

"Well, I just can't have people around who know about this. It would be hurtful to my… profile. The media hate me as it is. It's tough to be this successful. It's frowned upon by the media. I may as well be a murderer as be a rich and successful business man for all the papers care. But if this information that I was in possession of this 'lost' Rembrandt came out, then I fear they would turn on me completely. It would be ugly and I don't like ugliness." he shook his head. "I like beauty."

"I don't want the painting Nicolay and I don't want to tell anyone about it. Who would believe me? Who would I tell?"

"Then what was all this about?" Alva asked, "Please, enlighten us."

Janet focussed her attention on Nicolay. As dire as her situation was, she felt a terrible, coldness toward Alva right now. She didn't like being taken for a fool. "It was about putting a theory to the test. Seeing if I could solve a puzzle." Nicolay motioned for her to expand on this. "I found a letter from Weiss to someone I knew once. It had a coded message about the painting. I solved it. That's all. That's all I wanted to see. If I could solve the puzzle. Nothing more."

"Then why were you seeing if you could lift it off the wall darling?" Alva asked indignantly.

Before she could answer, Nicolay cut back in. "It doesn't matter anyway. I made the mistake of thinking it was secure. It wasn't. It isn't. I will sort that out with my team. But whether you were trying to steal it or not. I can't have you walk off this ship with this knowledge. Unfortunately for you darling, I do not know how to wipe your mind. So…" he paused, "the only thing I can do is not allow you back on dry land. Ever." he said with finality. He didn't look saddened by this news. "I have had to call my colleague. Dimitri will come and deal with you. I cannot promise you that things will be pain free. Or quick, but who knows. Be nice to him."

He walked to the door to the corridor, pulled it shut and locked it. The key went in his trouser pocket.

"We are going to go and await Dimitri and then we'll leave you with him." Nicolay said. Janet couldn't think of anything to say to this news. The pair of them left the living room toward the back deck. Nicolay took the key from the inside lock, pulled the door closed behind them and then locked it from the outside leaving the key in the door. He didn't make eye contact with her. They went around the side of the yacht and she could hear their footsteps going downwards toward the back of the yacht.

"Fuck." she put her hands over her eyes as if to hide from this news. "Brilliant you idiot. Bitch!"

She got up and looked at the lock and wondered briefly if she could break the glass in the door, but it looked extremely sturdy. She looked around the front room. It was minimalist. She wasn't sure if this was how it always was or if it was like this for the party. There were a few tables with drawers, she looked through them but there was nothing that could help her situation. Perhaps, she could learn to play herself a lament on the piano. She continued to pace the room like a beautiful caged leopard. Running through escape plans and scenarios in her head. It was no good. She was too upset at being taken for a ride by Alva to think straight. She sat back into the sofa and rubbed her head all over like this might somehow help. She stared into space. She wasn't sure for how long.

A deep burbling grew from the side of the boat and a black speed boat pulled up at the low rear deck. Janet guessed this was Dimitri. He was tall, dark, unshaven. He made eye contact with her momentarily through the glass doors. She shivered. There was nothing behind his eyes. No emotion. No feeling. They could have been the dead eyes of a corpse hanging on the end of a rope. He strained to lift what looked like some type of anchor out of the speedboat and placed it onto the rear deck. The anchor was the size of a coffee table. Attached to the anchor was a chain and on the end of the chain was a pair of hand cuffs. He climbed on board and moved the anchor slightly to examine the decking. He wiped a spot away as if he had scratched the varnish.

He walked across the deck and sat down at the table on the rear decking area and checked his watch. After a few moments, Nicolay and treacherous Alva appeared and they all spoke for a minute. The double glazed pane of the doors meant she heard nothing of the conversation. All that came across was the grim-ness of their faces. Then the pair walked to the rear of the yacht, got onto the speed boat together and sped off back in the direction of Nice. Nicolay drove. Alva looked back briefly and smiled but it was a smile filled with pity. In a way, Alva's smile was much more worrying than Dimitri and his anchor. Clearly, Janet thought, they didn't want to be on board when Dimitri did whatever he was going to do.

Dimitri unlocked her cage and slid the double doors apart slightly.

"Janet. Hello. We are to have a little chat." he said and walked in to the living area pulling the doors closed behind him. He didn't lock them back up. "Please, make yourself comfortable."

Janet did as requested with a fair amount of trepidation.

"I'm Dimitri. An acquaintance of your host. I'm on your host's inner circle." he said with just the slightest hint of Russian inflection at the back of his throat. "You, Janet are not on his inner circle. But, you have some information which only those on the inner circle should know about. This information concerns a painting in the private study." he smiled with some crooked teeth. "Does this make sense so far Janet?"

She nodded. Trying to listen to what he was saying, but at the same time, trying to keep her senses about her and figure out a possible way out of this.

"Janet, you have a letter which has details about this private study. Yes?"

She nodded but he paused awaiting a verbal answer.

"Oh, yes, I do."

"Janet, where is the letter?"

It was annoying that he began every sentence with Janet...

"It's in Barcelona."

"Janet, why would it be in Barcelona?"

"That's where my house is. It's where I live."

He shut his eyes for a second as if computing this information. He walked to a table at the side of the room, opened a drawer and took a pen and an envelope out. He gave them to her. "Janet, do you see that anchor out on the deck back there?" he motioned toward the door. She nodded. "The anchor weighs around two hundred kilos. Shortly, I am going to handcuff you to the anchor Janet and it is going to pull you to the bottom of the Mediterranean." He paused as if awaiting a reaction.

She resolutely refused to give him one, apart from the fact her face was going hot.

"I'm not really sure what will happen to you after that." he added. "Janet, you need to write your address down on this envelope. I will check you live where you say you do. If you write the correct address down for me. I will make this easier on you. I will do this by knocking you unconscious before I put you in the water. Do you understand? It will be much preferable to go into the water conscious."

She nodded in agreement. Although she didn't really want either.

Well there was no point to lie she thought to herself. She weighed up her options and there seemed to be very few. She wrote the address down on the envelope. He took the envelope and went out onto the rear deck locking the door behind him, caging her once more. He sat and made several phone calls over the course of fifteen minutes, then simply sat with the phone on the table and waited. He lit a cigarette and smoked it staring into the distance.

She weighed up her chances of escape. She thought about just trying to hit him or kick him in his balls and then get into the study and make a phone call. Slim chance, but a chance all the same. Also, he probably knew how to get into the study. But if she could just make a call to the police. Or she could try to push him in the water. Again. Slim. She had to try. She decided when he came for her, she would act scared and defeated. Deflated. But then she could try to kick him in his balls. It was the one last defence women had against stronger men. If she could make contact, she knew he would go down. He would struggle to fight her for at least a few seconds. What else did she have? Nothing really.

His phone went. Terrible ring tone she thought to herself. Focus Janet! He walked in and she looked down at her feet. He stood over her.

"So I think you gave me the correct address. There is indeed a Janet who lives at this address. So thank you for that. I can now make this easier for you. But I'm afraid now is the ti…" She extended her right foot upwards towards his crotch and unbelievably made contact. She felt the soft flesh of his balls compact. She didn't just make partial contact, she made full ball crushing contact. He dropped to his knees. His eyes shut tightly for a second. Then opened wide in disbelief, but she was up scooping herself to the side toward the open door. She pulled the door shut behind her and went to lock it, but the key was not in the door. She ran around the side of the yacht toward the rear to find another way into that central corridor. She ran as fast as she could, looking through the side window into the living space, she saw he was getting up off the floor. He was struggling and having to help himself up with the sofa. She found a door at the other end of the yacht and it was open, she flew down the corridor and into the study, pulled on the book and the book shelf opened. She slide in and pulled it closed behind her. She couldn't believe her eyes, there was no phone on the desk. She was sure there had been a phone on there. Why would you have an office or study without a phone?

She could hear him in the outer study now. Muffled but she could hear the angriness in his voice. He obviously didn't know which was the actual book. He was trying them all. She could hear him muttering loudly to himself about how he was going to enjoy drowning her. She searched frantically through drawers but there was no phones, tablets. There was nothing she could use to communicate with the outside world. She felt the small walls of the study closing in on her and he no doubt homed in on the book that would let him in. The book that would seal her fate. She turned to look at Rembrandt. He stared back at her once more, there was nothing that he could do for her, but his look said he felt her pain.

And then she heard the click. The wall swept outwards. She saw his face, hot and angry. His lips stuck in a snarl. He grabbed at the back of her neck. His grip was like a vice. It was almost paralysing her, her legs went half limp. She would never escape this now.

"There will be no more nice Dimitri Janet" he told her squeezing even harder "there will now only be pain for you. From here until you are at the bottom of the ocean. Gasping for air but only drinking salty sea water."

He manoeuvred her toward the rear of the yacht. Her feet barely touched the decking. She simply saw it passing under her.

He pushed her to the floor on the low rear decking. Her world of pain had begun. He transferred his grip to her left hand and it was handcuffed within seconds. Then her right. She stared down at her fate. A shining, brushed steel anchor. She took some deep breaths. It would do no good.

Then she saw a movement toward her. A man in denim shorts. Running at the pair of them. Dimitri turned at the last minute and the man hit him at full force knocking him into the sea, but Dimitri grabbed his arm and pulled him with him and the pair were in the water. The man in denim shorts surfaced quickly and was on top of Dimitri. She felt she recognised him somehow. She couldn't quite place him, but she immediately got a bad feeling in the pit of her stomach. Was it Charlie from Edinburgh? That would not make any sense at all. She craned her neck to see. He was holding Dimitri under the water. It was Charlie. She wracked her mind to figure out how he could be here, but her mind was a mess right now.

An arm reached out from the water and hit Charlie around the side of the head. Then Dimtri's head bobbed back up from the water. He sucked in air and went to head butt Charlie and contacted on his nose. His nose erupted with blood and Dimitri started swimming back toward the deck and Janet. He leaned up over the edge and grabbed at the chain attached to the anchor and Janet and started to pull it toward the edge. She knew if it went in, there would be little she could do to stop it pulling her down. She pulled back against him, but he was just stronger than she was. The anchor scraped across the deck shredding the varnish off the wood with its machined edges. He had his feet against the side of the yacht for purchase and leaned back. She grabbed onto a handle at the side. He managed to get the anchor onto the edge of the deck. Half of it dropped into the sea and the other half clung onto the edge. Charlie grabbed Dimitri around the neck with his left arm and pulled tight but this only helped Dimitri to get the anchor into the sea and it dropped with a huge splash yanking her attached arm toward the sea. The hand cuff tore at her wrist hacking the skin off against her wrist bone. Blood poured down her hand and dripped into the sea. Waves splashed up at the wound with a salty sting. She clung on, but its weight was hard to work against and she could feel her grip loosening on the rail. Dimitri reached up toward the edge of the yacht and pushed upward against it shoving himself and Charlie down under the water. They disappeared out of view under the yacht. She felt faint as if all the strength had been drained from her and hung on to the handle as much as she could but her grip was sliding further down under the strain. She hooked her elbow around the rail in a final attempt to hold back. She tried to see where the two of them had gone but there was now no movement. They must have been under water for a minute. Then, something rising to the surface. It was the dark mop of Charlie's hair. He shook his hair off like a labrador just out of a stream and pulled himself up onto the deck. He leaned back into the water and grabbed the chain attaching Janet and the anchor. He heaved it onto the side.

"Is he gone?" she asked.

Charlie was breathing deeply and covered in blood down either side of his face. "No, he's right there." He laid down flat on his back and pointed. Dimitri was floating face down a few metres out.

"Shit!" She jumped.

"I wish to fuck he wasn't though." Charlie added matter-of-factly.

"Turns out I can hold my breath for longer than him; I'm a good swimmer. That's what it all came down to. Who was that?"

"Dimitri."

"Who the fuck is Dimitri?"

"He's someone who works for Nicolay Zestakova?" Janet came back. "Anyway, what the fuck are you doing here and why am I even speaking to you? Do you remember drugging me in Edinburgh by any chance?"

He turned to look at her. Regret in his eye. "Well you did steal two and a half million from the people I was working with."

"Was?"

"Yeah, was." he emphasised. "I'm no longer working for them. And don't worry, I don't want the money back. I did. That's why I'm here in Nice, that's what brought me to Nice. That's not what put me on this boat though. That was worry about you. A gut feeling that you were in trouble on here. Which turned out to be bang on."

"So confused. I don't understand what you're saying."

"It's a long story, but let me get you out of those hand cuffs first. Do you know where there might be a paperclip?"

"Drawers in the table in there possibly." She gestured toward the living area.

He came back a minute later.

"I saw this on TV. Not sure if it works."

He stuck the paper clip into the back of the hand cuff and the clasp pulled open. Janet pulled back away from the anchor. Charlie got up and dived back in. He swam to Dimitri and pulled his body back toward the rear deck. Then he held Dimitri's hand up to Janet.

"Cuff him can you?" Charlie asked her. She snapped the cuff around his wrist. Charlie climbed back onto the deck and then pushed the anchor over the edge. Dimitri immediately begin heading wrist first toward the bottom. In seconds, he was inverted. His feet poked briefly from the surface of the water. His legs became merely two dark floating shapes. Then he was gone.

Charlie popped open the first aid box that was attached to the side of the rear deck and gave some basic first aid. An alcoholic wipe, then gave her gauze to hold over the wound and then he wrapped a bandage around the wrist and secured it with tape.

"How did you get on this yacht?" she asked him.

"I paddled out here on a canoe I rented from Nice. Took me about an hour. I'm guessing I've lost my deposit by now."

"Where is the canoe now?" she asked confused.

"It's tied to the side of the yacht. Then I managed to get on board just a few minutes before Igor. Luckily I tied it on the other side of the yacht so he obviously didn't see it. I managed to sneak on board whilst you were in there with the man and woman who locked you in. Was that Nicolay?"

"Yes. OK, right, start from the beginning please. I'm so confused by all this. I'm really thankful that you saved my life just now, but how the fuck did you end up here? On this boat: in Nice: now?"

"Depends what you call the beginning. If we're gonna be straight with one another, where is the beginning for you? How did you come by the bag of cash? If you can tell me that then I can probably fill in some gaps for you too."

There didn't seem much point now to not tell him. She told him everything she knew about Joseph which wasn't much. It felt good to get it all out. Purged. The reason she'd been in Edinburgh. The meeting with Joseph and going with him to Glasgow. She now understood now why he was so keen to get out of Edinburgh. She explained how much drugs and drink they consumed and how she thought that was the cause of Joseph's death. They came across her as she was leaving the hotel. The car was Joseph's.

Charlie explained how he had come to be part of the gang and how they had managed to steal the painting from the auction house by posing as the secure courier company. How after Joseph had delivered the painting to the contact, Joseph had then double crossed them to take the money himself leaving other members of the gang at the motorway services.

He explained how they had tracked her down to Edinburgh using Joseph's phone which she had and that he was talked into drugging her in Edinburgh by the gang, but how he regretted it. She just gave him a look which said 'sure' and nothing more for now. How they had followed the phone to Brighton. Then he went on to explain how he'd tracked her down to Barcelona.

"Again, I'm not proud of it but I tracked you down through your mum. Her email password is Janet1. She led me straight you at Barcelona Airport."

Janet came back, "Nice work. Hacking and following an old lady."

"I'm not proud. I *did* really want that money back. At the time. But I'm over that now."

He spied Dimitri's cigarettes on the table and took one out and offered her the packet. She accepted. He dropped the lighter out from the packet and lit their cigarettes. Then laid back for a second, shut his eyes and inhaled. It all tasted more of salt and blood than tobacco but it gave him a hit he needed.

"I only smoke after sex and near death by drowning experiences." Charlie quipped.

"So carry on." Janet told him. She leaned back and breathed the smoke in deeply. It hurt her lungs but it felt good. This was the first cigarette she'd smoked since the night all this started.

"Where was I? Ah, yes. I was supposed to just keep an eye on you until Carl came out here."

"He's the bald one right?" Charlie nodded. "That fucker gave me a real slap. Nice guy."

Charlie explained that something had happened back at home, delayed them and then she had started on her road trip to Nice so he'd been told to just tail her. He explained that another man was following her too and was watching the yacht on the mainland just outside of Nice. He explained he had no idea who he was or why he was following her. He told her what he looked like but she had no recollection of seeing him. Charlie missed out explaining how the man had been in her Barcelona house. None of this sounded good, but allowing her to have the stranger in her house whilst her mother was there was pretty inexcusable really.

"I thought I'd managed to remove all the traces of my old life. Anything that might lead you to me. I knew there was a possibility you would try every which way to get to me. Well, get the money."

"But I'm over that now. I really am. When I was on the mainland watching the yacht with you on. I felt you were in danger and it made me feel like a wanted to protect you."

"You're the one I need protection from." she said with a cold sneer.

"I can understand you saying that, but really my mind changed. If I could do anything to wind back time to the point in Edinburgh before I dropped that Rohypnol in your drink. I would. We were getting along really well."

"Were."

"So what was so important on this yacht? Am I right in thinking there is something on this yacht that you're after?"

She stood up. "Perhaps this is something you can help with." She guided him round the side of the yacht and to the inner central corridor, through the outer study which was now a mess with books all over the floor and to the secret inner study. He looked mystified. She leaned against the desk and pointed toward the wall. He looked at the painting. Then looked up close at the rough oil strokes that made up its surface.

"Is this an original?" he asked.

"Look at the inscription on the rudder of the boat."

He crouched down and leaned in close to the surface on the far right of the painting and read out aloud "Rem… brandt". His eyebrows raised and he stood back to take it all in better.

"That is 'The Storm on the Sea of Galilee' by Rembrandt from the early 1600s. It was stolen from a museum in Boston along with a load more paintings. Vermeer. Manet. No one knows who did it. None of the paintings have ever been found. Until now. It disappeared in 1990 and now it's here in this secret study where only a single oligarch can view it. Sick eh?"

"Bet there's a hefty reward for this now." said Charlie.

"Yeah five million dollars. But I don't want the reward Charlie. This is worth fifty mill'. To the right person. I don't want first class money Charlie. I want private jet money."

"Ok, good point." he was nodding.

She explained how she had come to find the letter at the bottom of the bag of cash and how she had cracked its code and wanted initially to put her theory to the test. See if it held water.

"But now that they tried to kill me. I wanna take it. I want that to myself."

Charlie was mesmerised by the painting.

"That's Rembrandt in the middle with the pink hat on." she said knowingly. "So they say."

He stared into the storm.

"Christ?" he pointed at the character to the right of Rembrandt. She nodded. "You want me to help you get it off the boat?"

"I do, but how the hell can I trust you?" She asked him. Genuinely reaching for a way. An olive branch to grab. "I did this on my own. I'm not gonna let your 'gang' have it. OK?"

"I don't know yet how I can regain your trust. But give me a little time and I might just show you. If I do, I'm not doing it for 'the' gang. I'm not working with them." he shrugged his shoulders to show her he was genuine. "Maybe if I come up with a plan for getting this off to start with. Do we need to go soon? Are those others - Nicolay - likely to come back shortly?"

"I have no idea. I don't want to stay her for long." She said looking him up and down whilst his eyes were on the painting.

"I think it would be good to get off this boat as soon as possible. Is there another rib or jet ski or anything?"

"Rib? Don't even know what that is, let alone where there would be one."

"I mean another small boat for getting to the coast."

She shook her head.

"I doubt we could drive this thing away or dock it anywhere, it's too big, so we're gonna need a way of getting off it somehow. We may need to use my little canoe but it would be a struggle and I don't want to risk it with this," pointing to the painting, "this painting is a little big for it. Plus we'll be spotted by your stalker. Unless we could wait until dark. But that's too long."

"Yes, that's hours away. I think they could come back before then. They're probably on their way back now. They've probably called Dimitri and figured out things have gone wrong."

"OK, can you take a look around the boat for…" he thought for a second, "them or anyone approaching us and for a jet ski or some life raft or something? See you at the rear of the of yacht."

"Quickly. What are we doing with the picture if we do manage to get it off this yacht?" she asked.

"I don't want it ok. I just want off this yacht and I want to help you. If the picture happens to come off with us, then it's a bonus, but it's up to you what you do with it. Clear?"

She nodded. Janet looked for a few minutes but saw nothing of note and no one approaching. Yet.

Charlie took considerably longer. He was half looking and half thinking. Trying desperately to come up with a plan. He looked in the bridge briefly, but as geeky and technical as his mind was, there was no way he could figure out how to get the yacht going. Too many buttons, dials, nobs, wheels, sliders.

He got to the rear deck where Janet was looking over the sides of the yacht.

"Anything?"

"Not really." she replied. "Except… how good exactly are you at swimming?"

"I'm pretty good. What you thinking? I'd struggle to swim back to shore and it would take too long."

"That." She said pointing further out to sea.

He looked out to where another three yachts were moored about a half a kilometre south. "Another yacht?"

"No. Not another yacht. Looks what's attached to the back of the far right one."

"Oh, yeah, good thinking." He could see a little

inflatable with an outboard motor attached to the back of the yacht. "Do you think it will have the keys in it?"

"One way to find out. You said you were a good swimmer."

"Jesus. This is gonna' take me about half an hour and I wanted to be off here before then. Can you find something to wrap that painting in? Curtains or a bed spread maybe. And on the off chance they come back, I suggest you hide out and keep a look out for me. Make sense?"

"Ok, will do. Get going!" she said with a mix of urgency and impatience and then. "But be careful, please. Ok?"

"Anything else?"

She didn't reply and set off down toward the back of the boat at a pace.

She found a blanket which would wrap several times around the painting and a rope which she cut to a sensible length. She wrapped the painting to double thickness and then secured the rope around it.

Back on deck, she checked the coast was still clear. So far so good. No speedboats heading toward them, but also she couldn't see Charlie swimming anywhere. He was probably too small to see by now. Out this far, the azure blue gave way to a dark, almost black, blue. Charlie's dark mop of hair could well just blend into this. She hated herself but he was really attractive to her. In spite of Edinburgh. There was no doubting he was attractive physically, but it was his charisma, his intelligence that made up the whole package. After he'd climbed out of the water with soaked clothes clinging to his body, she'd been able to see he either looked after himself or was just naturally muscular.

She continued to scan for movement toward the yacht. Minutes seemed to be hours. She was not breathing naturally again. Almost holding her breath. Then she faintly heard a motor. The distinct sound of a propellor under water. There was a speed boat heading towards the yacht from the direction of Nice. She ducked out of view. It was a long way off. She couldn't see who was aboard. She spun around to the direction Charlie was in but still could see nothing.

"Come on Charlie!"

Then she saw something move from Charlie's direction. He had got the speedboat and was coming back. She looked back in the direction of the other boat. It was close now but she couldn't see who was on it still. She ran up a deck so she could get a better view while trying to stay out of sight. The speedboat got to the Still Waters and continued past heading out to sea.

Charlie made it back and tied up the commandeered speedboat to the Still Waters. The boat was basic with an outboard motor but big enough to hold them and the painting. Charlie was able carry the painting alone to the speed boat. She untied the rope and threw it into the boat.

"Hang on a second." She said. "I need to check I've not left anything." She stood there and thought looking around. Aware someone had just died here. Okay, he'd probably not be missed by many, maybe Nicolay and would probably never be found, but still she wanted to be sure she was leaving nothing behind. "Okay." She climbed onto the speedboat. Once on the boat, she realised those few seconds had served a dual purpose. He could have just hit the accelerator and taken off with the painting. He didn't.

"Where are we going?"

"Well not back to Nice because, you have a stalker there. I just wanted off the yacht as soon as possible. Do you have any ideas?"

"Do you know where my car is?" Janet asked.

"Yes. It's near your hotel." Charlie replied still out of breath.

"Okay, we drop you off. You swim ashore, get the car and meet me at the far end of the Promenade des Anglais. I'll just have to ramp the boat up on the beach."

"Okay. Can't think of anything more sensible unfortunately, so let's do it." He pushed the forward on the throttle.

She slipped her hotel key card from her back pocket. "Can you get my bag. It's not unpacked. Can't remember my hotel room number, but take the stairs to the second floor, turn right and then it's the furthest room on the right. My car keys are in the bag, but check."

Charlie handed over control of the boat and jumped off the boat at the far corner of the Promenade. He wasn't sure if he'd be able to walk or not. He bobbed under the water and had to swim back to the surface.

"Be as fast as you can!" She called after him. He turned in the water and gave her a look. Janet turned across the shore toward the airport where she could see planes landing in the distance. She pushed the throttle forwards. She would go to the far end as they had described and wait to see her car pull up. The picture leaned against the back seats of the speed boat.

. . .

Charlie swam to the shore and was very aware of people on the beach staring at him. It hadn't helped that Janet had set off with a roar attracting onlookers. He came up out of the sea trying to look like he belonged there, like what he was doing was natural. Bond after a swim. On his way back to his hotel and a Martini cocktail. It wasn't natural. He looked nothing like Bond exiting the sea. More like a drunken, half drowned tramp. He walked up the narrow pebbled beach. Pebbles and stones shooting out under foot leaving him stumbling in his exhausted state. It must have looked like he'd been thrown off the speed boat by his girlfriend.

Once on the pavement, he set off and ran toward the hotel trying to look as unobtrusive as it's possible to look when your clothes and hair are soaked to the skin and you're running when everyone is strolling gently. 'Just look like you're out for a run' - he told himself.

He was sure the stranger would have been watching what happened on the yacht from shore but now, he was nowhere to be seen. So far. He wasn't sure how good the stranger's binoculars were and whether he would have been able to see Charlie's face in enough detail to recognise him back on shore. He also wasn't sure whether the stranger knew of the location of Janet's hotel or car. He only remembered seeing him at the dock and on the coast as he tried to follow the yacht. Perhaps Charlie was in shock a little? He had just killed a man with his bare hands after all. He pulled up to a walk. In the hot sun and rested his hands on his thighs. He was steaming. Vapour coming off his shirt and hair. People stared more. It had been self defence and more importantly, defence of Janet. The guy was going to drown her. It was not cold blooded. He set off again, trying not to think about Dimitri. He tried put his face out of his mind. For a few seconds it bobbed in front of him. Under water, his eyes wide. Charlie saw his mouth open. A gasp. He knew at that point that Dimitri was done for. He held on a little longer. Charlie kept his mouth closed, his eyes burned and his chest cramped as Dimitri was drained of his strength. Of his life. Muscles and brain shutting down without oxygen.

As Charlie reached the hotel, he paid particular attention to the direction in which the stranger had last been seen, but he couldn't see him. On the doorstep, he had a last look around. Nothing. As fast a runner as the stranger was, if he had set off running back at the time they set off back from the Still Waters, he probably wouldn't be back to Nice yet. Thankfully, he had stopped dripping now. Just steam rose from him. Charlie went for the room. Stick to what he was supposed to be doing.

. . .

As Janet reached the far end of the Promenade, she cut the engine and the speed boat slowed to a stop. Then realised that she was baking and with the wind no longer on her face, she was burnt. Hopefully Charlie wouldn't keep her waiting for long. He had to swim ashore, get to the hotel, grab her bag and car key and then drive over here through the traffic of Nice. It was probably four or five miles. Although it was only one road really. Her eyes were fixed on the road nearby. Where she would hopefully see her car soon. She didn't even have sunglasses with her now. Had no idea where they could be.

As time went by, she started to wonder how on earth they would get rid of this painting. Perhaps they should go for the reward. At least that way, she could be sure that people would once again see this work of art. The boat drifted around a little. Plus five million was five million. Not to be sniffed at. An aeroplane was coming in to land overhead and the noise was incredible. She felt the boat lurch side to side with a wave and then a bang and thud as another speed boat hit hers. A man jumped from the other boat into hers. Steadied himself.

"Hello Janet." he said calmly.

She did not respond and tried her very best to stay calm herself.

"So it looks as though you were right Janet." Reaper patted the large package leaned against the seats at the back of the boat. "I'm not so sure I'd have been able to fill in all those gaps on the letter. But you're a clever girl aren't you?"

"So you broke into my house in Barcelona?"

"Took me a while to find the letter tucked away in that book though. Anyway, I'd love to chat more but I'm going to take this now." His hand was on the painting. She said nothing.

"Then what you going to do with it?" She said half trying to stall for time. In the back of her mind though, even if Charlie got here now, there would be nothing he could do from the shore. If she was going to do anything, she was going to be doing it alone. And she needed to do it soon. "Do you even know what it is?"

"Of course I know what it is. Do you think I'd have followed you here from Barcelona just for the fun of it?" He picked up the painting by the rope that held the package together and looked to his boat but it had drifted a little now. "Move to the side Janet." He put the painting back down.

She shook her head.

"I know you and your accomplice just killed a man on that yacht, but to be honest it seemed like you had luck on your side. When I last killed. It was something I did on purpose. I planned it. I almost enjoyed it. But I'm not planning on murdering you Janet, but if you get in my way, I can't promise that I won't."

She sat to the side of the driver's seat. Reaper sat in the driver's seat and pushed gently on the throttle to move the boat closer to his. As it got close, he turned the wheel back and it gently nudged up side by side against his boat. Reaper jumped up, grabbed the rope on the painting and stepped effortlessly to the other speed boat.

"I actually came to you because of the cash I assume you stole from Carl and his little sidekick Dan, but I'm happy to leave you with that. I'm pretty fair like that. A fair trade."

"You'd be better off with the money. I'm not so sure you'd be able to get anywhere near the value that painting is worth. It's not something you can sell on down the pub like a mobile phone you nicked." Janet spat at him

"I think you under estimate me love. You know nothing about me. You don't know who I know. I have contacts."

"Sure you do."

"Anyway, I'd love to chat more, but I'm off now. Oh, final word of advice for you. Carl and his little buddy - Dan have your address in Barcelona, so I imagine they'll be paying you a visit soon once they get over the very sad loss of their pooches. I wouldn't stick around to see them. They're scum. Just saying." He set off. He looked back briefly.

Janet sat for a second. Thinking about options. She was not prepared to accept this state of affairs but she wasn't really sure what she could do. She shifted back over to the driver's seat and pushed forward once again on the throttle, then turned the wheel and aimed for the other speed boat. She suspected as her engine was much larger than his that his boat was not as powerful. She caught him quickly. He looked around at the noise and she hit his boat at an angle on the side. His boat lurched to the left and he was knocked off his boat and into the water. She looked back to see him bobbing about and looking in her direction.

    She half expected that his speed boat would just stop, but it just carried on its way. It speeded up. She had turned it slightly so it was now facing the beach head at the end of the airport runway. Another aeroplane was coming in to land overhead. She felt she could almost touch the underside of it. Feel the heat from the jets. She slowed her boat a little as the boat closed in on the beach. The other boat kept up its speed and hit the rocky beach abruptly coming to a stop. The stranger had forced her hand now and she jumped out of the boat into knee deep water, grabbed the painting from the beached boat. It's propellor was grinding against the rocks. Spinning but getting no further. She started in the direction of the Promenade des Anglais scrabbling over the rocks while trying to check on the whereabouts of the stranger. He was swimming toward the shore. She reached the road as he was getting out of the water. The painting was starting to weigh heavy in her arms now. There was no sign of Charlie in her car. She started heading back along the road in the direction of the port end of Nice where he would be coming from. She was aware she was on the wrong side of the road too but it was a wide and busy dual carriageway at this point. There was a crossing up ahead. The stranger was now out of the sea and close to the road. He was moving quickly even with his wet clothing. She couldn't wait for the crossing and had to get over. She waited for a gap in the traffic and set off across. Cars flew past blasting their horns in anger at her stupidness. The road was divided into a dual carriage way by greenery and palms trees. At half way across, she looked back and saw that the stranger was still gaining on her. She was at a terrible disadvantage with the painting which seemed to be growing in size and weight as she became more tired. She panicked and decided to try to get all the way over. A car clipped the corner of the painting and once again, she was blasted with the horns of several cars and trucks. She tried to run faster but it was like a sprinter taking on a tired marathon runner. She couldn't focus but heard a horn beeping up ahead. Without slowing down, she tried to focus again on where the noise was coming from and then she saw her Porsche. Charlie pulled up with the hazard lights on. More horns blasted as they swerved around her car.

As she got to the car, the door flew open and she pushed the picture into the back seat.

"Drive!" She shouted at him whilst pointing up ahead to the stranger. "Get past that fucker!"

Charlie saw the stranger up ahead in the middle of the road under the palms. He hit the accelerator and they were off. The stranger stood in the middle of the road with his hands on his hips shaking his head at them as they flew past.

"You okay? What the hell happened?"

"Just get going. I'll tell you later. I take it that was my stalker?" she asked.

"Yup. That's the fella. You don't know him then? Where we going Janet?"

"Road trip to Barcelona?"

"You sure? Your stalker knows where you live. As does Carl."

She shut her eyes momentarily. "Okay, guess not then. I'm running out of places I can go. Any suggestions?"

Charlie thought for a while as he drove in no particular direction. "Okay, how about London via the tunnel? And a stop over in Paris?" he raised his eyebrows. "London is somewhere we can shift that." He motioned back to the painting with his head. "Paris because, we'll need to break up the journey."

She pushed her head back into the seat, breathed deeply and forced a smile. "Okay. Paris. That will give you about eight hours to talk me around Charlie."

The End

Rate, review and recycle.

Please rate and review the book on Amazon.co.uk and pass onto another reader.

Thank you for your support!